THE BOY FROM SNOWY RIVER

AF583767

Fred Silcock grew up in the racing game, rode as an amateur jockey and became a racehorse trainer. Today he lives at Mt. Macedon in Victoria and is much involved in the breeding of new varieties of daffodil and private research projects. A keen student of Australian natural and rural history, he is a descendant of Capt. Eber Bunker, the first man to take whales in Australian waters.

THE BOY FROM SNOWY RIVER

FRED SILCOCK

ARCADIA

The perfect illustration on the cover is by Pieter Zaadstra,of Zaadstra's 'White Church' Art Gallery, 918 Frankford Rd, Glengarry, Tamar Valley, Tasmania. The author wishes to thank him and also Barry Oakley, Kate Daniel and David Bonsall for their kind assistance.

© Fred Silcock 2017
First published 2017 by ARCADIA
the general books' imprint of
Australian Scholarly Publishing Pty Ltd
7 Lt Lothian St Nth, North Melbourne, Vic 3051
Tel: 03 9329 6963 / Fax: 03 9329 5452
enquiry@scholarly.info / www.scholarly.info

ISBN 978-1-925588-06-4

ALL RIGHTS RESERVED

Cover design Wayne Saunders

For Marjory and Hazel

Part One

One

Like all streams that rose in the nearby hills and white-topped mountains beyond, the creek below Brian Drury's overnight camp was icy and shallow, stony and noisy, the water hurrying onwards to the Murray River. Drury, too, was on his way to the Murray, to the towns of Wodonga and Albury. His station, Foxhow, on the Snowy River, was now many days behind him. July was nearly at an end.

Drury was a stallion-man, a man who at this time of year took to the road and offered the service of his stallion to any breeder, big or small, willing to pay the fee of five-guineas per mare. This year, 1880, was the twelfth of his seventy-four years that he had gone out in this way and would not see the Snowy again until near the end of November. His stallion this year was the same as last year's, Kilrenny, a bay with black legs. His other stallion Lanarth, that had bred so many fine horses, including racehorses, was retired.

Some men travelled pretty ponies, some took the feathery-legged Clydesdale or the sturdy Percheron. Drury was a Thoroughbred-man and argued that there was no breed of horse on earth not improved by a dash of Thoroughbred blood. He preferred black-legged horses, for white on legs often ran into the hoof and white hoof was not as strong as black. This enterprise did not earn him much money but it paid its way. He had prospered as a cattleman and seller of horses to the British Army in India and financially was not a poor man. The breeding of good stockhorses was his great interest and he believed that the stockhorse ought to become a breed in its own right and to bring that about the way to go was through the Thoroughbred. These annual excursions he referred to as his *grand tours*.

In the dark away from the fire he could not see the two wagon horses but the tinkle of the bell strapped to the neck of one told him roughly where they were. Seated on the old wooden chair he never travelled without he leaned back and stretched his legs and again put the mug of tea to his lips. He thought about tomorrow and the route he would take to Yarrimba station; he would go the longer way, following the red, gravelly soil that was less likely to bog him at this time of year than would the black soil of the shorter way. He thought of the repairs he ought make to the yard before he left. The yard had been built years ago. He put his fingers into his beard and scratched his face and thought of how in Wodonga he would let barber Flinn loose on him; and he thought of the laudanum he would buy to ease the pain when his hip ached too much. He turned his head at the sound of Kilrenny's whinny.

The stallion, no longer as still as stone, moved out of the shadow at the far end of his yard. He lifted his head high and with ears pricked began to walk quickly. Reaching the fence he stopped. The breeze, at times from the north and at times from the east, had brought to his nostrils the scent of a mare in season.

Drury stood.

Kilrenny turned and started along the fence. Reaching the corner he swung around and with quickening strides started back the way he had come, head up and pointed into the breeze. He stopped and reared high enough to bring his breast into contact with the top rail.

Drury heard the sound from the rail – part creak, part groan. It was a yard whose rails were slender, a yard he had made years earlier and which was more bluff than capable of holding in a horse bent on escaping. If the horse broke out Drury knew he might never see him again; or the horse might put a leg between the rails and perhaps strip a tendon or shin, or worse. He damned the wild or stray mare he knew was out there. He damned all wild horses and stray mares. Wild horses: the inbred mongrels he saw as the scourge of the southern part of the range. He went to the wagon, drew a heavy rope halter from under the seat and hurried to the yard.

Catching hold of the stallion's mane with one hand to support him he managed at first try to slip the halter onto Kilrenny's head. He tightened the throat-lash and tied it. He followed rather than led Kilrenny as the horse again strode along the fence. The corner posts were the strongest of all and when the first one was reached Drury rushed the rope around it and finished the tie with three half-hitches.

He got through the rails and out of the yard and faced the stallion. He knew the mare had scented the stallion and would keep coming. Kilrenny's whinnying would help guide her.

Drury went to the front of the canvas-covered wagon and from a hook above the seat took a lantern and lit it. He went to the back and leaned in, rummaged in the darkness and drew out the Lee Enfield.

He searched again and brought out a small tin with bullets in it. He walked to the fire, looked across it at Kilrenny then turned towards the belt of straggly saplings on the other side of the fire. He judged the distance between the saplings and Kilrenny to be about seventy-five yards.

He got a piece of twine and with the lantern and rifle went to the saplings and chose a spot. He tied the lantern above his head, high enough to allow light onto the rifle sights. He turned down the flame.

The pale firelight barely reached the stallion but it was enough. The mare would go straight to him. The restless blur he could see was Kilrenny. Any similar blur would be the mare. The cold air made his eyes run and he blinked often to clear them.

The mare he wished he did not have to see he now wished would hurry. He never liked shooting horses but in this case what else could he do? Then, there she was. He put his cheek to the rifle butt and sighted. She was coming towards the fire, not towards Kilrenny. He waited for her to turn side on. But she did not turn. Again he blinked to clear his eyes. Suddenly there was a flash, something at the mare's side had glittered for a moment and then was gone. Drury lifted his head and saw the form on the mare's back.

Cradling the rifle in a bent arm and carrying the lantern Drury, his anger increasing, stepped from the trees and strode towards the horse and rider. "What're you here for – the stallion?"

"Yes." The voice was not a man's.

"Why'd you have to come at this hour? Why didn't you come in the daylight?"

"It was daylight when I started."

Drury reached the fire. "Well, it's not daylight now. Who sent you?"

"Nobody. Me."

"'Nobody. Me'. And who's 'nobody, me'?"

"Jem Tyler."

"Have you got five guineas?"

"Yes."

"Dismount and get the saddle off her – smartly. We'll sort out the rest later."

From behind, Drury looked the boy over and judged him to be aged about fourteen. He wondered when the boy's brownish hair last saw a comb. His trousers certainly hadn't been made to fit him and his boots were too big. His coat, without buttons, was old and had been part of a man's dress suit and was held closed by a cord around his waist. As the boy began pulling off the saddle Drury noticed the unlit lantern hanging from a metal D at the back. He guessed the glint he had seen when he was aiming had been a reflection off the glass.

Carrying his lantern Drury led the way. He had the sliprails down by the time the boy caught up.

"Wait here," snapped Drury, "and don't come in till I tell you." He handed Jemmy the lantern.

Standing at the side of the mare Jemmy saw the stallion's nearside foreleg as it positioned itself. He saw the misshapen hoof, the thickened, slightly bowed tendon above the fetlock. "He's got a bad leg. I don't want a foal with weak legs."

"You won't get a foal with weak legs. Now be quiet. I've got enough here to bother with. Don't speak again."

When all was done, Jemmy followed Drury's hand direction and led the mare away.

After replacing the sliprails Drury took the lantern from the boy and pointed towards the fire. Kilrenny was quiet now and Drury's aggravation began to subside. He fell in behind the boy and looked the mare over. 'No quality' was his impression. The coarseness of her head fascinated him; he thought it ass-like but with ears too short for an ass's. She was small and not in the best of condition and had long since seen her best years. Her colour was yellowish-brown, paler around the muzzle. Her legs he approved of: they were fine-boned below the knee and hock and were black. The other black began in her tail, merged at the butt and ran in a streak along her backbone and flooded into the short scraggy mane that fell on both sides of her neck.

Two

At the fire Jemmy turned and faced the man and waited to be spoken to.

"Now what's the story to all this?" asked Drury. "What did you say your name was?"

"Jem Tyler."

"Does anyone call you Jim?"

"No. My born name is James but my real name is Jemmy."

"If you say so. What's the rest? Where've you come from?"

"Jindabilla station."

"Jindabilla? That's near six or seven mile up."

Jemmy put a hand in his coat pocket and took out five sovereigns and a silver crown.

Drury took the money and looked at it in his hand. "I'll write you a receipt before you go. How did you know I was here?"

"A stockman from Jindabilla was riding boundary saw you a few days ago and said you'd be camped here tonight."

"You hungry?"

"A bit."

"You drink tea?"

"Yes."

"When did your mare last drink?"

"She wouldn't drink at the last stream."

"She might drink now. Take that pail and go down to the creek and fetch as much as you can carry. Plait your reins through the spokes of that wheel. She'll stand."

Jemmy began tying the end of the reins to a spoke.

"I said plait them – don't tie them. Leave them loose. If you tie them and she gets a fright and pulls back you could finish up with a broken bridle. It's easier to catch a loose horse if it's got a bridle still on its head and reins dangling instead of lying on the ground. Didn't they teach you that at Jindabilla?"

"No," Jemmy answered nervously. "I knew before. But I forgot."

"For your own sake, best not forget again. Maybe not much here to frighten a horse tonight. But you never know. I saw a horse bolt one night when an owl landed on its back. If you want to tie her up securely, use a rope halter over your bridle. Off you go now and get the water. I'll see if I can find a nosebag for her. Not much in the tuckerbox, for man or beast, till I get to Yarrimba."

Drury watched the boy walking away and thought about the name – Tyler. There was a George Tyler in trouble over an assault in a grog shop on a goldfield between here and the Snowy. Drury knew the man who had been assaulted. There was a warrant out for Tyler's arrest.

Three

Drury held out a sack and Jemmy took it.

"That's the most I can offer you to sit on," said Drury.

Jemmy spread the bag and on the ground about a step from Drury's chair.

The two thick slices of bread Drury had cut he put on a plate and handed to Jemmy.

"There's a fork there," said Drury. "You can do the toasting – that's about all the bread's fit for. But to go with it I've got the best beef dripping you've ever tasted. If Epicurus were around today he'd pay me a fortune for the recipe."

Jemmy ate and enjoyed. He saw Drury looking at the mare and said, "She's half thoroughbred."

The man pursed his lips and drew in breath. "Who was telling you?"

"Mister Archbold, who owns Jindabilla. I bought her from him for a pound."

"A pound? You were robbed. Five to ten shillings at most is what she's worth. You've put a five-guinea-a-service stallion over a five shilling mare. That's not what a wise man usually does."

"But she's a willing goer. She got me here tonight, and she'll get me home."

"Anyway, why does a boy like you want to breed a horse?"

"I'm a station hand now but I want to be a stockman, and I want to have good horses."

"Good horses and good stockmen do go together, I grant you. But why go to all this trouble? There are stallions on Jindabilla that would have been all right."

"The Jindabilla stockmen say there's no stallion there that's as good as any that you'd have."

"I couldn't argue with that – certainly not if I were still taking out

Lanarth." Drury paused. "Your mare's old, you realise? There aren't many more foals left in her; and there's a chance that tonight's mating was not successful. Bear that in mind. You can never ever be sure till a foal actually comes along. If she's not in foal, you don't get a refund. That's policy. But, in your case, if she's not in foal I'll give you a free return service, for her or any other mare you'd like to bring along. That's the best I can do."

Jemmy nodded.

"How long have you been on Jindabilla?"

"Not long. I come from Quartz Creek – mostly."

"I know Quartz Creek. Is Hagley still doing the timber there?"

"Yes. My mother cooks for the men."

"How old are you, son?"

"Thirteen."

"Tell me – I'm curious – how does a boy your age come to have five guineas in his pocket?"

"Gold."

"Gold? What – you hold up coaches or you own a gold mine?"

"No, no, no. I find it. I pan and I get some sometimes."

"Where do you do this, at Quartz Creek?"

"Yes. I get only little bits, the fine stuff. Nobody looks there anymore. They say it's all gone. I find what they missed. The Indian hawker who comes around buys it off me. A tree fell over once and I panned the dirt that came up on the roots and got nearly half a sovereign's-worth. I've had a few strikes like that."

Drury poured the last of the billy tea into his mug. He watched as Jemmy finished the second piece of toast. "Would you like more? I can stand you another slice if you want it. What did you think of the dripping – as good as I said?"

Jemmy nodded then shook his head. "I'm full, thanks."

"How much money have you got left?" asked Drury.

"A shilling."

"Tell you what I'll do with you: I'll refund you five shillings, because of the long way you've had to come. I can't make it any more than that. If it were to get around that I'll take less if children bring the mares, everybody'll be using kids to bring them. You understand what I'm saying?"

Jemmy nodded.

"As for the stallion's leg," Drury went on. "You were concerned about it and I've taken your money so I'm bound to tell you about it. You were smart to spot it. But my advice is: don't let it worry you. He had that leg when I bought him and I know how he got it. There was a time when it wasn't like that. He was a racehorse, but only for a short time. He had his first and last race as a two-year-old. He was trained and raced on iron-hard summertime tracks, the kind that strain and tear the ligaments and tendons of many young racehorses. As they heal, injured tendons or ligaments thicken and never work properly again. Best not to let it happen in the first place, by not asking too much of your youngsters. This young-'ns can take plenty of walking and trotting but galloping is the problem. So, for this colt, his racing career was over soon after it started. That, perhaps, was lucky for me. If he had turned out to be a good racehorse, probably I'd never had been able to buy him as cheaply as I did. He's a four-year-old now and an ideal type for what I want him for. He's not overlong in the legs, which is what you want if you're turning cattle or working amongst timber; he's deep-chested, got a good shoulder, strong hindquarters and not too long in the back, which is what you want in stockhorses; and he's got a good eye, the kind that usually denotes intelligence and good temperament. But don't think I'm against racecourses. They're great proving grounds in some respects. Any horse that can win at Flemington or Randwick is a horse that you could take out of the stable and ride a hundred miles in a day if you had to. Now that's the kind of horse we want in our stockhorses."

"Is his name Kilrenny? Someone said it was."

"Yes, and I bought him in Melbourne."

"I've heard of the big horse market there – Kirk's Bazaar."

"That's where I bought him."

Jemmy stood and drew from inside his coat a folded piece of newspaper. He unfolded it and held it out to Drury. "I brought this to show you."

Drury took the piece of paper and squinted, then put his hand into a side pocket of his shortcoat and brought out his narrow, wirerimmed spectacles and put them on. "What have we got here?" He turned the paper towards the fire and after a few seconds began to smile. Jemmy stepped closer.

"I know this horse," said Drury, still smiling. "And I know who the jockey is. This is Grand Flaneur, and the man on top is Tommy Hales."

Jemmy had watched Drury's eyes and saw they had not gone to the writing at the bottom of the picture. He knew now that this man really was the great man of horses that the Jindabilla stockmen said he was.

Still looking at the picture Drury spoke again. "I was at Flemington the day this colt won his first race. He was a two-year-old then. After that race he showed lameness and, wisely, his owner spelled him and didn't bring him back till he was a three-year-old. That's where he's at now. He hasn't been beaten so far. If he starts in the Victoria Derby, he'll win. Mark me."

Jemmy listened, waiting to hear what Drury would say next.

"I'll tell you a little story that was told to me, and I believe it," said Drury. "The man who told me saw it happen. Flaneur was being walked home from the track one morning, stableboy on his back, other horses all around him. There was a strong wind blowing and a sheet of newspaper came hurtling along, tumbling and going this way and that, blowing under horses' bellies and between their legs. One horse bolted. Other horses were rearing and plunging and cannoning into one another. The paper came to Flaneur and wrapped itself around one of his forelegs. Flaneur lowered his head, looked down at the paper and kept walking, the sheet still clinging to his leg. He knew it couldn't hurt him. Now that's intelligence – good temperament. Oh, to have brains like that in your horses. The paper came off after a while and blew on and frightened horses behind. It hadn't frightened Flaneur. With brains like that, if Flaneur were a human he'd become a statesman, could be a prime minister."

Jemmy waited for more story, but none came.

Drury handed back the cutting. "I'm pleased to have seen that. Thankyou. Tell you what you should do, though: get a piece of thick paper or cardboard and make a cylinder and keep the picture inside it, rolled up. If you keep folding and unfolding it, it'll break up along the creases and fall apart."

Jemmy nodded.

"A man who came to Jindabilla said a big lord in England has offered a high price for Flaneur and Mister Archbold said the government should make a law to keep Flaneur in Australia."

"Why's that?"

"He said Flaneur was too valuable to bloodstock breeding here."

"That's something Archbold would say," scoffed Drury. "Not much of the broad thinker in that man. As a sire, Flaneur couldn't go to a better place than England, for the sake of Australian bloodstock as well as England's. The best of our colonial mares are not as good as the best English mares, and that's a fact. In England, Flaneur would be put to some of the best mares in the country, in the world, and, in time, offspring from those matings would come out here and in that way our bloodstock would be improved. You can tell Archbold I said that – and tell him what a fool I think he is. No, you'd better not. He's the sort of man who might dismiss you for insolence. For the sake of your job, say nothing. But you can quote me to whoever else you'd like."

When Jemmy had put away the picture, Drury spoke again. "I've got to send you on your way soon. It won't be long before the boy over there starts coming back to life. When that happens I want your mare as far away from here as you can get her. You've got a long ride ahead of you anyway, and the sooner you start, the better."

"I know some shortcuts. But I've got to pick my way – the ground's rough. I've got to get off and lead her. That's why I brought the lantern."

"You got enough kerosene?"

"Yes. It's here." He tapped the coat pocket with the bottle of kerosene in it. "I didn't want to leave it in the lantern in case it leaked out onto her skin."

"Good thinking. Raw kerosene can burn skin, even a horse's."

Drury relit his lantern, got a pen and ink and began writing out the receipt, using the floor of the forward end of the wagon as a table. "What name do I put here – James or Jem?"

"Jemmy."

Handing Jemmy the receipt and the five-shilling crown, Drury said, "I've put on there that you're to get a free return service if the mare isn't in foal."

"Thanks."

"I'll help you saddle."

Jemmy did not move and hesitated before he spoke. "Do you need anybody to work for you – a boy?"

Drury did not hesitate. "No."

"I can harness."

"I'm not surprised. But I don't need a boy. You were meaning yourself?"

"Yes."

"You've got work."

"I'd sooner work for you. I could help you a lot."

"I'm sure you could, but I'm not in need of help. Besides, your mother and father would have to be willing."

"My mother would be willing. I could bring in the wagon horses in the morning; and I can find horses in the bush. I can bell and hobble and iron shirts; and I can sole a pair of boots. And I can tell the time and count up to a hundred and say the Ten Commandments."

"That's as sterling an application for a job as I've ever heard, I've got to admit, but I'm not in need of a good man at the moment. I suppose you can read and write too?"

"Not yet. That's next."

"I'm pleased you've got it on your list. It won't do you any harm."

"If you changed your mind one day, would you remember me?"

"I will."

"You said you know Quartz Creek. Do you go near there sometimes?"

"I do, and I'll be near there in about a fortnight."

"I'll be there too. If you change your mind, that's where I'll be."

"What does Jindabilla pay you, just out of interest?"

"Two shillings a week and keep."

"That's about the going rate for a boy. If you worked for me, I'd do you two shillings a week better. I'm only saying 'if'. That's better pay than the bowmen at Agincourt got – sixpence a day and no Sundays off. And working for me wouldn't be as risky as Agincourt. I'm only saying 'if'. If I were to need a boy, I'll think of you. That's the best I can say. Now on your way."

The mare was saddled and Jemmy mounted.

Drury watched the boy go.

Jemmy was about to enter the stand of saplings he had ridden in through when he heard Drury's voice.

"Wait a minute. Come back."

Jemmy turned the mare. Had Mister Drury changed his mind, or made it up, about taking him on? He started back, watching Drury moving towards the rear of the wagon.

Drury pulled out an old felt hat that had had the brim cut off. Holding it close to him so that the biggest of its contents, a shoeing hammer and pincers, wouldn't fall out, he went to the sack Jemmy had been sitting on and emptied onto it everything that was in the hat, including horseshoe nails and a buffer. He turned the hat inside out and belted it against a wagon wheel. Then he turned the hat right side out again and waited for Jemmy.

"Put this on," said Drury, handing Jemmy the hat. "This'll keep most of the chill out. It's better than nothing. After you make your next lucky strike, buy yourself a hat – a first step to keeping yourself alive if you're getting around at night in this country. When you're finished with it, don't throw it away. If we meet again, give it back to me."

Four

Jemmy kept count of the days since he had met the stallion-man and decided at the end of a week that he could wait no longer. If Mr Drury did call at Quartz Creek to take him, he wanted to be there, and he wanted to be there early in case the man came sooner than expected. Though he knew there was more chance Mr Drury would not come, he was determined to cling to all possible hope. Arriving home sooner than he might need to was a worry, for either his father might be there or might turn up. That, too, was a chance he would have to take. If his father discovered him not to be still at Jindabilla there would be trouble. He kept his plan secret for there were men at Jindabilla who were friends of his father's and who might try to stop him if they knew what he was up to. So that nobody would think he had no more than wandered away and got lost and they went looking for him, and maybe caught up with him, in the dark of the morning he crept to the bedside of Charlie Dench and woke him and told the barely conscious youth that he was going and asked him to milk the cow.

A sack held all his belongings and he was easily able to hold it in front of him across the mare's withers. He rode bareback. Every saddle he had ever used was borrowed.

The shortest distance from Jindabilla homestead to Quartz Creek was thirty miles he had once heard his father say. He did not want to push the mare to try to do the trip in one day, seeing he would have to walk her all the way. He decided he would go the longer way and ask Ellerslie station to put him up overnight. He had never been to Ellerslie but knew the direction it lay in. When he came upon good grass he let the mare graze a while but could not stay long for he needed daylight to find the Ellerslie homestead. In the late afternoon he saw the homestead, about a mile away. A haze was beginning to settle around him. He thanked his luck and Jesus and God.

He rode towards the out-buildings and yards and when got to them rode towards a man he saw standing and looking in his direction.

"Is this Ellerslie?" asked Jemmy.

"It is," replied the whiskery-faced Joe Pollard, head stockman.

"I'm passing through. Could you put me up somewhere for the night, and let me put my horse in a paddock?"

"That we could do," said Joe. "Where are you headed?"

"Quartz Creek."

Coming back from putting the mare in a paddock Jemmy and Joe introduced themselves. Joe picked up the sack Jemmy had thrown down and slung it over his shoulder.

"How long you been on the track?" asked Joe as they walked.

"Since this morning."

No sooner had Jemmy spoken than he halted and bent forward in pain.

Fearing the boy was about to fall, Joe dropped the sack and swept Jemmy up in his arms and walked quickly.

"I can walk, I can walk," insisted Jemmy. "It's gone now."

Joe put him down. "When did you eat last?"

"Last night."

"You've got an empty-belly pain. We can soon fix that."

Joe led the way into the cookhouse.

"Got a traveller here with empty-belly pains," said Joe to a big bald man wearing a grey, sleeveless flannel undershirt. "Hasn't eaten all day."

"Sit down, son" said the cook. "You're not at Death's doors. All you got is collapsed intestines. We'll get em filled out in a minute." He looked at Joe. "Butter some bread for him, Joe. The mutton's ready enough on the outside."

Joe began cutting one of the fresh loaves on the table and the cook went to the oven and started slicing pieces off the outside of one of the legs of roasting mutton.

"You know where the butter is," said the cook to Joe.

Jemmy ate and the men watched him.

"Eat as much as you like," said the cook. "But leave some space – dinner's only an hour away. We eat well here. By the time you're ready for the blankets you'll be as full as a tick."

At dinner he met the rest of the station staff, stockmen and station hands, eight in all. He was given a bed in the main hut. The bed was like the others, wooden triangles for ends with sacks lashed to the outside poles and straw-filled hessian mattresses with a blanket on top. He slept in his clothes and pulled over him the one blanket he owned. Over the blanket he let a man put a kangaroo-skin rug.

In the morning after breakfast the cook gave him two thick mutton sandwiches wrapped in newspaper. Joe rode with him to the side of a hill and pointed out the start of a track that Joe said should see him close to Quartz Creek by near the end of the day. Once he got near Quartz Creek he believed he would be able to find his way even if darkness did catch him.

"Make sure you stop now and again and graze your mare," were Joe's last words. "Empty horses can get stomach cramps too."

Five

Though he could not see the sun Jemmy knew it was ahead of him and high enough to ensure a few more hours of daylight. The tallness of the timber around him was comforting. He was now in territory he could deal with. A wide stump, the top of which had long been cut down, was reassuring. He was further relieved when he came across a track that he could tell a snigged log had been dragged along not many days ago. Downhill from now on and he must come to the creek, and the mill, or the main track to it.

The Quartz Creek rush of '65 in the Warooka hills southeast of Albury was ended within three years. The alluvial deposits were the first to peter out. The deep leads lasted longer. The last mine to close was Pilcher's Reef. So profitable had it been and so certain were the owners that the best gold had not yet been reached that they built a brick house for the manager. But all the gold thought to be in the mine was never found and the mine closed. The house was now owned by Murdock Hagley who cut and milled timber and sent it by bullock wagon to Albury and Wodonga. Jemmy's father once worked at the mill but had left. Mrs Tyler had stayed. She assisted Mrs Hagley in the house and cooked for the mill's six single men.

Jemmy came to where he could see below the orange-brick house and the shingled-covered mill and huts and log stacks. He rode closer, swung away at one point and stopped in the bush above his mother's hut, which she shared with her three daughters who were all younger than Jemmy. He threw down his sack, dismounted and tied the end of the reins to a thin sappy branch. He knew the mare was too tired to soon become anxious at finding herself alone in a strange place. He put down his sack beside her and for good measure took off his coat, heavy with his scent, and threw it over the same branch as she was tethered to. Carefully he made his way towards the hut.

Reaching the hut he crept to a window and peeked in. He could not see his father. He could hear young girls playing, squealing, and young boys yelling. A game was going on. Though his father was not in the hut he might be nearby, perhaps with some of the mill hands, who by now might have knocked off. Cautiously he made his way towards where he could hear the squealing and yelling and saw his sisters and other children, chasing one another. His eldest sister, Annie, saw him and ran to him. All the other children began to follow.

Annie, aged twelve and in muddied laced-up boots, was smiling as she ran. "How long are you back for?" she called before reaching him.

He put a finger to his lips. When Annie stopped he asked, "Is Dad here?"

"No."

"Has he been here?"

"No."

Soon other children, eight of them, were surrounding him.

"Where's Mum?" Jemmy asked Annie.

"Up at the house," said Annie.

"See you after," he said to Annie. Backing away he turned to the others and lifted his hand in a gesture of hello and 'see you later'.

At the knock Margaret Tyler went to the backdoor and opened it.

Jemmy smiled and was silent.

Margaret's mouth opened as if to let out a gasp, but no sound came. Then sound came, a long, loud sigh. She threw her arms around her son and held him. She kissed the top of his head. When she released him she left her hands resting on his shoulders and took a step backwards. After a short silence and without taking her eyes off him she took him by the hand and led him into the kitchen and closed the door. Margaret was small and of neat build with long dark hair fastened at the back. She had a pretty and pleasant face and was aged in her early thirties.

"Where've you come from – Jindabilla?" Margaret asked.

"Yes. Annie said Dad's not here. He isn't, is he?"

"No. I haven't seen him in months. Have you?"

"No."

"He's in trouble again – do you know?"

"Yes."

"The police came here."

"I know the trouble. I was with him."

"Don't tell me any more about that, now."

"I don't know where he is, either. He took me back to Jindabilla and told me to stay there till he came for me. I've left Jindabilla, and if he knows …"

"You don't have a job there any more?"

"No. That's why I've come back – to ask you about another job – a better one – and I want to take it. But I mightn't get it. The man mightn't come. But he might. If he doesn't come, I'll go back to Jindabilla and say I'm sorry."

"You went without speaking to anybody – to Mister Archbold?"

Jemmy nodded.

"He mightn't take you back."

"I know."

Margaret became silent.

Jemmy did not wait for her to ask about the other job. He pulled out a chair at the table and sat. His mother seated herself opposite, and listened. When she thought he had finished she sighed.

"You know this man might not come?"

Jemmy nodded. "But he might."

"Don't build your hopes up, my darling. From what you've told me, the chance he'll come is only slight."

"But he gave me the hat, and said not to throw it away."

Margaret could find no more to say on the matter. "We'll see," she said with another sigh. Then she said, "I'll have to go soon and see to the men's dinner. But we can all eat up here tonight, and you can sleep up here too – it'll be alright. The hut's getting too small for us all. The girls are growing. The Hagleys are away for a week." She looked at his shirt and trouser braces. "Where's the coat Burt Bray gave you – you've still got it?"

"Yes. It's with the mare. And I'd better go and get her."

They got up together and outside went separate ways.

Jemmy found the mare near where he had left her. She had pulled free of the bough and was grazing. He caught her, put on his coat and shouldered the sack and led the mare away. He knew a spot where there might be good grass, if the teamster's bullocks had not been on it lately. He was sure Burt Bray, the mill foreman, would lend him a long rope.

That night they ate in the kitchen of the house. The kitchen was bigger than the whole of their hut, and warmer, and Jemmy's sisters enjoyed the evenings there when the Hagleys were away. Though there was no lack of talk between Jemmy and his mother, Margaret purposely did not tell her son that even if the stallion-man did come, if she was not favourably impressed by the man she would not consent to Jemmy going with him. Also she did not again speak of how remote she thought was the chance that the man would come.

There was another contingency she chose not to speak of, one which Jemmy too was aware of but did not bring up: George's anger if he learned Jemmy had defied instructions and left Jindabilla. It was Margaret's hope that the stallion-man episode would soon come to an end and Jemmy would return to Jindabilla and ask to be reinstated, even if he had to beg. At Jindabilla her son would be safer than he might be in many another place. Likely he would be better off there than wherever his father happened to be. The matter allowed Margaret another thought. If this Mister Drury was a good man, if she could feel sure that he was, with him might be a better place for Jemmy than with either his father or back at Jindabilla.

Six

The two weeks since Jemmy had seen the stallion-man ended. July was coming to a close. Eight more days and the month would be August. Mr Drury had not given an exact day that he would come, if really he decided he would come; but if he was going to come he could be a few days late. He might have struck a patch of bad track or road or a wagon horse might have gone lame or he might have found more work for Kilrenny than he had expected.

Another week passed and Drury had not appeared.

Jemmy woke in the dawn and lay wondering if the stallion-man too might be awake, maybe harnessing up, maybe getting ready to come to Quartz Creek. That a week more than a fortnight had gone by was not a good sign, Jemmy admitted to himself. If after another week Mr Drury had not come he would know the man was not going to come. He watched his mother moving about the hut and when she left to go and make breakfast for the men he got up and dressed. Margaret had not started out so early this morning for it was Sunday and the mill was not working. As his sisters would when they got up, he dipped from the pot of oatmeal his mother had set to cook at the back of the stove. After eating, he went out and took the mare to water. She not always drank of a morning.

Near ten o'clock he got his pan and went to the mill to borrow a mattock. He carried in his pocket the flattish, white dentifrice jar with black writing on it and which was as smooth and seamless inside as it was outside and had no cracks that might trap specks of gold. As he entered the long wooden-roofed mill he heard the sound of Silas Linger's file sliding over the teeth of the huge circular blade at the far end. He walked towards the sound, passing the long leather belt, sagged and at rest, leading from the steam engine to where Silas was working. Always he had liked being there when the machinery was started up, seeing and hearing the noise of it all, the grunting of the engine, so slow at first, and the wobbling, flapping and smacking of the top of the belt as it at first hit the underneath part. A few times Mr Hagley had let him put his hand on the lever as it was pushed to switch the belt across to the driving wheel.

He chatted a few minutes with Silas and left with the mattock.

Where the bush allowed, Annie ran. She knew her brother had gone to the creek and when she came to a high bank above the stream she stopped. She looked up and down but could not see him. She called. "Jemmy, the man's coming." Again she looked up and down and did not see him. She called again. Then she saw him, on the other side, running.

Seven

Bringing the horses to a halt at the end of the wheel-rutted roadway Drury looked about the clearing, broad enough to bring around the biggest team of bullocks. He saw the mill and logs and sawn timber and huts and the orange-coloured brick house. He drove on.

He had not seen where they had come from but to the left and right and front of him children, seeming excited and welcoming, began surging towards him. He estimated there to be near a dozen. He halted again and waited. One runner, a boy who certainly would reach him before anybody else, he believed he recognised.

Puffing, beaming, Jemmy looked up at Drury.

"Mister Tyler, I presume," said Drury. "I've come for my hat."

"For me, too, I hope."

"Yes, for you too, if you're still available."

"I am."

"And where might I find your mother?"

Jemmy pointed to the house.

From his seat and over the top of the gathering, some members of which were at the horses' heads patting them, Drury looked towards the house. He saw a woman standing before the open front door. He lifted a hand. Mrs Tyler waved back.

Drury climbed down, fixed the wheels and reins and let Jemmy and Annie lead him away. Some of the other children followed.

"You can come into the kitchen," said Annie before they reached the house. "Mister and Missus Hagley are still away. They might be back tomorrow."

"Where's Kilrenny?" asked Jemmy.

"He's at Burrumbooka station, waiting for us. Another week's work there should finish us up. Someone else is handling him while I'm away. It's been two days to here and it'll be two days back. Your mare, what's become of her? Have you been able to put her somewhere?"

"No," admitted Jemmy. "I could leave her here if I have to. But I don't want to. If she can't come with us then she'll have to stay. Annie will look after her. This is Annie. She's my sister."

Annie and Drury smiled at each other.

"We can leave her at Burrumbooka," said Drury. "Would that suit you?"

"Yes."

As the visitor and the children who chose to escort him neared the house Margaret went back to the door and closed it and walked out to meet the man she assumed was Mr Drury. After the formalities Drury was steered to the back of the house and into the kitchen.

By slightly more than the hour that Drury and Jemmy's mother spent talking Margaret had made up her mind. She was approving of Jemmy going with the man. They talked for not much longer when Drury announced that he should be on his way, that he wanted to reach in daylight the site he had camped at last night. The final words on Jemmy came quickly and the matter was settled.

Most of the children who had welcomed the visitor were now reassembled for the farewell. Jemmy's sack was stowed and Jemmy's appearance with the mare was awaited. They watched Jemmy coming, leading the mare by a short piece of rope tied around her neck.

"If it wouldn't be too much trouble, Mister Drury," said Margaret, "would you make him wash his hands and comb his hair before he comes to the table, even if only in the evenings?"

"That would be no trouble. No heath-dwellers allowed at my table."

"Could I ask another favour?" said Margaret. "Would you hold his wages till he's got enough to buy some new clothes – good, hardwearing stuff? He's badly in need of more clothes."

"That, too, won't be a problem. In fact, we might be able to attend to that fairly quickly. He's a member of the firm now and entitled to a refund on the money paid for the stallion. So he's already got five pounds in the bank."

Margaret's expression satisfied all Drury's expectations of thanks.

"I'd like to ask one other favour," she said reluctantly. "Take the cost for it out of his money. Would you make him take two teaspoonsful of cod-liver oil once a week?" She put her hand to her chest. "It's supposed to be good for keeping away the bad one – consumption. You can get it from the Indian hawkers."

“I’ll see to it.”

“Thankyou.”

Before Jemmy reached them Drury pulled from the back of the wagon a cotton-rope halter. He looked at the mare as she came up and thought no better of her than he had the night he had first seen her. He was an admirer of the fine-sculpted head of thoroughbreds and Arabian horses. He doubted he had seen a coarser or uglier head than this mare’s. For the sake of present company he kept his thoughts to himself. When she reached him he began putting the halter on the mare. “For now, Blink Bonny, this can be your tiara, not that nasty old piece of tow.”

As he turned away from securing the rope lead to the rear of the wagon Drury glanced at the mare’s black hooves. He bent and lifted the leg nearest him and inspected the underneath of the hoof. “When was the last time she had shoes on?”

“I don’t know. Not since she’s been mine.”

Drury dropped the hoof but kept looking at it. “Interesting. Very interesting. You walked her here from Jindabilla?”

“Yes.”

“It’s hard to believe, but there’s the proof.” He glanced at the other hooves. “Great hooves.”

Unhurrying, Drury let the farewelling take its course and at the end, reins in hand, climbed into the driver’s seat. “Buda and Pest – Albury and Wodonga – here we come.”

Reaching where the track was about to turn Drury spoke. “Are you a gambling man?”

“Oh, no,” said Jemmy, certain his answer was what his new employer wanted to hear.

“Pity. If you were, I’d have bet you a penny to nothing that if you looked back you’d see your mother standing where we left her, and looking this way. Go on, take a look.”

With one hand Jemmy gripped part of the frame holding up the cover over the wagon and leaned out.

“Yes, she is.”

“Well, give her a wave – a good one. Better still, get out and do it.”

Drury stopped the horses.

Jemmy got out and waved.

Margaret began waving.

When his mother stopped, Jemmy stopped.

Jemmy turned, gave a last wave and climbed back onto the seat, puzzled at how Mr Drury knew his mother would still be standing there.

Eight

With near half a mile behind them nothing so far said could have passed as conversation. Jemmy was nervous, excited and happy, hardly able to believe that he was here, sitting beside Mr Drury. He knew of the towns of Albury and Wodonga and that a bridge across the river led from one place to the other. He gathered that on the way there would be stations and other places they would call at, and there would be many people waiting to bring their best mares to Kilrenny.

"Swagman ahead," muttered Drury.

Jemmy saw the figure, about a hundred yards away. He could see the bulges that were part of the man's swag and could see the man had a beard. When he last saw his father he did not have a beard. But his father might have a beard now. Speaking as he moved, Jemmy turned and climbed over the backrest and into the covered part of the wagon. "I just want to look in my bag for something," he said. From the back he called, "I've got to go into the bushes for a wee. Don't stop. I'll catch up." He slid over the backboard and onto the road.

Keeping pace with the wagon Jemmy remained behind it. Then he took a chance and darted into the bush. He went deeper and deeper then turned, caught glimpses of the wagon and kept level with it. He made no sound.

Drury and the swagman stopped and briefly chatted before going their respective ways. From his accent Drury thought the man a German.

The boy should have been back by now, thought Drury. He stopped and looked about him. Then he saw Jemmy, waiting on the side of the road ahead, almost as far away as the swagman had been when they first saw him.

Jemmy waited for the wagon and, after looking to see if the man walking was turning around, hopped on without Drury needing to stop.

"What was all this about?" asked Drury, amused. "Was that fellow one of your creditors? You were avoiding him, I'd say."

Jemmy did not answer, and did not know what a creditor was.

In the late afternoon they reached the spot Drury had wanted to be at before dark.

The horse work came first – the watering at the creek, the putting on of the nosebags and afterwards the hobbling and belling. Next would come the fire making. Wood gathering was a duty Drury intended quickly educating the boy to. He would teach him to always watch for kindling and dry, short pieces of wood as they drove. There was a permanent place in the wagon for the keeping of dry wood. If the boy could handle the wood job well, that would say a lot. For dinner tonight there was fresh beef, potatoes and cheese.

They drank tea after dinner. Beside the fire Drury sat on his chair. Jemmy sat cross-legged on the sack he had once before sat on. With his tea Jemmy ate a piece of one of his favourite dishes, bread with sweet condensed milk on it.

"I've been thinking," said Drury. "Seeing we're going to be living so closely together, I think your always calling me 'Mister' will get on my nerves. You have my permission to call me Brian. Think you can handle that?"

"Yes. But sometimes I might forget."

"It might take some getting used to, but you'll make it, I'm sure."

"Will I call you Mister if somebody's around?"

"No. Keep it the same all the time."

They were still sipping tea when Jemmy spoke next.

"Back at the Creek, why did you call my mare Blink Bonny?"

"Oh, that was just a, a sort of salute, like when you meet somebody for the first time and you say 'pleased to meet you'. Later you might find that you're not so pleased to have met them, but till you know the worst, you always start out by being courteous. Does she have another name?"

"No. But that could be her name. I don't mind. What does the name mean?"

"Ah, the great Blink Bonny, the most famous mare in English turf history. She was only a little thing, probably not much bigger than your mare. She won the English Derby and broke the record. Not many fillies win the Derby. Mostly at three years of age colts are better developed and race better than fillies, but she beat them. A few days afterwards she came out and won the Oaks. She became the mother of a colt named Blair Athol and he, too, won the Derby. There are men in England who still say that

Blair Athol was the greatest racehorse ever bred. Later he was sold to a stud and had to be walked there from miles away. All along the roadsides people waited and cheered him. There might never be another horse the equal of him."

"How do you know about horses in England and what the men there say?"

"I read."

Nine

The day had come when after weeks on the road and visiting stations they picked up the main road leading into Wodonga. The road now behind them, if they had turned that way, led to Melbourne. The road in front of them, if they kept to it, would take them to Sydney, across the Murray. Cottages on small acreages, out-buildings and huts, were becoming more frequent.

The biggest building to be seen ahead was the Colonial Hotel, two storied and made of timber, and when the track leading in to it came up Brian drew on one rein. Bypassing the front entrance he drove into the muddied yard at the back, where there were stables and a bath-house.

"Ho there, Brian," called a man from a doorway that led into the hotel's kitchen. He was the stableman and keeper of the bath-house.

"Ho there to you, Rupert," replied Brian, passing the reins to Jemmy.

"Heard you were on the way – heard a week ago," said Rupert, walking towards the new arrivals.

"You're intelligence wasn't wrong. Here we are. You're well, I hope?" said Brian not yet attempting to climb down.

"I am indeed. What's your pleasure today – the usual?"

"Yes, a feed for the horses, plus one for each of us, and a bath."

"You've got an offsider, I see."

"Yes. This is Jem Tyler."

Rupert gave Jemmy a salute and Jemmy returned it.

"What's the latest racing news from the cities?" asked Brian. "What's the latest on Grand Flaneur?"

"He won the Sydney Derby – if you haven't heard – then he come'd out and won the Mare's Produce Stakes. The papers say he'll come south for the Victoria Derby or Melbourne Cup, or both."

"Not both, I hope – not for a three-year-old."

Brian turned to Jemmy. They grinned, delighted at the news of Grand

Flaneur's victories, and the vindication of Brian's predictions. For weeks they had found talk of Grand Flaneur everywhere they called at but till now nothing from a source likely to be as reliable as Rupert. Wodonga was on the telegraph.

They bathed, fed themselves and the horses and were on the road again within two hours.

The next stop was in the township, at barber Flinn's. This was the first time a barber had cut Jemmy's hair. He liked what he saw in the big mirror above the bench in front of him. In the mirror he watched as Flinn's assistant combed then trimmed Brian's beard. Afterwards they went to the shop of John Nobelius. Brian addressed the draper as "Nobbie". When they left, Jemmy was the owner of more new clothes than he had ever had in his life. There were clothes for best and clothes for work, and two pairs of boots – one for best, one for work.

Then they crossed the river and were in the municipality of Albury.

Fry's livery stable and the Caledonian Hotel, on opposite sides of the street to each other, were where they next stopped. Fry's was where the horses would be kept, the Caledonian was where Brian and Jemmy would stay.

After a lot of hearty talk at Fry's they crossed the street and walked into the bar-room of the Caledonian and after a lot more hearty talk, between Brian, the proprietors, Gordon Ettershank and his wife, and the one barman on duty, the two set off on foot for the office of the *Border Post* where Brian lodged an advertisement telling that the thoroughbred stallion Kilrenny was available for service at Fry's stable.

On the way back they called on the saddler in Kiewa Street. The saddler did not hesitate in saying he would take all five stockwhips Brian had made and that he should drop them in as soon as he cared to.

Back at the Caledonian again, Brian led the way to the bar and ordered a pot of beer for himself and a cordial for Jemmy. Ettershank, a Scott, served them. Jemmy listened when Brian asked about the tariff required for "the lad here" seeing they were going to share a room and that Jemmy wouldn't eat as much as an adult. A deal was soon done.

They were still at the bar when Angus, Ettershank's second son, came up at the other side of the counter and waited for Jemmy to drain his glass. They looked at each other but did not speak. Angus had hair that was so dark-red that if you were not standing close to him you might think it was black. He took the glass when Jemmy emptied it, left and went to the bench along a wall in the larger part of the room, collected the few empty glasses there and carried them away to be washed. The chore completed, he came back to Jemmy and said across the counter, "How old are you?"

"Thirteen and a half, nearly. How old are you?"

"I'll be that soon."

Ettershank and Brian regarded the exchange.

"The young ones always introduce themselves," observed Ettershank. "There's never a need for us to bother."

Within the week, Jemmy had more new clothes. A day when the rain seemed as if it would never stop he walked with Brian out into the street. Brian was hatted and wearing his long coat made of oiled linen. Jemmy had a sack across his shoulders and another over his head. They went to Agnew's general store. When they left Jemmy walked with a stride that matched Brian's. The rustling and crackling made by the new oilskin coat seemed to Jemmy like music. The hem of the coat almost covered his boots and the sleeves were rolled back near half the length of his forearm. On his head was an oilskin hat of a kind he had never seen before and which Brian said was called a sou'wester and that seamen wore them. Over each arm he carried a wet sack.

"All my five pounds must be gone now," said Jemmy.

"When it is, I'll tell you."

A day came when in the afternoon Brian appeared at the stable dressed in his dark grey suit and black bowler hat. He was off to visit the widow of an old friend, he told Jemmy, and also told him where he could be found if anybody came for Kilrenny.

A mare for Kilrenny did come and Jemmy set out at a jog. He turned corners and came to a wooden cottage with the picket fence that he thought was the one. He had no sooner stopped when he saw coming towards him in the street a charge of about a dozen white geese, necks outstretched and wings extended, hissing as they ran. He hastened backwards, but the geese kept coming. He did not slow in his retreat till he had opened up more than a few yards distance between himself and them.

The birds stopped, remonstrated a while longer then began wandering back the way they had come, around the corner.

Cautiously Jemmy made his way back to the cottage, stood at the gate and called out Brian's name, at the same time watching for the geese. He did not want to go to the door and knock, in case the geese came again and this time caught him behind the fence. He had never had geese accost him before and he was not sure how best to handle these. He watched the front door of the cottage. Nobody came. He called again and nobody came and he wondered if he might have the wrong house. He decided that the back of the house was where he ought to try next. If the geese were far enough down the road he would make a run for the back, call out, then run for the front if he saw the geese returning. He looked around the corner. The geese were far enough away to persuade him to put his plan into action. He ran to the fence at the back of the cottage, called out and looked to see the reaction of the geese. The geese started on their way, half running, half flying. He now thought the fence might be a help to him and he vaulted it and hurried to the backdoor and knocked and called Brian's name. Brian opened the door. The geese were now at the fence. Without Jemmy telling him, Brian knew he was wanted, also he noted the problem of the geese.

"Go and wait for me at the front gate," said Brian.

Brian went back into the house, said a hurried goodbye to the lady and within the minute was standing with Jemmy looking over the gate at the geese. The geese were looking at them and still hissing and bobbing their outstretched heads.

"How did you get past them when you came?" asked Jemmy.

"They weren't here then. What we've got to do is outsmart them. Think you can outrun them for half a minute?"

"I'll try."

"Here's what we do. You go over the side fence there, draw them away and keep running down the street and let them nearly catch up to you, then you wheel around and head back up to here – fast. By then I ought to be far enough up this street for them not to want to bother with me. Then you run your hardest and catch up with me. When they think they've driven us off, they'll stop. I know all about geese – they chased me more than once when I was your age."

Jemmy went over the side fence and began his run, geese following.

Brian opened the gate and hurried off.

At what he thought was the right moment Jemmy came around in an arc and ran his fastest. The geese adjusted and kept after him. Jemmy made the next turn and saw Brian and ran towards him.

Brian stopped and looked back. "They've stopped. You can slow down. We've beaten them."

But Jemmy didn't stop, not till he reached Brian. He looked behind and saw the geese had desisted. He grinned at Brian and they walked on.

"We handled that well between us, didn't we?" observed Brian. "I took care of the strategy and you supplied the action. We were a good team."

Jemmy grinned again. "I reckon we were."

Ten

The month was still October and Jemmy was enjoying Albury and was pleased the stay was to last into November, till after the running of the Melbourne Cup. The job at present left him with so much time to himself. There was no wood to gather, no fires to light, no horses to bell and hobble and go looking for in the dark and cold of the morning, no harnessing and unharnessing and no cooking to help with. The wagon horses were now out on grass and needed no caring for, though their paddock was not so far away that a horse could not be soon fetched if needed for the buggy to take Brian somewhere. Mostly all he had to do was muck out Kilrenny's loose-box, groom him and three times a day take to him the feeds Brian prepared. Brian exercised him every day, either by riding him or lunging him on a long rein in the big yard at the back of the stable. The easier life off the road and the better-quality fodder was agreeing with Kilrenny, and Brian, sometimes after running a hand over the horse's rump, would say that he could see the horse's condition improving every day. The better diet and warm stable at night was hastening the shedding of the stallion's winter coat, giving way to a shorter, shinier coat for the coming summer.

Often Brian was not present when potential clients came to view the stallion and Jemmy would officiate, taking off the rug and leading Kilrenny about and letting the men see how well the horse walked and remarking on the fine head and intelligent eye, as he had heard Brian say to other people. One man said he was impressed that the stallion could be handled so easily by so young a boy. "That shows his good temperament," Jemmy put in. He liked Edgar Fry and sometimes helped with the harnessing or saddling of horses that went out on hire. There was a regular coterie of men, not always the same ones every day, that often drifted in and talked with Mr Fry and the stable hands and imparted news and told stories that everybody would laugh at. Boys around his own age came in at times and wanted to be given tasks to do with horses and for no pay. Mr Fry always obliged.

Most of the work he had to do with Kilrenny was during the morning, including Saturdays and Sundays. Between noon and four o'clock he had little to do, and a full afternoon off was never difficult to arrange. One Saturday afternoon a family named Henderson, friends of the Ettershanks, took him and Angus to a football match at Wodonga. Another day he went to a tannery where Brian bought kangaroo hides for his plaiting work. One day they went to the races and the winner of the main event, the mile-and-a-half handicap, was won by a horse sired by Lanarth. Brian was so elated that he offered the winner's owner a free service for one of any two mares the man cared to bring to Kilrenny.

Often in the afternoons when he was not needed at the stable till four o'clock he would go to the school that Angus attended and wait and walk home with him and some of the other boys. These walks home could be rowdy affairs with plenty of skylarking and wrestling and teasing of girls if any happened to be close by. The only girl he had so far learned the first name of was Heather. He knew her name because once Angus had called out to her, "How's the weather – Heather?" She turned and replied, "Good for fishing – flat-head." The other boys laughed and Angus chased one, caught him and put a headlock on him and dragged him to the ground. But the boy got away and ran off, still laughing, and Angus threatened to 'get him tomorrow'.

Angus loved playing cricket and football. He despaired of ever convincing Jemmy to bowl, not throw, a cricket ball. They used a wooden box as a wicket and played in the street outside the hotel. Jemmy reckoned that bowling overarm was stupid; throwing was better. Furious, Angus yelled one day, "Alright. Do what you like. Shoot it out your bum if you want to, but you won't get past my bat."

Jemmy noticed that though Brian never went to church he went to other meetings that church people went to. They were a certain kind church of people, called Methodists, he learned. One night Jemmy and Angus sneaked to the doorway of a hall that a meeting was being held in and listened. There was a man on the platform talking, and the talk did not seem to be about God and nobody was praying.

Sometimes he had to go to the hotel to fetch Brian when he was wanted at the stable. If Brian was not in the bar-room drinking and talking he might be found in the parlour, reading, or upstairs out on the balcony, reading. Sometimes Jemmy found him in a chair, dozing, a book or collapsed newspaper in his lap.

Brian read all the newspapers that came his way, the local weeklies and monthlies, journals and magazines, many of which had come from

Melbourne and Sydney; and there were some that came from England. The stacks of books, journals and newspapers in their room never stopped growing. Some were for taking back to Foxhow, Brian said.

Fascinated, Jemmy would watch Brian's face as he read, see the occasional smile or the eyes narrowing or widening. Jemmy had learned that he should not interrupt at these times; a question asked was usually met with silence or a frown or both. Once, so intrigued was he at Brian's concentration he asked what the writing said. "I'll tell you when I'm finished," answered Brian without looking up. Jemmy never did learn what that writing said. But there was news that, after it was read, Brian never failed to pass on: it was news about Grand Flaneur or the latest successes of champion jockey Tom Hales.

What Jemmy had had in mind to do for some weeks he now set himself to do as soon as he thought the moment was a good one. What he had learned about Brian was that the old man took more kindly to requests or was less dismissive of him when not overly occupied with matters that for one reason or another he was giving more than a little bit of time or thought to. Jemmy had the piece of paper ready in his pocket. One day as he was crossing the street he saw Brian above, sitting on the balcony and not reading. He hurried up the stairs and out onto the balcony.

"Everything alright over the road?" asked Brian as a greeting.

"Yes."

Jemmy saw the folded newspaper on the floor beside Brian's chair.

"Any good news today?" asked Jemmy.

"Ordinary stuff – nothing much." Brian took off his glasses. He had been snoozing and had forgotten them.

"Could you still read if you broke your glasses, or if you lost them?"

"Only the big print. But in case that happens I have a spare pair."

"If you broke them too, what would you do?"

"Wait till I could buy a new pair."

"You might have to wait a long time, if you were on the road, say. If I could read, I could read to you."

"Yes, that's right, you could."

"In case you break your glasses, why don't you teach me to read?"

Brian hesitated. He answered carefully. "That's a task I don't think I'd be up to."

"I'm a good learner."

"I know you are. But being able to read and being able to teach somebody to read are two different things."

Jemmy put a hand into a trouser pocket, took out a small piece of paper, unfolded it and held it out to Brian. Brian took the paper. On it he saw in childish pencilled writing the words Jem Tyler. The words had been copied from a piece of paper his mother had once given him.

"I wrote that."

"Did you?" Brian studied the writing. "That's very good. In the hands of the right person, a school teacher, I'm sure you'd soon learn to read and write. I couldn't teach you, though. Can you write other words besides these?"

"No. But I bet I can write any words you show me."

"I'm sure you can. But that's not the way it works. You've got to learn about sounds at the same time. There are sounds that go with letters, or groups of letters, and you have to learn about those sounds."

"What have sounds got to do with it? Nobody talks while he reads or writes, unless he wants to."

"You do have to understand the sounds, take it from me." Brian raised the piece of paper and studied it again. "Let's take what you've got here." He handed the paper to Jemmy. "How many sounds would you say are there?"

"Two: 'Jem' and 'Tyler.'"

Brian shook his head. "My count is seven."

Unbelieving, Jemmy took back the piece of paper and stared at Brian. "Just a word a day – one word – or every two days?"

"I told you, it doesn't work like that. You have to have special charts. If we'd been better prepared, we might have been able to squeeze in a month or so of schooling for you while we're here. But there's no time now."

Jemmy would not believe that Brian could not teach him to read. That his name had seven sounds in it he would not believe. He was sure there was a reason Brian would not teach him. Maybe the reason was that it was just not a good day to have asked. Maybe a better time would come. He would wait.

Eleven

The Victoria Derby run at Flemington had been won, but nobody in Albury yet knew the name of the winner. Albury was on the telegraph but there was never any telling how long the delays might last at the relay stations.

That evening in the bar-room of the Caledonian there were many more patrons than usual. This was always the case on Derby night. The Caledonian was one of the places in Albury that news of the race arrived first. Next Tuesday evening, after the running of the Cup, the crowd would be bigger than tonight's.

At the bar and in a louder voice than his usual, Brian declared, for the benefit of anybody able to hear him above the hubbub, "If Grand Flaneur started, he won."

Nobody challenged.

"I'll put it another way," said Brian, spoiling for discussion. "The only way he could not have won was for him to have not started, or if he fell over or by other intervention by the Lord himself, whom I have no reason to believe is a racing man."

"Get out with you," scoffed a man on the other side of the bar.

Looking directly at the man, Brian said, "I tell you, if he started and didn't fall, he won."

"That's one way you could put it," said another man, "I'll put it another way. You never know what can go wrong in a race. If Flaneur had bad luck in running, the colt from St Albans – Progress – could have come in first."

Brian shook his head and wagged a finger. "Bad luck aside, Progress could never beat Flaneur."

"If Flaneur won, what price him for the Melbourne Cup?" said the other man.

"If Flaneur raced today, he won't start in the Cup," asserted Brian. "Owner Long isn't that stupid. Long's got a head on his shoulders. If Flaneur started in the Derby, Long wouldn't race him, a three-yearold, three days later, and over the hardest two-miles any horse can be made to run. Long's a smart man. He'll save him, as a four-year-old, for next year's Cup."

"He's accepted for the Cup," said the man.

"That would be to baffle the bookmakers," responded Brian. He paused and finished the last of his whisky. "Long's a big bettor. If Flaneur accepted, he'll be scratched. You'll see."

"But there have been three-year-olds win the Derby and Cup double," said a man standing beside Brian and who had been listening.

"I know, I know," conceded Brian. "But what happened to them afterwards? Most of them hardly ever won another race; they were ruined: raced too hard too young, raced to death, burnt out. Long's got his head screwed on the right way."

Behind the bar Gordon Ettershank looked up at the clock. The time was nearly half-past seven. He glanced about, looking for Angus. Angus, on duty, was not in the room and Gordon guessed the boy was outside. He took a small pad from beside the glasses on the shelf above his head, tore off a page, picked up a pencil and went to the doorway. He saw his son and Jemmy talking to two boys on the verandah.

"Go to the *Border* office and see if the Derby result has come in," instructed Gordon. "It ought to be in by now. Whoever you see, ask him to write it down. Don't you write it, let him. If it's not in, wait for it."

Angus and Jemmy ran off.

The information was in and they got it and ran back to the pub.

There and back they ran all the way.

Jemmy, grinning, found Brian and stood beside him as Gordon rapped the bottom of a beer pot on the counter and called for attention.

Quickly the room quietened.

"Gentlemen, the winner of the Victoria Derby is... Grand Flaneur."

A cheer went up. Drinking was not long postponed.

Twelve

The first Tuesday in November, Cup Day, came and since early morning people in thousands had been converging on Flemington racecourse. They came on foot, on horseback and in almost every kind of vehicle that could be drawn by horses. They came by train from the city, to a station on the racecourse, or up the Maribyrnong by steamer. Many had come from distant parts and had begun their journeys days or weeks before. There were many who had come from other states, by trains and ship. The men who were managing the hotair balloon in the centre of the course had been readying their apparatus since before dawn. The balloon, attached to a rope, could be let rise to a height of three hundred feet. The attached basket could hold eight passengers. For five minutes aloft the charge was half a crown per person.

At around the same time as they had run off to the office of the *Border Post* on Derby night, in the night after the Cup Jemmy and Angus set out for the same destination. They were not long away.

Again Gordon Ettershank tapped a beer pot on the counter and asked for quiet.

"Gentlemen, Grand Flaneur has won the Melbourne Cup."

The cheering was louder than that on the night after the Derby.

Jemmy went to Brian and waited.

Shocked, Brian could do no more than shake his head.

"You look as if you've been poleaxed," said a man standing on the other side of Brian.

Still shaking his head, Brian turned to the man. "I didn't think Long would do it. I didn't think he would do it. Lord, help the colt now. They'll race him to death, nothing surer. A three-year-old, especially if he's run in the Derby three days before, should never be saddled up for the Cup. They'll break him down, that's what'll happen. The die is cast – they'll break him down. When he went lame as a two-year-old Long spelled him straight away rather than risk seriously injuring his legs. Now this. What's got into Long?"

"Long's a gambler," said the man. "What more do you want to know? He'd have backed him for the double. The odds would have been good – Derby and Melbourne Cup, not something every horse can do."

"I never doubted that Flaneur could do it, if he had to. I just doubted that Long would ask him to do it."

Brian drank on, but unhappily.

Morose and with a hip that was aching, he looked at his watch and saw the time was close to nine o'clock. For today he had had enough of everything, including liquor. Limping slightly, he left the bar and walked into the hall and towards the stairs.

Jemmy caught up with him.

They climbed the stairs together, Brian with a hand on Jemmy's shoulder.

Inside the room Brian lowered himself onto the edge of his bed He looked at his boots and contemplated their removal.

Jemmy changed into his nightshirt. He turned to Brian, who had not moved since sitting down.

"Do you want me to unlace your boots?"

"If you wouldn't mind," muttered Brian, "And take them off too."

With boots off, Brian swung himself onto the bed and let his head fall back on the pillow. "Would you get that overcoat of mine in the closet and throw it over me. I'll undress when my strength comes back, or I might go downstairs again later, if I feel better."

Jemmy did as asked. When he looked again Brian's eyes were closed.

From his bed and through the glass of the door that opened onto the balcony Jemmy saw a low moon. He could hear the hum of the voices below in the bar-room and now and then a burst of collective laughter. The sounds seemed to come up through the floor, and up the stairs and through the closed door. Then he heard the cracking of stockwhips in the street. He rose quickly, went out onto the balcony and leaned over the rail. There was a group of men on the road; he could clearly see them in the moonlight. He recognised the two who were swinging the whips; they were young stockmen he had seen in the pub earlier. Their whip handling was the fancy stuff. One of the whippers held a rolled-up page of newspaper in his left hand and cut it in half with a swing of his whip held in the other hand. His partner showed he could do the same trick. Stockmen visiting town did not as a rule bring their whips. But often Dan Perry and

Jack Staker did and were never backward in providing entertainment if they were asked. Tonight's moon provided as much light as they needed. Standing well apart, each man rapidly passed his whip from one hand to the other, cracking loudly every time. The hotel crowd began flowing onto the street.

Jemmy had the best view of all.

"The Sydney Flash," called an onlooker.

And so the Sydney Flash was demonstrated: three sounds in quick succession: one in front, one at the back and one above the head. The performers obliged again and again.

The crowd cheered and clapped.

A man carrying a pot of beer in each hand emerged and presented the drinks to the crackers.

After they drank, the entertainers resumed, their whips constantly passing back and forth from the right hand to left.

"Give us the Melbourne Cup, boys," called somebody.

A cheer of encouragement went up.

"The winner gets two pots, the loser, one," came a voice.

This was a race the two stockmen had put on for the first time last year. A steward and a starter and a judge were appointed. Two empty jam tins, got from the pub kitchen, soon arrived.

The steward, accompanied by the starter, stepped out thirty paces along the roadway. The two whippers followed. The tins were placed on the ground. The starter called "go" and the whippers moved in. Whoever whipped his tin to the imaginary line adjacent to the judge would be declared the winner. To the barracking of the watchers the tins were started on their way.

Jemmy leaned farther out from his grandstand.

Hardly at any time did the tins go in a line as straight as intended.

The distance had been about half covered when somebody called out, "Bluebirds."

The sound from the barrackers suddenly abated. The whippers had not heard and kept at what they were doing.

"Bluebirds," came the voice again.

The whippers heard this time and stopped. They looked in the direction everybody else was looking in and saw at the end of the street and coming towards them the mounted constable McGinty.

The constable was taking his time. He wanted to be seen. His way when approaching an unruly gathering was to proceed slowly. Often the mere sight of a policeman and the allowing of a minute or two of grace was enough to restore orderliness.

The whippers ran into the crowd.

Jemmy saw them. The crowd parted to let them through. The whippers vanished under the balcony and Jemmy leaned farther out but could not see them. But he could hear their laughing voices and he ran along the balcony to see if they would come out at the other end. He watched them hurry to their horses tethered at the side of the hotel and mount. On the street they heeled their horses to a gallop and at the same time began cracking their whips. A laugh went up from the crowd.

The crowd stepped back to get out of the way of McGinty, in pursuit.

In Gaelic for "clear the way", somebody yelled "*Faugh-a-ballagh,*" and the crowd began moving back to get out of the way of McGinty, now coming through and at more than a canter.

A man was calling out wanting someone to bet him that McGinty wouldn't catch either of the offenders.

At the end of the street the stockmen swung right. Still cracking their whips they swung right again at the next corner. Another corner came up and the riders turned right again. To the delight of the crowd outside the pub the course of the chase could be followed by the sound of the whips and occasional glimpses of the participants across the vacant allotments on the other side of the street and which ran through to the next block. At the next corner the two defiers of the law took another right turn, bringing them back into Olive Street.

Behind them came McGinty.

Cheering broke out again as the riders passed.

"McGinty's gaining," somebody reported loudly.

Someone called after the policeman, "What'll it be, Constable, whisky or beer – I'll have it waiting for you next time you're passing."

The next crossing came up. This time Dan and Jack, now one behind the other, did not make a turn but rode straight ahead.

McGinty's horse was a good one, and fresher tonight than those of the larrikins he was chasing. He knew who these disturbers of the peace were, had had trouble with them before. Now he gained on them quickly. He ranged up beside Jack, seized the near rein of his horse and brought the animal to a halt. No sooner did McGinty let go the rein than he caught Jack by the back of the collar.

"Are you going to come peaceably," said McGinty, "or have I got to drag you off and march you past all your mates at the pub?"

"I'll come," agreed the subdued Jack.

The apprehension of the other villain did not overly concern the policeman. He knew where he could find Dan when he had the time to go and get him, or might hand the job on to another officer.

Nobody had had a better eye-view of events than Jemmy and when it was all over he went in to see if Brian was still in the room or not asleep and tell him what had happened. He found Brian fast asleep.

The talk at Fry's next morning was about little else than Grand Flaneur winning the Cup and the police chase involving the two young stockmen. Jack Staker had spent the night in jail and been charged with being drunk and in charge of a horse and furious riding in a public place.

Thirteen

With Cup Day now nearly a week behind them they were on the road again. Another few days and they would be close to Burrumooka station. The route they were taking was more direct than the one they had taken after they had left the station nearly two months ago. Jemmy was anxious to see his mare, now named Blink Bonny. He wanted to see how much bigger her belly now was. Still with him was the fear that she might not have got in foal the night he had taken her to Kilrenny.

Word had reached squatter Hector Judd that Brian was on the way and he sent out a man to run Bonny into the home paddock.

The travellers arrived in the early afternoon, a time Brian liked to arrive no matter where he went, and Hector and his wife met them on the driveway.

As the greetings and chatting went on at the bottom of the steps Hector noticed the boy looking away and out into the paddocks.

"Your mare's over there," said Hector, pointing.

"First things first," said Brian to Jemmy. "Unharness and turn out, then you can go."

He found Bonny, not hard to pick out amongst the other horses. She paid no attention to him as he approached and she kept grazing. Nearly all her dull winter coat had fallen out and in every other respect she looked well. The long rest and plentiful spring feed had made her wider across the rump and back. He decided not to try to pat her, in case she suspected he was trying to catch her and therefore might move away, he went only close enough to get a good view of her belly. He was disappointed.

That night Brian dined and slept in the homestead. Jemmy dined with the stockmen and slept in the main hut. Next day Bonny was run in and the station's farrier trimmed her hooves. As he belted the toe knife with his hammer to remove as much surplus hoof as possible before the rapping, the farrier remarked on the toughness of the hoof. For the long trip to Foxhow Jemmy thought Brian would recommend shoes for the mare, but he didn't. This was strange, Jemmy thought. He had even suggested shoeing.

The following morning and not long after daybreak they were on the road once more. Kilrenny was placed beside the wagon horses and Bonny behind the wagon. The mare and stallion showed no special interest in each other and Jemmy thought this might mean Bonny was in foal.

As the morning wore on the warmth that came with it was making Jemmy drowsy, but the thoughts of the good times in Albury still came. They had never ceased to come for as long as they had been on the road since leaving the town. Sometimes they entered his dreams at night. He thought of the Panoramic Theatre he and Angus had seen. This theatre was in a big tent and you looked through a slot in a thick curtain and on the other side was a turning thing like a huge barrel and it had on it pictures of places in other countries and moved around as you watched and the first picture you saw came back after awhile. One entertainment he sometimes thought of only because he could not understand why Brian had taken him was at a hall where an Englishman who Brian said was famous wore strange clothes and talked strangely. The talk, Brian said, was the language of Shakespeare. Everybody had clapped. Other kinds of memories came too. The news came through that soon after the Cup Grand Flaneur had raced again, and won. This had put Brian in a bad mood. Jemmy wondered if this might be part of the reason why there seemed to be a whole lot of change in Brian's mood since they left Albury. Brian had not been talkative yesterday and was less so today, so far. Maybe his hip was hurting more?

The morning wore on and was nearly passed when the sight of a shady spot ahead made Brian take a look at his watch. Reaching the spot he reined in under the trees and stopped. Nosebags were put on the horses and while Brian began taking the necessaries from the tucker box Jemmy made a fire for the billy. Brian sitting in his chair and Jemmy on his sack they ate bread and cheese. They were on tea when Brian broke the silence.

"There's a fork coming up. Do you know where we are?"

"Yes."

"If we take the left prong, you know where that'll take us?"

"Yes."

"Quartz Creek," added Brian, "and that's the road we're going to take. I'm taking you back there and leaving you with your mother."

Jemmy was bewildered. "But …" When he found his voice again he asked, "Why? Am I sacked?"

“I’ve given this matter a lot of thought – a lot, and for much longer than a day or two. I can’t fault you as a helper, but I think your life with me, the way it would be from now on, would be no good for you. At your time of life you need people around you, family: mother, father, brothers, sisters, uncles, aunties and whoever else you’ve got, or just friends. At Foxhow, I’m the only one you’d be with for days or weeks on end, and that’s no good.”

“You told me I was a member of the firm.”

“You were, while you’ve been with me. With me, from now on, is no place for you. Somewhere where you can go to school is where you ought to be.”

“There ain’t a school at Quartz Creek,” protested Jemmy.

“That may be, but the situation would be worse if you came to Foxhow. You’d be so far from family that you’d be almost an orphan.”

“No, I wouldn’t. Lots of boys go away to work. Foxhow isn’t in another country, and my mother won’t mind.”

“If you must work, working closer to home would be better for you; for preference on a station where there are plenty of people.”

“Anyway, I don’t want to go to school. They hit you with canes.”

“No. Only bad boys get the cane, and you wouldn’t be a bad boy.”

“I’m too old to go to school.”

“No, no-no-no-no-no. You’re a perfect age.”

There was no more argument Jemmy could think of to put up. The shock settled in. He could hardly believe his life with the stallionman was now over.

“For any good it might do you, and it just might,” said Brian, “I’ve got a reference written out for you. I’ll give it to you later. You don’t understand what’s happening but your mother will. Next year, if you’re free, we might join up and go to Albury together again.”

As they began again making ready for the road another silence set in. This went on till, after about half a mile, Brian broke it.

“Now be a good boy and go to the back and get your gear ready.”

Jemmy stood and climbed over the backrest.

Brian listened to the rummaging, thankful that the boy had accepted the situation. There was more he had to say but the worst was over.

The fork in the road came and Brian pulled to the left and kept going.

The packing up he had listened to he could no longer hear. He could understand Jemmy's not coming forward again and sitting with him. For Brian the sadness of the situation had been with him for weeks. Giving him the determination to not falter was the belief that what he was doing was right. He wished Jemmy would come forward and sit with him. He decided he would break the ice.

"The track's narrowing," called Brian, pulling up. "I think we'll put Kilrenny at the back with Bonny. Would you fix it?"

Brian waited.

Jemmy did not answer or appear.

"Alright, sulk if you must. I'll do it." Turning as he climbed down he glanced into the back of the wagon. Jemmy was not there. The flaps at the rear were apart and the mare, too, was not where she ought to be. Puzzled, Brian went to the other side of the wagon. He looked down the road behind. There was no sign of horse or boy. Frowning, he got back into the wagon and went on to where the timber was thin enough to allow him to make a turn. On the way down the road he looked into the bush on both sides. At the fork he looked along the other prong. There they were, Jemmy astride the mare and near a quarter of a mile away. He stirred the horses to a trot.

Gaining on him, Jemmy heard the wagon. He did not turn or stop.

Brian made a trumpet of his hands and called out. "Hey there. Hold on."

Jemmy stopped, turned the mare and waited. Across the mare's withers he held a sack with belongings in it.

"Where do you think you're going?" said Brian angrily as he reined the horses in beside the boy and pulled up.

"I dunno. Down this road, somewhere. But I'm not going back to Quartz Creek."

"Oh, yes you are."

"No, I'm not. I don't have to go where you tell me – not any more. You're not my boss now."

Flustered, Brian struggled over what he thought he should say next."You haven't got all your clothes there. What am I supposed to do with what you've left? They're too small for me to wear."

"This is all I can carry, and what's left ain't mine anyway. I'm not a member of the firm any more."

Brian grew angrier. "If you're not going to Quartz Creek, you've got to have a plan to go somewhere. Use your head."

"I'm not going back to Quartz Creek."

"Well, I can't go to Quartz Creek without you. I've got to show you to your mother, or she could think I've abandoned you or murdered you and buried you in the bush somewhere. Now I've had a new thought these last few minutes. I might be able to arrange for you to go and board with a family I know in Albury for six months and you could go to school. It would be for only six months but that would be enough time for you to learn to read and write. I know how much you'd like to be able to read and write. I'd cover the expense. But we'd have to talk about it with your mother."

"I'm too old to go to school."

"Too old, my eye. There was a Frenchman named Rousseau, a very clever man, and he said that children shouldn't be sent to school till they were aged fourteen as it wasn't till then that they came to any real interest in learning. You're at a perfect age to go to school. You'd learn in six months more than you might have learned over years before that. Have I got to explain again? With me as your only company you could finish up with boundary riders' disease, talking to rocks or trees or ants. Too much on your own sends some people mad."

"It hasn't sent you mad."

"But I can read. That's the difference; that's what stops me from going mad. You can't read."

"That's because you wouldn't teach me."

"I can't teach you. I've told you why."

They stared at each other.

"I'd better get going," said Jemmy. He turned the mare.

"Wait on, wait on," called Brian, his voice the loudest Jemmy had ever heard it. "Come here, come here."

Jemmy stopped, turned and rode back.

Almost spitting the words, Brian said, "I've let you push me harder than I've ever let any man. I'll make you an offer, my last and final. Take it or leave it. If you leave it, I'll go to Quartz Creek and tell your mother what you've done, that you don't care if she has to worry about you, that you've deserted her. I will take you to Foxhow, on a three-month's trial – three months and no longer. After that, if I'm not satisfied with the situation

– whether you are or not – I'll send you packing. That's my offer. What's your pleasure? Take it or leave it?"

"… I'll take it."

"There's more," said Brian. "We still go to Quartz Creek, for your mother's sake if not yours. You're going to see your mother whether you like it or not."

Jemmy hesitated then nodded.

"There's a saying," continued Brian, "Beware of the fury of a patient man, and I'm nearly at the end of mine today. Now hitch your mare and get into this wagon before I throw you in."

Fourteen

It was three weeks and a day since they had left Albury. Not only was Quartz Creek behind them but so too was the Braywood homestead. Braywood was the nearest station to Foxhow, the two properties separated by the Snowy River. The homesteads of both were a long day's drive or short day's ride from each other. In early summer the Braywood cattle being taken to the tops for grazing would pass through Foxhow, and when Foxhow cattle were ready for market they would go with Braywood cattle.

His father, much to Jemmy's relief, had not been at the Creek when they called. He could not tell Brian that his fear of his father was the reason he had not wanted to go back there. If his father had been there, there would have been trouble and an end put to any further life for him with Brian Drury. He had been ordered to stay at Jindabilla and not only had he disobeyed but had gone to another job; that would have earned him a thrashing. He was further relieved when they left the Creek on the same day as they arrived. He thought of how pleased his mother had been to see all his new clothes, not forgetting to show her the oilskin and the sou'wester. He did not speak of his being on trial with Brian for three months and he wondered if Brian had spoken to her of it. He could tell she was eager for him to stay with Brian. Knowing how clever his mother was and what she wanted for him, he doubted she would have mentioned his father to Brian. Driving away this time he didn't wait for Brian to tell him to look back and wave to his mother. After his last wave he began watching the road ahead. He had not forgotten the swagman that had come along, and who he thought might be his father, the first day he had driven away with Brian.

Everybody they saw at Braywood welcomed Brian. Chester Tweedie, who owned the station, was the most bow-legged man Jemmy had ever seen. Jemmy thought that if Mr Tweedie's knees could be brought closer together he would be taller. Fresh beef was put into clean hessian chaff bags. A crate of hens was lashed to the side of the wagon, and two bluish, long-haired dogs joined the caravan. The dogs had become ecstatic at the sight of Brian. Blue Boy and Blue Peter were their names, Jemmy was told, but afterwards he heard them called only Boy and Peter.

They were nearing the river and through wide breaks in the trees Jemmy saw in the distance the outline of the Snowy Mountains.

"Is Mount Kosciuszko over there?" asked Jemmy.

"Yes."

"Can you tell which one?"

"Not from here. It doesn't stand out like the Matterhorn or Everest. See the line of bumps? One is higher than the others; that's Kosciuszko."

"Where did you get the name Foxhow?"

"It's the name of the village I was born in, in England."

"How old were you when you left?"

"Five."

The dogs were first to reach the crossing. They walked a few yards into the water and returned to the bank.

Observing familiar landmarks on both sides of the river, Brian made a judgement. He believed the water flowing over the bar would, at its deepest, come up to not much past the horses' bellies. He judged the current not too strong for what had to be done. There had been times when he had waited days before crossing. He stopped, called in the dogs and they leapt up onto the footboard.

The horses went forward. Reaching the water's edge they showed hesitancy.

"Righto, boys, hit those collars – hard." A tap on the rump from the end of the whip handle assured the horses that any refusing would mean consequences.

Swifter and swifter came the water. It began climbing the wheel spokes and the horses' legs. The horses threw up their heads when their faces caught splash. The fowls fluttered and squawked when water shot up through the bottom slats of the coop.

Brian drove an angled course, pushing the horses into the increasingly strong current; in this way there was less chance of a horse being swept off its feet. A horse down was the worst that could happen; this could bring down one or both of the other horses. Momentum had to be kept up and regularly Brian let the tip of whip handle drop on the rumps of the haulers.

Bonny was tied at the back. Being smaller than the other horses the water began to no longer pass under her belly and the current was pushing against her side. Suddenly the whole of her body sank and with neck outstretched she began to swim, the current pushing her downstream. But the halter rope was preventing her being washed away. Water was coming through the floor and Jemmy climbed into the back and began picking up things and putting them on top of other things.

Brian, aware of what was happening behind him, called out, "We're going all right. We'll be out of the worst in a few more strides."

Because she was almost on an angle to the wagon, Bonny struggled to keep her nose above the water that was pushing into her face and she constantly snorted to clear her nostrils.

At last the water stopped coming through the floor. Jemmy saw nothing of what was happening at the front. The mare was now claiming all his attention. More of her head suddenly appeared above the water, then came her mane and the line along her back: her hooves had found bottom again. She struggled to keep her feet as more of her body began rising from the water.

When they came out of the river they were on Foxhow.

Foxhow's fifteen thousand acres lay between the Snowy and the Prapunga. The Prapunga, one of the Snowy's offshoots, rejoined the mother river miles downstream, nearly at the town of Fitzford.

The wagon horses, their flanks heaving, were kept at their task till flat ground was reached. After a rest, they were sent forward again. The dogs raced ahead and soon disappeared. Jemmy had been amazed at how long they could go missing before suddenly reappearing and before going missing again.

Through stands of timber and in and out of dense bush then sparse bush and across grassy stretches the caravan made its way along a track with wheel marks still visible. Since leaving the flats Brian constantly assessed the growth of the grass around him. If reasonable follow-up rains came the season would be good.

"A few fresh pats," commented Jemmy.

"Yes, I noticed them. We might even see a beast or two before we get home. Keep a look out for One-eye."

"A bullock or a horse?"

"A big old brindle bullock that I've never sent to market."

"Why?"

"He's been too useful over the years. He's a leader. When we go to the tops, he leads the way. When we come down, he leads the way again. He knows the way, both ways."

"When will we be going?"

"Shortly after Christmas."

"We're too far from Kosciuszko to go there, aren't we?"

"That's right. The most we'll see of Kosciuszko is the water that comes off it and flows down our two rivers and floods the flats."

"How many will we be taking?"

"Around a couple of hundred."

"Two of us can handle two hundred?"

"Yes – with One-eye's help. There was a time when I'd take up a thousand. Of course, I might have to run a few more now – to pay your wages."

Jemmy thought hard about Brian's last remark. If Brian meant to get rid of him in three months, why would he speak of running more cattle to pay wages? Was this a sign that Brian was thinking of keeping him on?

"Who helped you last time?"

"The Braywood boys. Different times they've got men to spare down there. One way and another Braywood and Foxhow work in with each other. Chester is a good neighbour – none better. There'll be Braywood boys up here when the yard-work's on."

They came to the last rise before the sweep downwards, at the end of which lay the mix of buildings that made up the homestead. The biggest of the wooden-fenced home paddocks ran away into lightly timbered hills.

At the yards they stopped and Bonny and Kilrenny were led away separately.

They drove on and stopped near one of the doorways of the stable which, like all the other buildings, had a bark roof held down by poles over the top. Taking an end each, they carried the coop of hens to the doorway.

"We won't let them out till just on dark," said Brian. "That way they won't go far."

"Where will they roost?" asked Jemmy.

"Inside, up in the rafters, away from foxes. They know where."

The hens out of the way for the time being, Brian gave the next direction. "We'll go to the residence now and unload as much as we'll need tonight and turn out the horses. I want to get most of the beef into the pickle, quickly. It's getting too late to do much more today."

Jemmy had not heard the word 'residence' before but thought it might mean the place where they would sleep.

The big hut they came to had a verandah at the front and glass windows each side of the door. On the verandah was furniture for sitting on.

They got down and Brian gave another order.

"There's a ladder around the back at the chimney. Go up and throw the boards off the top."

Jemmy found the ladder leaning against the chimney and went up and after tipping off the rock on top threw down the boards, which he guessed had been put there to keep possums and stray birds from getting into the hut. When he got to the ground he looked for Brian.

As he entered the hut Jemmy's gaze went everywhere. The floor was earthen, dry and hard. There were glass windows in all the walls. Catching his eye was a tall red-glass lamp standing on the table. The lamp was the most elegant he had ever seen and the colour was not paint but seemed to come from inside the glass. There were four beds, in twos, one above the other, each side of the fireplace but far enough back to allow for a chair on either side of the fireplace. The chairs were for leaning back in and had armrests and cushions. The mantelpiece had chisel marks along the front and on top were lots of things including a stopped clock with Roman numerals. Near a window was a large bookcase with glass doors and inside were lots of books. A pile of dry wood and kindling lay at one side of the fireplace.

Looking at the wood Brian said, "That's not the wood I left. Someone's been – the Braywood boys or Tom." He walked to a shelf and looked at an enamel mug turned upside down with a spoon sitting inside the handle. "Tom's been. His sign's here."

"Who's Tom?"

"Tom Halpen. You'll meet him. He stays a while when he comes. He's a prospector."

"Is there gold on Foxhow?"

"None that Tom ever found. And I've never looked."

To and fro they went from the wagon and hut. Getting the meat into the pickle was the chief priority. After they took the wagon away and unharnessed the horses and turned them out Jemmy was told to take himself off and look around but to stay within call.

"There's enough glow to tell you where the sun is," said Brian. "When it's gone behind that hill over there," he pointed, "let the hens out. Don't shoo them, just open the hatch and let them find their own way out."

When the hatch was opened the hens cautiously left their prison. They were brown birds, crossbreds, speckled and not big and largely were descended from English Game, one of the keys to their survival. Not only did the Game blood make them masterly foragers but made them able to rise sufficiently in flight to save them from an attacking fox. Many a pursuing fox had leapt into the air to bring one down and had missed.

He walked into the stable with its high wooden-slab sides. There were single stalls, ten of them, with a lane in the middle and at the end two railed loose-boxes. The doorway near the loose-boxes took him into the tackle room. The walls and ceiling of the room dripped with all manner of gear. There were not many saddles, though plenty of racks for more. Where there were brass buckles they were tarnished and bits and stirrup-irons that were not plated were rusty. Much of the leather was dry, hungry for oil. A lady's side-saddle caught his eye and he went over to it.

The next doorway took him into the forge, a roofed place open on one side. Sets of rusty horseshoes tied together with string hung from nails on the walls and on posts. The anvil was slightly hollow in the middle. The bellows were so big that he thought two of him could fit inside. The pole that worked it had wired to the other end an iron cog that must have come out of a huge machine and acted as a counter balance. He pulled down the pole. Black dust from the hearth shot up and he turned his head away quickly and spluttered and spat.

He went back to the long hut with its kitchen at the end. There was a long table with benches on both sides and a fireplace and chairs at the other end. It was a table for ten or twelve men and there was dust all over it. Dust was on everything. He went into the kitchen. The doors of the big black-iron oven were open. He looked inside and saw a possum curled up.

It was near dark before they sat down to eat.

The dogs, their bellies full, were stretched in front of the fire. Till the nights became warmer they would be allowed to sleep inside.

Brian decided upon no more chores tonight. He took the red-glass lamp from the table and put it on a stand at the side of one of the big chairs. Beside the chair was a small table on which he had put some of the papers and magazines brought back from Albury. His spectacles sat on the top of the pile. He sat and made himself comfortable.

Jemmy did the same in the other chair.

The matter of where Jemmy would sleep had been settled earlier. His bed was to be the top one across from the lower one in which Brian slept. The chest on the floor at the end of the beds on Jemmy's side was to be Jemmy's.

"This chair," said Brian, "is always mine, no matter who visits. You can sit in it if you want to, when I don't want it. The chair you're sitting in is yours, unless Tom visits. That's always his chair when he's here. If we have a visit from anybody else that's more senior than you, it would be good manners to offer him your chair. Is that all right with you?"

Jemmy nodded. He knew the last question was not really a question but a case of 'that's the rule'.

"Say 'yes,'" recommended Brian. "You nod too much. You want to try to break yourself out of that habit. If there's a word that can be used, use it instead of nodding."

Jemmy nodded.

Brian sighed and said no more. He put on his spectacles and took the top magazine from those beside him.

Jemmy looked across at the bookcase then back at Brian. Brian was still turning the pages of the *Illustrated London News*.

"How did you get that book cupboard up here without breaking the glass?"

Brian looked over his spectacles.

"I took the doors off and packed them in straw."

"Are there pictures in any of the books?"

"In some. But you'd have to search."

"Can I go and have a look?"

"I'm sure you can – you've got two legs. If you want permission, you should say 'may I have a look?'."

"May I have a look?"

"Yes, you may. You may take books from the case any time you like. But always put them back in the places you took them from. If you put them on the table, first make sure the table's clean. We might set up a lamp or candle there for you. But not tonight."

Fifteen

In the morning the grass was wet and the rain Jemmy had heard in the night was gone and a fine day seemed on the way.

For this morning, the harness-horses became saddle-horses and Brian and Jemmy rode out to find and bring in other horses.

"Will we see Lanarth today?" asked Jemmy as they rode away.

"We might. He's out there somewhere. If we don't see him today, we'll see him another time."

Five horses were brought in. Jemmy was told he should pick two as his regulars. He was certain of one he wanted, a chestnut, a son of Lanarth and named Ochre. These horses had to be shod and Brian wanted to do two today. The two selected, one of them Ochre, were taken to the forge.

A hole was scraped in the charcoal in the hearth and kindling put into it and lit. Carefully Brian raked charcoal over the flames. After a wait he gently worked the lever above the bellows and the fire responded.

Jemmy was sent to the wagon to fetch two sets of shoes that had been made up at Edgar Fry's forge during some of Brian's spare time in Albury. Now they had to be fitted, their shape altered to neatly fit the shape of the hoof they had to go on.

"And bring the apron and tools," Brian called after him.

The leather apron Brian put on went from his waist to almost the tops of his boots and in the middle of it was a long split that allowed for the holding of a horse's leg between those of the shoer.

From the old hat Brian took a horseshoe-nail and held it out to Jemmy. "Look at the point and tell me which is the front of the nail and which is the back."

Jemmy took the nail and examined the point. He looked and pronounced, "No difference." He suspected Brian was joking with him.

"Is that so? You put a nail into a hoof backwards and you'll soon know all about it. Look again."

Again Jemmy looked. He shook his head.

"Look again, closely. You'll see one side of the tip is flat and the other side is angled, sloped. It's slight but the angle's there, and it's damned important."

Jemmy studied the nail again. "Yes, yes, I can see it."

"The side with the bevel must always face the inside. That little bevel steers the nail towards the outside of the hoof. If you drove the nail in the other way around, you'd soon know about it. The nail would go into the quick and the horse would pull his leg away so fast he might castrate you – and might give you a clout on the head for good measure. And into the bargain you'll have a lame horse, a horse you can't use. And the flat sides of the nail play a part too. A lot of science in a horseshoe nail."

The hooves were readied, trimmed with the toe knife made from a piece of buggy spring sharpened on one side and made to cut by belting it with a hammer; afterwards the underpart of the hoof was rasped to level and smooth it.

Boy and Peter ran off with the pieces of hoof thrown to them.

When a hot shoe was placed on a hoof Brian blew the smoke away so that he could see if the shoe needed to be narrowed or widened. Scorch marks on the underside told him where more levelling was required. He would talk as he moved backwards and forwards between horse and anvil.

"Always remove any burnt hoof. Burnt hoof is dead hoof and a layer of that under a shoe can lead to a loose shoe."

Jemmy was let finish the driving home of a few nails and shown how to break them off and ready them for clinching. He was shown how over-heated iron would "burn" and become clinker and be useless.

After the first horse was finished Brian decided he needed a cup of tea.

"If I don't go up," asked Jemmy, "can I – may I – stay here and have a bang on the anvil with an old shoe?"

"Yes. Take what you like from that stack of old ones over there. There's enough heat still in the fire for what you want to do. But don't touch the lever. There's a knack to it. The balance is a bit fine. It's like me, near ready for the next world."

In the hut and as he sipped Brian listened to the ring from the anvil. There wasn't much rhythm in it and he smiled and wondered what strangely shaped pieces of iron he would find when he went back.

That night Jemmy found his first book with pictures and he took it back to the chair by the fire. The pictures were drawings that he could hardly believe could be so perfect. The first pictures were of people in strange clothes, and there were men wearing helmets and carrying shields and swords and spears. He came to a picture that puzzled him and he dwelt on it. It showed a woman in a dress like a short robe that did not cover the bottom part of her legs or shoulders or arms. The woman was holding up a baby by one leg and in her other hand was a short sword. He could see the fear in her face. Clinging to her legs were two older children. Coming towards them were men with shields and drawn swords. It seemed the woman was going to kill the baby. He was moved enough to interrupt Brian's reading and took the book to him.

"Is the lady here going to kill the baby?"

"Yes. And she's going to kill the other children too. She's Queen Isadora and she's a Spartan and those soldiers are Athenians. After she kills the children she's going to kill herself. She doesn't want herself or her children to fall into the hands of the Athenians."

"Why?"

"She was the widow of King Theramus of Sparta. Sparta and Athens were at war. If the Athenians had captured her and the children they would put them to death and might not have done it in a very nice way. The Athenians had killed her husband. Killing her children and herself was the only way she could ensure that the soldiers couldn't kill them cruelly."

"Why did the soldiers want to do that? A woman and children couldn't hurt them."

"That's the way life was lived in those places in those days. If the children had been allowed to live, or if they had escaped, they would have been honour-bound to one day avenge the killing of their father and mother. Revenge played an important part in life in those times – thousands of years ago. If you killed somebody, it was wise to wipe out the entire bloodline, for safety's sake."

Jemmy was puzzled and unhappy at what he had been told and he took the book back to his chair.

Sixteen

The game of cribbage began taking up part of some evenings. This was more at the behest of Brian than to the liking of Jemmy. Brian was surprised at how well the boy played. It was a game Jemmy enjoyed but at the moment had no desire to indulge in it much, not until he had finished exploring the contents of the bookcase. He searched for books with pictures.

One night he went back to the chair with his fourth book and on opening it soon came to the first picture. The picture was of a Chinese-looking man mounted on a small horse and dressed in a kind of armour he had not seen in any other pictures of men in armour. Strapped to the man's side was a sword in a scabbard. In front of the saddle was a pouch with a bow poking out and behind one of the man's shoulders were the tops of arrows. Quickly he turned pages and came to the next picture; it was of a group of men attired in armour and astride horses, horses similar to those in the first picture. Some of the men held spears pointing upwards. One man held up a shaft with three crosspieces at the top with ox-tail tips, nine in all, hanging from the arms. Again Jemmy quickly turned pages to find the next picture, and the next and the next. Then he went to the front and started again. There were many pictures and very few of them did not have horses, always the same kind, small with short, shaggy manes and heads not fine like those of thoroughbreds, or Arabian horses he had seen in pictures. He put aside his qualms about interrupting Brian's reading and took the book to him.

"Would you tell me what the name of this book is?" He held the book upright in front of him.

Brian leaned forward and read aloud the words on the cover. "*Travels with the Armies of Subedei Bahadah*, by Bembeedok of Bukhara, translated by Wilbur H. Morrow."

"Who was Subedei Bahadah?"

"One of Ghengis Khan's commanders."

"Who was Ghengis Khan?"

"The greatest horse thief in history."

"Bigger than Ned Kelly?"

When Brian got his laughing under control he replied, "Compared to Genghis Khan, Ned Kelly never got out of kindergarten. Kelly stole horses in ones and twos, or dozens at most; Genghis Khan stole them in thousands. This book will tell you. Once, he sent his son Jokee on a mission – gave him a small army to take with him. Jokee came back with a hundred thousand horses, plundered from a neighbouring country. This son killed, or threatened to kill, everybody who tried to stop him."

"One man stole a hundred thousand horses?"

"He had an army helping him."

Jemmy could not immediately think of a next question, then said, "That must have been all the horses in China."

"No. They were from the other side of China, the other side of Mongolia. Genghis Khan was a Mongolian, not a Chinese. He stole horses, and everything else he came across, from everywhere he went, and he went a long way. Some say that if time had allowed, all that might have stopped him reaching Britain was the English Channel."

Jemmy opened the book at the picture whose number he had noted. He turned the book and held it out in front of Brian. "This horse and all the others in the book look like Bonny."

Without taking the book Brian studied the picture. "...I'd have to agree, I suppose. They're ugly little brutes. And, from what the book says – and I've read it – they were tough, like Bonny. But, likely, that's as far as it goes."

"If my mare looks like them, she could be one of them. Where these horses came from, she might've come from."

"She might not have, too. All she might really have in common with them is her height – the Mongols' horses were ponies, and Bonny, if she doesn't measure 'pony', that's fourteen and a half hands from hoof to wither, she goes pretty close to it. I've never heard of any Mongolian ponies reaching Australia. I've never seen a Mongolian pony, and I don't know anybody who has. This artist, too, might never have seen a Mongolian pony. He might be guessing. You've got to be careful of pictures in books. I went home to England once and in a gallery I saw a painting of Mary, Christ's mother, dressed in a long, blue satin dress. Mary, mother of Christ, dressed in blue satin, and the dress was European-style. Could Mary truly have dressed like that?" Brian shook his head. "In other galleries I saw paintings of Biblical characters wearing European clothes. In one gallery

I saw a painting of Adam and Eve and both of them had belly buttons, navels. Adam and Eve were not born of woman, so they wouldn't have had belly buttons. You've got to be careful of all paintings or drawings you see in books, or in art galleries."

Jemmy was confused. But there was one question he wanted to ask. "How big is a 'hand'?"

"Officially, four inches. Any horse under fourteen and a half hands is classed as a pony."

Brian went on. "It would be good if your mare had come down from Mongolian ponies. Those ponies were great little animals – that book tells all about them. They could survive under conditions so hard that many other kinds of horses would have died. In a forced march, they could do eighty miles in a day – off grass. Their hooves were so hard they didn't need shoes; this allowed them to walk on ice without slipping. This made the Mongols the only invaders ever to successfully campaign in Russia in the winter. Frozen rivers between forts became like highways. They could find grass under snow like no other horses could. That book will tell you."

"Bonny has got tough hooves."

"I don't think that entirely proves your case."

"But some Mongolian ponies might have got to Australia without anybody here knowing about it. There might have been a shipwreck."

"I wouldn't bank on the likelihood of that." Brian shook his head. "You say your mare's half-thoroughbred. If she is, isn't that enough for you, without any of this Mongolian stuff?"

"No, not if there's more. I want for her every honour she's entitled to."

Brian sighed.

Jemmy went back to his chair. He looked across at Brian, who was about to recommence reading. "When you finish all your books from Albury, would you read some of this book to me?"

"… I'll think about it."

Seventeen

Brian could plait by lamplight or firelight, but to strand a kangaroo hide he used only the best light, daylight. He took from a shelf one of the rolled-up hides he had brought from Albury and spread it over the end of the table nearest the window. From the same shelf he took a large pair of tailor's scissors, put on his spectacles and trimmed the hide into an oblong shape. Then he took from an old balsawood cigar box a small penknife whose blade, due to continuous honing, was now shorter and thinner than it once was. Into the tip of the thumbnail on his right hand there was carved a V-shaped notch that he never allowed to grow closed. Gripping the knife in the same hand, he let the edge of the blade fit into the notch and, starting at the outside of the hide, he began cutting the leather in continuous strands about an eighth of an inch wide.

At near noon he downed tools and left everything where it lay. There was much preparation yet to be done before he could start plaiting. He made tea in a pot and took from the cupboard bread made yesterday and half a wheel of cheese wrapped in oilcloth. He went to the doorway and called out to Jemmy.

Jemmy had been put to work in the tackle room, oiling leather. He heard. He was running as he passed through the tackle-room doorway, the dogs at his heels. They raced towards the hut. He stopped at the pail on the verandah, wet his hands and began rubbing soap on them.

"Wipe them on the towel, not your pants," said Brian from the doorway.

The handtowel was a piece of hessian made soft by long soaks in hot water and soap.

Jemmy saw the leather and tools on the table. He did not ask but hoped a whip was being made for him. He was alarmed, too. Brian had mentioned plaiting at night. If Brian plaited at night, that might mean less reading from the Mongol book.

By one o'clock they were in the saddle and riding across a flat area of about half an acre near the hut and at the bottom of a slope.

"Wouldn't here have been a better place to build the hut?" said Jemmy.

“Yes, it would have been, if a hut was what I intended for here. Once, there were other plans for this site.”

“Plans for a house, a big proper one?”

“Yes.”

“Might you still build it, one day?”

“I don’t think so.”

Houses bigger than huts Jemmy linked to men with wives and children. He was curious – Brian had never mentioned if he had ever had a wife. He had often wondered about the lady’s side-saddle in the tackle room.

“Have you ever had a wife?”

“Yes, a long time ago,” Brian answered curtly. “Let’s keep our mind to our riding.”

Slung across Brian’s back was a telescope in a leather case.

Before the end of the next hour they were behind twenty or more cattle and moving them along quietly. The dogs were not to be seen; they were searching for more cattle. Searching out cattle rather than rounding them up was what they were meant to do. On a muster in scrub they were out of sight much of the time but were never far from the musterers. Often it was their barking or a startled beast bellowing or crashing through timber that told where the dogs were.

Coming out of thin timber and onto a grassy clearing Brian drew a halt and looked across an open tract about half a mile wide. On the other side was a low hill, flat on top except for boulders and thin timber. Brian dismounted, gave his reins to Jemmy and walked to a tree. At the tree he put the telescope to his eye, using the trunk to steady the instrument. He saw no cattle, including none lying down or standing amongst trees. He walked back to Jemmy, at the same time whistling loudly for the dogs to come. Boy and Peter appeared and Brian drew cords from his saddlebag and put them on the dogs and tied them to a sapling. He turned to Jemmy.

“Tell you what I want you to do,” said Brian. “Trot over to that hill.” He pointed. “Keep to the bottom and to the right; go to the other side and work your way along the back and see if there are any cattle there, or fresh signs. Work your way to the other end and come round and come back here and tell me what you’ve seen. Clear on that?”

Jemmy almost nodded. He replied with a yes.

It was near twenty minutes before Brian saw Jemmy next. He was so disbelieving of what he was seeing that he put the telescope to his eye.

Jemmy was behind cattle, six or seven head, and coming this way.

The cattle began to settle down in the open and Jemmy found himself not needing to ride so much from one side to the other to keep them bunched. They had given up trying to escape him. He was pleased with himself. When nearly to where he had been despatched he saw Brian riding toward him.

"I think I've got One-eye," called Jemmy.

Brian swung in behind the cattle. His voice came in a roar. "Well, why the hell didn't you leave her there, and the others? Why the hell didn't you do as I told you to do? Who's supposed to be master on Foxhow, you or me?"

They stopped and faced each other.

Jemmy was almost unbelieving of what he was hearing. "I thought this was what you wanted me to do."

"Is that what I told you to do?"

"No, but I thought ..."

"I only wanted to know what was there. I wanted to leave that area for another day. Who's in charge here, you or me?"

"You are."

"Oh, I am, am I? I was beginning to think you were. If I'm master, what did the master tell you to do? I didn't tell you to pick up cattle if you saw any; I only told you to see what was there."

"I thought you would have wanted me to bring them," pleaded Jemmy.

"All I wanted to know was if there were any cattle there. Why do you think I didn't let the dogs go with you? In future, listen to what I tell you to do. Just do as you're told. Hear me?"

Crestfallen, Jemmy nodded.

The new cattle, one of them One-eye, were driven in the direction of the others. The dogs were released and all moved on.

Though Jemmy had not been told, the muster was not intended to bring in cattle but to move beasts from some localities to other places from where they would be inclined to drift downwards towards the river flats, and to see where other cattle might be and could be moved on another day – all in preparation for the making up of a mob to go to the tops later on.

The remainder of the ride went with less said than Jemmy thought would have been the case if earlier he had not made Brian so cross. What had happened was worrying him. He made sure not to nod or shake his head when he was spoken to. He thought of the trial period he was in and how black a mark he might have earned himself.

That night there was no reading from the Mongol book, and Jemmy did not ask for it. He was not convinced that necessarily Brian was punishing him. Maybe Brian just did not feel inclined and Jemmy thought he should be careful not to risk aggravating him.

In bed, Jemmy tried to think only of the stories about the Mongols and their ponies, of the game Jokee's father made his soldiers play, making thousands of them spread out in a big circle, maybe a hundred miles round, and drive ahead of them and into a circle all the wild animals they came upon and in the end killing only one and letting the others go, all to teach the army coordination, Brian had said. He wondered what kinds of wild animals there might have been. But his thoughts kept returning to Brian being so angry with him that day and what he could do to make amends.

"Are you asleep, Brian?"

"Nearly."

"I'm not."

"So it seems."

Jemmy slipped from beneath the blankets, dropped to the floor from his top bunk and went to Brian's bed and sat on the end. "I'm sorry for what I did today and I won't do it again."

Brian knew what was being referred to. "We'll hope not. Maybe I was a bit too gruff. You're a pretty good lad when you're at your best, I've got to admit. Let's forget the matter and start afresh. Back to bed now."

In two bounds Jemmy crossed the room. With both hands on the edge of the bunk he sprang and threw himself onto the bed. He was no sooner under the blankets than his thoughts returned to the Mongols and Jokee. What would the drove of a hundred-thousand horses look like? How did Jokee do it: did he straggle them or divide them into mobs; might the drove have taken weeks, or months, to come in? If Genghis Khan was the greatest horse thief in history, as Brian said he was, Jokee must be the greatest drover in history. He thought of Bonny and Brian saying she reminded him of no breed of horse he had ever seen before. Brian also admitted he had never seen horses that looked like those in the Mongol book. Mongolia was where Bonny's ancestors had to have come from, this had to be, the proof was there, in the book. If the truth were know, Bonny might have come down from one of the very horses that Jokee rode. He wondered how many horses Jokee himself owned.

Eighteen

Another book with pictures began claiming Jemmy's attention. The illustrations were of more than horses but parts of them: innards and muscles and bones, and there was a picture of the skeleton of a horse with names beside all the bones. It was a thick book with gold printing on the black front-cover. On the blank page inside the cover was some handwriting in ink and the date 1877. The words in ink were a person's name, he believed, and although the name was handwritten he thought it had a similarity to the one on the cover. He turned from one to the other and became convinced they were the same names. He took the book to Brian and asked the name of it.

At the sight of the book Brian smiled. The book was *Veterinary Notes for Horse Owners*, by Captain Horace M. Hayes.

"Now turn the cover and see the ink-writing that's there."

Brian did as requested.

"Is that name the same as the one on the cover?"

"Yes."

"I know that the name of the man on the front is the name of the man who wrote the book. But why did he write his name inside?"

"That's what people do when they make you a gift of a book."

Jemmy's eyes widened. "You knew him, and he gave you this book?"

"Yes. He was a vet in the British Army in India, and that's where I met him."

"What did he look like?"

Brian chuckled. "Like any one of fifty other men I could name. He had a beard and he was a Briton. In the Army, all vets hold the rank of Captain."

That night Brian found he was not asked to read from the Mongol book. By the time Jemmy had fully indulged himself in his new find he knew that the Mongol-book reading period was near past and that a refusal by Brian was likely.

Brian was near ready for bed, but there was time to casually broach a matter he had been giving some thought to. He spoke again of his intention to go to the town of Fitzford for Christmas, with Jemmy accompanying him, of course. It was a plan Jemmy liked the sound of.

"I've been thinking," said Brian. "When we go to Fitzford for Christmas, it might be a good idea if you opened a bank account."

"What for?" Jemmy knew about banks and how Ned Kelly used to rob them.

"They're good places to keep your money safe."

"Not if Ned Kelly calls in."

"Kelly won't be robbing any more banks. He was due for hanging while we were in Albury. It would have been done by now."

"But other robbers might come."

Brian spoke a little on how banks worked, on how money was guaranteed even if the bank was robbed.

Jemmy asked no questions. He was suspicious of the whole idea. His money was best kept in his own hiding place.

"I'll leave you to think about it, and we'll talk again, later, before we go."

Nineteen

The middle of December came.

In the dark of early morning Brian and Jemmy led four horses from the yards to the stable and by lantern-light saddled them. Two horses were for riding, two received packsaddles. The lamp was put out and the horses led to the hut and tethered near the door.

The necessities for the three-day trip were not many and when the riders emerged from the hut for the last time they had on oilskins.

Boy and Peter read the signs and got to their feet.

As he mounted, Brian caught a glimpse of what he thought was the rim of Jemmy's gold pan protruding from under a flap of one of the saddlebags. He sighed. "Is that your pan I can see there?"

Jemmy, not yet in the saddle, saw he was caught out. He had not asked permission to bring the pan, so had not exactly gone against orders.

"I thought when we stop sometimes, at a creek, I could give a bit of dirt a try. It won't hold us up. I'll do it only when we're stopped and there's no work to do."

"Take it back. We're not on a prospecting trip. We need no more chattels than're necessary."

"I could tie it on the outside coming home and it wouldn't take up any inside room."

"You heard me."

Jemmy drew out the pan and put it beside the door.

"Put it inside – a gust of wind could blow it away. It could be a mile from here by the time we get back. Is there anything else that oughtn't be on board?"

Jemmy hesitated. "Only a book – one."

"Take it back."

Jemmy extracted the Mongol book and took it into the hut.

Brian called after him, "You can bring the cribbage board and cards, but that's all."

The sky was still starry and the air cool and slightly misty. A fine day was on the way. It was the sort of morning Brian liked to ride in. He wanted to be at the Prapunga flats by near eight o'clock.

They reached the flats in good time and after a while entered a forested part, much of the floor of which was strewn with old fallen branches and tree trunks, some covered with moss. Brian led along a path he knew. In places the bracken closed over the path and came up to the riders' knees. When the path could not be seen Brian rode with a slack rein and left the navigating to his horse.

They heard the river before they saw it. The ground became softer, almost spongy and the grass was plentiful. The spring flooding had done its usual job. Soon they would cross the river and no longer be on Foxhow.

"Once we cross we'll be climbing nearly all the time," said Brian.

Before the day was over they would again cross the Prapunga. Tomorrow they would meet it once more. Before seeing the Snowy again, near Fitzford, they would have crossed the Prapunga four times.

The plan today was to be at Hutchinson's hut by late afternoon. They needed to be there before dark for they had not brought a lantern, and amongst the tasks to be carried out was the gathering of wood. There should be dry wood in the hut, as was the custom, but it would have to be replaced, as was another custom. Squatter Hutchinson had built the small, slab-sided bark-roofed hut for the use of himself and men when taking cattle to the high plains for summer grazing. But such huts, and there were many of them throughout the ranges, were freely used by any traveller needing shelter.

They came to where they would cross. Brian looked at the ground around him. He halted and dismounted, handed his reins to Jemmy and began a wider inspection.

"Horses," said Brian. "Unshod."

Jemmy saw what Brian was looking at. "Many?"

"Hard to say, but enough to be a worry."

"Not Foxhow horses?"

Brian did not answer. Studying the ground, he walked towards the water's edge. "I doubt it. Not here." Brian looked across the river. "Maybe over there is where they're from ¬– visitors, wild mongrels."

"Could they still be here, in the timber somewhere?"

"Maybe, maybe not. But we haven't time today to go looking."

Brian mounted and they rode out into the ford.

Leaving the water, Brian studied the ground.

"If they are wild horses," said Jemmy, "and they're still on Foxhow, and there aren't many of them, would it matter much?"

"The few mares I've got left I don't want mating with mongrelbreds. Nobody in his right mind wants them getting amongst his stock. They're so inbred, for one thing. There's nothing like inbreeding to compound faults, the kind you don't want, and once you've got them they could keep turning up for generations."

"Mightn't some of them be good horses?"

"Think about what I just said."

The climb was steady till early afternoon. Then the terrain became steeper. The squat and spreading snow gums were becoming fewer. Then with about an hour and a half of daylight left to them they saw Hutchinson's hut and rode towards it. Around the hut and enclosing about two acres was a chock-and-block fence. The sliprails were up and there were no horses to be seen. Brian was pleased at this, for it meant the place was unoccupied.

Jemmy dismounted, put down the sliprails at one end and led his horses through. He put up the rails after Brian came through. He did not remount for the hut was close and he would walk. Brian handed him the lead of his packer and swung away.

Brian was pleased to find the grass, never plentiful here at any time, had not been grazed lately, which meant the horses would have full bellies by morning. The grass also meant that the fences were likely to be in good order and had kept out wild horses, and would keep his horses in. To be certain, he rode a circuit and found nothing amiss. There was enough water in the shallow pool at the lower end to serve the horses for tonight.

As expected, there was dry firewood in the hut. But wood used would have to be replaced.

"When we unpack," said Brian, "I'll hobble and you go for wood."

Though there were fences, hobbled horses were easier to catch than horses not hobbled.

At dawn next morning they were in the saddle again. The air was damp and chilly and they had on their oilskins.

Gaining a ridge they turned and followed it south. The foggy air was clearing. Jemmy saw away to the east the whitish glow that he knew would soon become orange. Everywhere thick cloud made unseen the valleys it lay in. Only the peaks, like islands, showed above these sea-like clouds.

The riders descended into a wide and deep pot of trapped cloud and Jemmy thought this must be like walking on the bottom of an ocean, the mist, like water, above him.

"I call this the Dell," said Brian. "It's nearly always like this."

They began climbing steadily and suddenly were clear of the Dell. Again they turned south.

They had gone not much farther when Brian halted, reined his horses half around and signalled to Jemmy to come alongside. They were at the brink of a drop from which cloud was slowly rising and passing over them. The ground before them fell away steeply and where the drop ended could not be seen.

"We go down here," said Brian.

Jemmy was disbelieving. "Horses can't go down there."

"These horses can. The trick is: keep them facing downward at all times. Don't ever let them turn side-on; if you do, their feet'll go from under them and you'll finish up at the bottom with a horse on top of you. We've got about a thousand or more feet of this, though not all of it is as bad as it is just here. Ready?"

"Isn't there another way?"

"None that I want to take today. If you'd sooner, you can go back to Foxhow and keep the hens company. What's your choice?"

"… I'm coming."

"Good boy. This way saves time."

Down, down, down they went.

At the bottom the Prapunga met them again and they crossed.

Jemmy looked back. Through the wispy cloud the side of the mountain appeared steeper than it had from the top. That the horses had coped with the descent surprised him. He leaned forward and patted his mount and gave his packer a thankful glance. Brian, in front, turned in his saddle and looked at Jemmy and was pleased. Jemmy thought Brian was about to speak, but he didn't. With packsaddles full on the return trip, Jemmy doubted Brian would choose this way to come. Going up, laden, would be different to going down, unladen.

Shortly after noon and no longer wearing their oilskins they crossed the Prapunga once more. At a grassy spot the horses were rested, hobbled and let graze. The riders ate and drank tea. The dogs swam, shook themselves afterwards and stretched out in the shade.

Two more ranges to be dealt with lay ahead. But they were ranges that mostly could be ridden through rather than climbed, if you knew the tracks as Brian did. Mount Wrath would be the first.

They reached the other side of Wrath at nearly four o'clock. The range after that would be Eilean. It was between these two they would camp tonight.

To soothe their riding muscles, and give their saddle-horses a respite, the riders again dismounted and walked beside their horses.

"What does 'compound' mean?" asked Jemmy.

"In respect to what?"

"You said the word yesterday when you said about wild horses.

You said there was nothing like inbreeding to 'compound' a fault."

"In this case it means 'to strengthen'. It means if two horses related to each other by blood have the same fault and are mated, the offspring would surely have the same fault and likely would pass it on to their offspring. If the fault were, say, pasterns too long or too straight, this could be passed on for many generations."

They rode for a time without speaking when Jemmy said, "I've been thinking ..."

"You want to be careful of doing that. You might explode."

Jemmy grinned.

"Go on. Let's hear what you were thinking."

"I was thinking: if inbreeding compounds faults, would it also compound good points?"

"Yes. And some breeders do that, but very, very carefully – it's called 'line breeding', and it's very selectively done. But it can still go wrong. Better for fools like you and me to stay away from it."

Jemmy said no more on the matter.

"I think you've got a soft spot for wild horses – softer than I have," said Brian. "If you want to own a lot of horses in a hurry, and you could round them up, you could lay claim to all the wild horses in these mountains and I think nobody would challenge you."

Twenty

Like Hutchinson's, the next hut, known as Lomond's, was slabsided and bark-roofed, but bigger. It had a table, two beds and two chairs, all bush-crafted, and there were wooden kerosene-tin boxes that had been converted into shelves and doorless cupboards. The beds were similar to those at Hutchinson's: the ends inverted Vs of rough timber with hessian sacks lashed from one side-pole to the other.

There was no horse paddock. Close to the hut was a well, the top surrounded by a square of short logs to keep kangaroos from falling in. Lomond himself had been dead for years. Most people had called him Ben, though probably that was not his real name. He was a Scot from the isle of Lewis, as far as anybody knew, and had given the names of Wrath and Eilean to the two mountains he lived between, and, locally, the names had been adopted though were not gazetted.

The horses were hobbled and belled and let go. Feed hereabouts was better than at Hutchinson's and the horses began to graze instantly. Such good grass meant that they would not roam far during the night.

On his way to look for wood Jemmy went to the nearby grave of Ben Lomond. When he returned he said to Brian, "That big piece of stone on the grave is quartz. I wonder where it came from. Quartz country is gold country."

"I don't know where it might have come from – maybe from where the grave was dug. But there's not time left for you to go fossicking today. Besides, if you could find anywhere in this valley where gold hasn't been looked for, you'd be lucky."

"But some might have been missed."

"The Chinese worked through here after everybody else left, and anything they missed wouldn't be worth looking for."

The bread for dinner was harder than last night's, even harder than it had been at breakfast that morning, but tonight with cheese melted over it neither eater hesitated.

The dogs, their bellies full of kangaroo meat, tired from the day's running, were curled up with their backs against each other near the fire. At Hutchinson's they had claimed the third bed. There would be no soft bed for them tonight.

After dinner the travellers sat and stared silently into the fire. Brian's eyes closed and his chin started to slowly descend towards his chest. Jemmy watched. A bell outside tinkled. Brian woke and quickly lifted his head. After a minute or so he went to his bed and spread over it a heavy blanket and arranged his oilskin to pull over him. Jemmy went to his bed. Again they would sleep in their clothes. They were sitting on the edge of their beds and taking off their boots when Jemmy spoke.

"I've been thinking about what you said about me and a bank account," said Jemmy. "I'll do it. But I won't put in all my money – just some. I'll see how it goes and I might put more in later." That opening such an account would please Brian had swayed him.

"You're being very wise. I thought you'd come around, after you'd thought about it."

"Are you sure I won't have to pay them to mind my money?"

"Very sure. We'll talk about it again tomorrow. Not tonight."

"Say the Kelly gang came and robbed the bank while I was there and took my money before I'd handed it over to the bank man, would I lose my money?"

"The Kelly gang is gone. Kelly's gone – gone forever. They hanged him. So it won't be Ned Kelly that steals your money."

"Say somebody else did it, would I lose my money?"

"No. Take my word for it. The bank would honour the payment you were there to make. Go to sleep. Tell you what I'll do, if it'll put your mind at rest: if you get robbed tomorrow when we're in the bank, or if the bank is robbed afterwards and you're not compensated, I'll compensate you. In fact, I'll compensate you even if you're robbed in the street on the way to the bank. Now that's all for tonight."

Jemmy lay on his back and watched the flickering images on the walls. He turned his head and looked at Brian.

"Can I ask just one more question?"

Brian sighed. "If it's about banks – no."

"It's not."

"If it's a brief question, and not about banks, yes. But ask properly. You know what I mean."

"*May* I ask you one more question?"

"Yes."

"Are there any churches in Fitzford?"

"What? Yes. Good night."

Curiosity lifted Brian above his weariness.

"Why do you want to know if there are churches? Do you want to go to a Christmas service?"

"I wouldn't mind. But I was thinking of something else. I'm not christened and I'd like to be."

"There are many people not christened. There's nothing strange about not being christened."

"I'd like to be christened. If you're not christened, you won't see the face of God when you die."

"Who told you that?"

"Barney Kelson at Jindabilla. He reads the Bible all the time."

"He might read it, but how well he understands it is another question."

"Have you been christened?"

"Yes. My parents took me along when I was a baby."

"Then you don't have to worry."

"I'm pretty sure I wouldn't be worried anyway. But there's nothing wrong with your being christened if you want to be. As for not seeing the face of God if you've not been christened, I have my doubts. Tom Halpen is as good a student of the Bible as anybody I know. When he visits again we'll ask him."

"I know I'm not too old to be christened. John the Baptist christened grown people, even old people, so you don't have to be a baby to have it done."

"Yes, yes, I know that. But there's more to it these days. Christenings are usually family affairs, and there's a godfather involved."

"What do godfathers do?"

"They guide you through your religious education. Usually godfathers are uncles or close family friends."

"Could anybody else do it?"

"I suppose so. I can't see why not."

"I'd like to get it done soon. Would you be my godfather?"

"Oh, no, no, no – I couldn't accommodate that. This is a matter you need to take up with your family."

"Mum wouldn't mind. My sisters aren't christened. Mum said she would like us all to be christened one day."

"Well there you are, the matter's taken care of. Your mother's got it in hand and you'll be christened in due course."

"If you'd be my godfather, I wouldn't ask you to guide me through my religious education. I wouldn't ask you to read the Bible to me."

"There are reasons why I wouldn't be suitable. A better man for the job would be Tom Halpen. You could ask him."

"But he mightn't come to Foxhow for a long time. You said he doesn't come much."

"True. Also, he doesn't go to Fitzford much, so there's another problem."

Brian rolled over and faced the wall.

"… I was thinking," said Jemmy.

"Well, don't – not any more tonight. If you must think, think of where you'll be sleeping tomorrow night, or what you'll be having for Christmas dinner … If you get up through the night to go outside, throw some wood on the fire, some of the heavy pieces. Goodnight and that's final."

Twenty-one

As on the other days, they were away in the first of the morning light and not long before noon they came to the Snowy. The banks were becoming higher and they rode towards the bend the other side of which was the town of Fitzford. The town had sprung on the side of the ford where a shepherd known as Johnny Fitz lived in a hut. The ford became much used when a gold strike in the mountains to the east came in 1860. The hut was gone, devoured in a bushfire, and nobody knew for certain what became of Johnny, and nobody round about knew if Fitz was all of his surname or only part of it. The diggings to the east were still expanding and the town had become a gateway and supply centre for prospectors, local squatters and the drovers coming over from the Monaro with sheep and cattle destined for the Melbourne markets. One story about Johnny was that in England he had been sentenced to seven years' transportation for the illegal use of a horse and at the end of the sentence received another seven years for the theft of a cow.

To enter the town the riders had to cross the ford or go over the bridge farther down.

Nearing the bend Jemmy saw men on the other side – two were near the water's edge and there were several others, with shovels, higher up and at the side of a wooden flume down which water was flowing. He could see the water spilling into the river at the bottom, could see the smoke and hear the chugging of the engine pumping water up to where the flume started.

One of the miners waved and the riders waved back.

Brian put hands to his mouth and called out, "There'll be none of the bend left soon."

The man nearest lifted his shovel. He was Rollo Austin and Brian knew him.

"We'll go along to the bridge," said Brian to Jemmy. "I helped with getting the government loan that part-financed it, so I use it now and again on principle. Before the bridge came the town used to get cut off for weeks when the river flooded."

They crossed the bridge and followed the road that curved to the left and led back along the river and into Victoria Street. The street started, or ended, at the ford. They made their way to the Royal Oak, the biggest of the town's five hotels, where they would stay. Though there was good stabling here, and a good stableman, the horses and dogs would be consigned to Peter Webber's livery stable farther down, near the corner of Albert Street.

They booked into the Royal and carried up their luggage, such as it was.

Christmas was four days away. Tomorrow evening there was to be a dinner that Brian was looking forward to attending. The dinner, held at the Royal, was the annual meeting, though no business would be discussed, conducted by the men who called the association they belonged to the Fitzford Sportsmen's Club. Brian was a foundation member.

Before going to Peter Webber's there was a place Brian wanted to call at, Henneberry's Store. He wanted to put in an order that would go out with the next wagon to Braywood, where he would later collect his purchases. Once, through delaying, he had missed a wagon by only hours. Also from Henneberry's he wanted to pick up his ordered newspapers and magazines. And he wanted to see Henneberry's noticeboard, to see if any visiting Methodist speakers were to give lectures while he was in town. The Methodist lectures, open to all, were always worth attending. He was never surprised at what the Methodists spoke on – anything from agriculture to the whaling industry or astronomy.

The front doorway of Peter Webber's stable was high and wide enough to admit the biggest of commercial coaches. Peter had the Cobb & Co horse contract at the Fitzford end of the Wodonga–Fitzford run – six horses in, six out, once a week. In good weather, with no bogging, the run between the two places took three days. This run Cobb & Co now had all to itself, due in no small part to the company's policy of changing horses every fifteen miles. Fresh horses meant fast coaches.

The strong sunlight at the doorway dazzled Peter as he turned towards the shapes of horses and riders coming in. He lifted a hand and shaded his eyes. Peter, a man of thirty-five, clean-shaven and hatless, walked towards the horsemen. His recognition of the elderly man, and the dogs, came with a rush. A smile broke across his face. "We've been expecting you."

Brian dismounted and he and Peter shook hands.

Peter took the lead of Brian's packer. "The wife said only yesterday that we'd see you today or tomorrow. Which way did you come?"

"Over the back – Wrath and Eilean."

"And you brought company," said Peter, turning to Jemmy, who was now dismounted.

"Yes," said Brian. "This is my head stockman, Jem Tyler."

Jemmy and Peter shook hands.

Peter turned away and called loudly. "Alfred."

A boy about Jemmy's age and size appeared in the back doorway, an opening as big as the one at the front. The boy advanced sullenly. He focused on Jemmy.

"He's bigger every time I see him," said Brian.

"He's finished school and he'll be working here from after Christmas. The little devil, he's insisted he finish his school holidays before he starts. But he's working part of today, to give him practice, I told him." Peter grinned. "He's not happy about it."

Both men laughed.

"Take one of those horses and give a hand," said Peter to his son, inclining his head towards Jemmy's horses.

Leaving the boys to introduce themselves, Peter and Brian, each leading a horse, walked away.

"What do you want done with them, same as usual?" asked Peter.

"Yes."

"The dogs too?"

"Yes. I'll get the chains out in a minute. The boy'll come every day and give them a run. And he'll give you a hand with any jobs you want help with. He'll spring to it. Just ask him. You'll find him a good boy."

The boys eyed each other. They didn't bother with introductions.

Alfred led the way to a long rail about chest height and threw the packer's lead over it. At intervals along the rail were items of harness and saddlery.

"How do you want this stuff put?" asked Jemmy as he commenced unsaddling Ochre.

"You can see."

"Just thought I'd ask first. It's your stable. Maybe you want it put somewhere else."

Alfred did not answer.

Brian and Peter talked as they worked and when they finished unsaddling led the horses towards the back doorway.

When the boys were ready they followed the men. They walked abreast.

The dogs, deciding at last to move from where they had flopped, rose wearily and followed.

"Who's Mister Drury to you: your boss or what?" asked Alfred.

"Boss."

"How old are you?"

"Fourteen next March."

"I'm fourteen now. How long you been working for him?"

"A long time. Months."

"What do you do?"

"Stock work."

"You're not a stockman," sneered Alfred. "You're not old enough."

"I didn't say I was a stockman. I said I did stock work.

"Probably you're only a rouseabout."

"I do a bit of that too. Got to. If you're the only worker on the place you've got to do a bit of everything. I do a bit of prospecting on the side."

"Have you ever found any?"

"Plenty."

"Have you got any gold to prove it?"

"None on me."

"Where is it?"

"Back at Foxhow – hidden. Sold some and bought a good mare – half thoroughbred – and she's in foal to Mister Drury's stallion. The foal could become a racehorse – could be worth a lot of money."

"You haven't got a mare," sniggered Alfred. "What's her name? Come on, what's her name – quick, quick, quick. If you're fairdinkum, you shouldn't have to think. Quick, quick, quick. What's her name?"

"Blink Bonny."

"Blink Bonny. Where'd you get that name? You just thought it up, now."

"No, I didn't. That's been her name for a long time. I named her after the famous filly that won the English Derby."

"Yeah? When did this Blink Bonny win the English Derby? Come on –

quick, quick, quick. If you can't tell me quick, you're lying."

"In eighteen fifty-seven."

"How do you know?"

"I read."

Alfred desisted.

"And if my mare's foal is a colt," Jemmy went on, "I'll name him Blair Athol, after Blink Bonny 's son that won the English Derby in eighteen sixty-one."

"I don't believe any of that," said Alfred. "What's your name, anyhow?"

"Jem Tyler."

They released the horses into a paddock and went back inside to where the men were talking.

"Your good wife," Brian said to Peter. "I'd forgotten to ask."

"She's well. Don't leave without you see her."

"Wouldn't dream of it. I'll do it now."

"Take your man with you. She baked this morning." Peter looked at Jemmy. "You might be in luck."

"Come, my boy, and meet a lady," said Brian.

The two walked to the side door that opened onto a path that led to the cottage.

Peter called after them, "Tell her to give you the coach papers. Take them with you. I've finished with them. There's some from Melbourne, some from Sydney."

Lizette Webber had long, dark, slightly greying hair tied in a bun at the back of her head. Her delight at who was standing on her doorstep was easy to see.

"Come in, come in. We knew you'd be along soon. And you've brought a friend." She beamed at Jemmy.

Brian took her hand and bowed as if he might kiss it.

Lizette's cry was half shriek, half laugh. "Oh, get out with you. Don't you go bowing at me. You're as bad as the boys I used to know down the coast."

Jemmy was introduced. He, too, took the hand that was extended and bowed slightly.

The visitors were asked to sit down. Lizette then went to the stove and pushed a big black-iron kettle onto the hottest part. Tea for the visitors was on the way.

Jemmy quietly watched and listened to the easy banter that was going on.

Lizette spoke with more than a hint of an Irish accent. Her parents came from Ireland and, up till she turned twenty, when she married Peter, most of the people she lived amongst on the south-west coast of Victoria were Irish emigrants. Her family were potato farmers near the hamlet that had been named Killarney, which was near the place called Belfast, which was on the Moyne river, all names that the settlers had brought with them.

The cake they had with their tea was plain, yellow from the Jersey butter in it.

Afterwards Lizette said to Jemmy, "Would you say no to a piece of date cake?"

"No. I mean I wouldn't say, no."

"I know what you meant."

She turned to Brian. "You'll be having Christmas dinner with us again, we hope?"

"My thanks. Yes. However, there is a problem: my protégé here."

She looked at Jemmy. "He's invited too, of course."

Jemmy smiled and nodded. "Thankyou very much."

Although the piece of date cake was served on a plate, once picked up it never touched the plate again.

Amused, Lizette watched. "You're enjoying that, aren't you?"

Jemmy nodded.

Lizette rose and began carving off another slice of cake. Then she cut a second and looked at Jemmy. "Another for you, and would you take the other piece out to Alfred? Did you see him in the stable?"

"Yes."

Jemmy stood.

"Take it in your hand," instructed Lizette, speaking of the slice for Alfred. "Send a plate out there and it'll never come back in one piece."

Lizette went to the door and held it open for Jemmy then went to the window and watched him walking along the path. She spoke without turning.

"What's the story to your lad?"

"The full story? God only knows. He comes from Quartz Creek. He's been with me a few months now."

"He's very polite, got a nice way about him."

"I think he can thank his mother for much of that, from what I saw of her. And I do what I can. Some credit to him, though. He's easy to teach."

"You weren't able to send him home for Christmas?"

"No. Transport's one problem; and he definitely didn't want to go."

"Did you notice the bow when he shook hands?" She smiled. "He copied you."

"Yes, I noticed."

"I wish somebody's good manners would rub off onto that heathen of mine. He wanted to wear a black armband for Ned Kelly."

"Jem's had no schooling," said Brian. "Can't read and write."

"That's a pity. Can't you do anything for him – teach him a word or two?"

"I could try, but I don't. I mustn't."

"Oh, why not?"

"There's more to this than you think. I've got myself into a predicament and I don't know what to do for the best. At Foxhow, with me, isn't where he should be. He should be with family, or with more people than there are at my place. He needs a village around him. He's a good boy, but he oughtn't to be with me. Going to school is what he should be doing. I fear the more I do for him, the more he'll want to attach himself to me. For his sake, I don't want that. And there's a father that he goes to a lot of trouble to keep away from. I've never met him, and I'm not sure I want to."

"If he has to work away from home, he could do worse than work for you, as unsatisfactory as you say it is. You'd have to be thankful of his company at times?"

"I am, I am, I grant you. But I haven't exactly escaped unscathed."

"What do you mean?"

"I've become a chatterbox, a sermonier. Nearly everything I say to him turns into a lecture."

"Maybe it's the teacher in you coming out."

"Maybe it's the bore in me that's coming out. I used to be a reticent chap."

"Reticent? You've never been reticent in your life, not as long as I've known you."

"Well, I'm worse now."

They chatted on and eventually the subject gave way to others. Brian asked about the health and doings of people they both knew. Lizette asked about his last stay in Albury. He asked what she had lately heard on the riding successes of Tom Corrigan, a family neighbour on the coast and now-famous steeplechase jockey.

***

"I know where there's plenty of gold," said Alfred.

"Where?"

"In a creek over there."

"How far away?" Jemmy was suspicious but curious.

"We could walk it – easy. Not far. I can get away, I reckon."

"I haven't got a pan, but I'd like to take a look."

Alfred went to his father and Jemmy hurried to the cottage and spoke to Brian.

Brian had no objection to Jemmy's going off with Alfred. "Here's a key. You know where the hotel is. Better go in the back way. We're both looking a bit rough for the front door. If I'm not there, take yourself to the bathhouse and get into some clean clothes."

Alfred led his gold-seeking acquaintance along a track that began near the back of the stable. At a road they crossed and took another track. They went into bush, came out and scrambled down a steep bank.

"Here," said Alfred.

They were in a mostly-dry watercourse whose banks were far enough apart to accommodate a river. But there had never been a river here, only a creek that had been widened due to gold seekers digging into the banks and the rains that followed.

"This place's been flogged out," declared Jemmy.

"Plenty of blokes still come here," insisted Alfred.

"They'd be new chums."

"Well, there used to be plenty of gold here."

They walked on, following the trickle that passed as a stream.

“There might be some that’s been missed,” said Alfred.

“There’s always some that somebody’s missed,” replied Jemmy. “But I reckon there’ve been a lot of blokes here looking for what’s been missed. But if I had a pan I wouldn’t mind giving it a go.”

“Dad’s got a pan. We could get that.”

“You want to try with me one day? If we find any we’ll go halves?”

“Yep.”

They kept walking.

“You’ve never had a go at gold?” asked Jemmy.

Alfred shook his head. “Any gold I ever go for, I’ll do it the way Ned did.”

“Who – Ned Kelly?”

Alfred grinned. “Let others find it then I take my share.”

Jemmy kept an eye open for where he thought might be good places to fossick in. They came to where there was a stretch of mud and they moved out to firmer ground. Jemmy stopped to look more thoroughly at an object sticking out of the alluvium ahead. He hoped it was what he thought it could be: a cradle for washing soil away from gold. If it was a cradle, the main part was buried in the mud. The shaft sticking out could be the lever. He began walking faster. Alfred let him go.

By the time Alfred caught up, Jemmy was barelegged and up to his knees in the mud. Reaching the wooden object Jemmy put his hand on the lever and pulled gently. The lever broke off. “It’s all rotten,” he called.

Alfred laughed.

At a pool Jemmy washed his feet and legs.

On they walked, Jemmy carrying his boots tied around his neck.

The banks on both sides became higher. They came to where the mud was suddenly arrested by a rough levy made of rocks. The water on the other side was clear. Cut into the side of the bank on the right was a foot track that led to the top. Jemmy could see at the top the upper part of a tent.

“There’s a camp. Let’s go up.”

“No,” said Alfred. “No-one’s there. It’s haunted. A man died up there. I’m not going. Come on, we’d better go back.”

“When did he die?”

"A long time ago."

"Wouldn't hurt to look."

"No. It's bad luck. I know where we can go – Billy Munro's." Alfred's mind was made up and he turned and started back the way they had come.

When Jemmy saw Alfred was not going to wait, he followed.

They climbed the bank and went into the bush and came out on a road, not the one they had earlier crossed. Nearly two hours had passed since they left the stable. They passed cottages that had lots of ground around them. Foraging hens made way for them and a few tethered goats took no notice.

"Keep your eye open for a bottle we can take pot-shots at," said Alfred.

"Yeah; a cod-liver oil one. Have you got to take cod-liver oil?"

"No."

"I do, and it tastes like rotten fish. Any geese around here?"

"No."

Ahead was a crossroads and through the trees on the right could be seen the backs of some of the taller buildings in the main street.

At the crossroads a man in a dark suit and bowler hat came out of the street on the right and kept walking. He disappeared at the other side.

"That was Brian," said Jemmy, breaking into a run. "Let's catch up."

Jemmy stopped and turned when he saw Alfred was not joining in.

"Didn't look like him, to me," said Alfred.

"It was. I'd know him a mile off. Come on."

"Nar."

Unhurrying, Alfred caught up. "There's nothing down that way, only the cemetery. Let's track him. That'll be more fun."

They stopped at the crossroads and saw the back of the man they had seen, a hundred or more yards away.

"That's where he's going, I reckon," said Alfred. "The cemetery."

Alfred led to the other side of the junction and into the bush.

They reached near to where the road finished at the cemetery entrance. Brian was already inside. Through breaks in the foliage where they were hidden, the boys watched.

Brian, seeming certain of his path, made his way amongst the headstones. He stopped at a grave and faced the upright stone at the other end. After a minute or so he turned and walked to the edge of a part where there were no headstones. As if expecting to see somebody, he looked across a grassy expanse that had been newly scythed. Long, green cut-grass lay on the ground. Then he turned and went back to the grave he had earlier stood at. After a time he turned away, took the path he had come in by and started back along the road.

The boys came out of the bush when they thought Brian was far enough away to not hear or see them. They dashed into the cemetery. Jemmy now led. He had seen the grave Brian had stood at and he went to it.

The grave had on top of it a broad stone slab. The weathered marble headstone at the end had curved shoulders that met at an apex in the middle.

"It's wide," commented Jemmy.

"That's 'cause there's plenty in there – four."

Alfred went on reading the headstone.

"Who are they?" asked Jemmy.

"Can't you read? His wife and children."

"Children, too? I didn't know he had any children. I knew he had a wife once."

They stood silently, looking at the headstone, Alfred reading it, Jemmy wishing he could read it.

"What're their names?" asked Jemmy.

"You can read."

"The writing's faded a lot. I can't see it properly."

"You must have rotten eyes. I can read it. The three girls are Henrietta, Maude and Gertrude."

"…What was Missus Drury's name?"

"Amelia Jane."

The ages of the interred and dates of their deaths Jemmy could read. Mrs Drury was aged thirty-two; Henrietta was ten; Maude seven and Gertrude five. They had died in 1860. The next shock came when he discovered how close the deaths were to one another. He mumbled, "They all died in two weeks. The same two weeks."

"There're lots of graves like that here – full of people, whole families. The fever that went around – flu – got 'em, Mum and Dad said. There're lots buried over there too." With a jerk of his thumb Alfred indicated the area where the grass had been scythed. "They came to Fitzford from all around because there were doctors here. Most of them came from the goldfields. If they didn't get better they finished up here." Alfred turned away. "I wonder what he was looking at over there."

They went to where the grass had been scythed and stood where Brian had stood.

"Can you see them?" said Alfred, crouching.

"See what?"

"Get down like me and you'll see – graves."

Jemmy dropped to one knee, lowered his head and looked out over the surface of the ground and saw the mound; they were low, all near the same length, width and height. "There's hundreds of them," he said, astonished. "They go right back to over there. And there's no crosses. Nothing."

"Yep. They're nearly all diggers. They just came to town and died. There're plenty of graves like this up at the diggings, too. No crosses; no names."

"I've seen graves on stations, but I ain't ever seen this many."

"Not many go in there now, 'cause the flu's gone. If it comes back though – "

They returned to the grave of Brian's wife and children.

"We'd better get going if we're going to Billy's," said Alfred.

The bunches of dead flowers on some of the graves gave Jemmy an idea. He remembered seeing yellow somewhere and soon saw the colour again, clusters of small round blooms growing at the sides of some of the paths between the graves. "Let's put some flowers on their grave." He began picking the yellow flowers.

"They're not flowers, they're weeds, pee-the-beds."

"That doesn't matter."

After picking enough to make a posy, Jemmy put it on the grave.

"If they'd buried Ned here, I'd look after his grave," said Alfred.

"I know someone who wouldn't – Brian."

They went to the road.

"Don't forget to look out for a bottle," said Alfred.

Twenty-two

They had slept well. Last night had been their first between cotton sheets since they were in Albury, months ago. This morning, clean from their bathing the previous afternoon and dressed in their best clothes, Brian and Jemmy stepped out into the street. They went to the barbershop. From there they went to the Bank of New South Wales branch in Victoria Street. When they left, Jemmy held in his hand a bankbook in which he had nervously signed his name. Before that, nervously, he had signed his name in a big book that the man on the other side of the counter put in front of him. The man had shaken his hand. As the man had reached to take the fifteen shillings Brian put a sovereign with it.

Next, Dilmond Percival the tailor was called upon. The call was only social. Percival was a shire alderman, and a member of the Sportsmen's Club, as was the next man they visited, Tobias Brumley the saddler. He too was an alderman. Both these men would be at the dinner tonight. Other calls followed.

They were back at the hotel close to noon and entered through the bar-room. Brian looked at each of the several drinkers at the counter.

The man he hoped to see was not amongst them. He asked Jemmy if he would like to have a raspberry cordial. Brian caught the eye of the barman and put his hand on Jemmy's head. The barman nodded.

Brian was seated in the lounge when Jemmy came in with his drink. Against a wall was a bookcase he had discovered the previous night and he went to it started searching for books with pictures.

From the corner of his eye Jemmy saw Brian lift his hand in a wave to an elderly man who had come into the room. The man was tall and sparely built and dressed in a black suit. His hair was more white than grey but his bushy eyebrows were black. Jemmy believed this was Cedric Hoy, the man Brian had been expecting.

Jemmy put back the last book he had opened, drank the remainder of the cordial and returned the glass to the bar.

Brian and Cedric were through to the dining room when Jemmy got back to the lounge. He followed.

Brian pointed to a table near a window. "Over there. We can watch the poetry of the street: see who's riding or driving a nice horse."

Seating themselves, Cedric replied, "You can watch the poetry of the street. I'll look after the poetry the cook puts on my plate." He noticed Jemmy standing beside them. He turned to Brian. "I heard you had a boy with you. Is this him?"

"It is. My head stockman, Jem Tyler."

"At least he's a handsomer than your last one."

"Don't let his angel face fool you," said Brian. "He's a dangerous man. He thinks like a lawyer, forgets nothing you say and will use it against you when you least expect."

The men sat but Jemmy remained standing. He extended his hand to Cedric and they shook.

"Sit down, son," said Brian.

Jemmy listened to all that the men said. He was finding himself not taking a liking to Cedric.

They reached the bread-and-butter-pudding part of the meal when Brian asked, "Have you done any more about the last of the Mount Ebony stock?"

"Yes and no. We've got all the cattle out, and most of the horses. But not the grey Arab. Can't get him. He can go like the wind and with no weight on his back we can't head him in a straight run. If we'd been lucky enough to get him early, we mightn't have bothered about the others. We'll try again around February, when the place is drier and they come in closer for water."

Mount Ebony station was a deceased estate and Cedric and his sons had been the successful bidders for the stock on the property.

The meal finished, Brian turned to Jemmy. "Laddie, Mister Hoy and I want to go somewhere and talk business. Why don't you go along to the stables and see Alfred? Give the dogs a run. Do anything you like. The rest of the day is yours."

Jemmy rose and turned to leave.

"Aren't you going to tell Mister Hoy how pleased you were to meet him?"

Jemmy was not pleased to have met Cedric but did as he was told. He turned to Cedric and straightened himself. "I'm very pleased to have met you, Mister Hoy." He put out his hand and Cedric shook it.

Cedric's eyes followed Jemmy. "Has he had any military training? The way he drew himself up I thought he was going to salute. I could almost believe he was pleased to meet me."

"Why shouldn't he be? He doesn't know you as well as I do." Brian grinned. "He's a good boy. He tries hard."

"Where did you get him?"

"He wandered into camp one night with an old mare for the stallion. I nearly shot him."

"He calls you Brian, I noticed," said Cedric, disapproving.

"I couldn't live in a hut with anybody, even a boy, calling me Mister all the time."

"Be careful. You know what familiarity can breed."

"Not much danger of that. He won't be with me long enough. But when I send him off, I'd like him to own a few good manners, if only in memory of me. There's not much else I can send him away with."

"Why bother at all, if you're going to get rid of him?"

"Good manners are easier to live with than bad. You know that. After me, he could go on to better things. I'd like to think he might.

He's got a lot to learn, and most of that will come from the adults he meets, if they'll be bothered with him. If you haven't noticed, adults respond better to children with good manners – will talk to them more, teach them more. Who bothers talking to people not courteous or respectful?"

Cedric took his watch from a waistcoat pocket. "About time we adjourned, to that other place." He meant the bar. "And the meeting's at two."

But he did not move. The meeting he had to attend was a shire council meeting, the last for the year, and it would be a short one, held in a reception room of the hotel. Cedric was Shire President.

"You said the boy's name is Tyler?"

"That's right."

"Any connection to the Tyler that the warrant's out for – the Tyler that assaulted Atha Bonwick at the Nelore diggings?"

"I think so, but I'm not sure. Probably father and son."

"What's the boy told you?"

"Nothing. Not a thing. He's been well drilled, and I don't quiz him. He might talk one day. He'll talk about his mother but not his father. I think he's too frightened of his father to break with the drill. I've met the mother, a good woman. I think she's having a hard time."

"They say Tyler's in smoke."

"That's where I'd be too if I were him."

"It was Atha's wife who pressed charges. She wouldn't let go. The police wanted to treat it as no more than a common fight in a goldfields' grog shop. It wasn't a fight, I believe. Tyler king hit him. Atha's never picked a fight in his life. He's been a pretty sick man ever since – gets abscesses in the ear on the side he was hit; goes nearly mad with the pain at times. Sometimes they think he's going to die. Then he rallies. If Atha were to die, what do you think Tyler's position would be?"

"I don't know, but I wouldn't like to be in it."

"Murder?"

"A tricky one, that. Manslaughter, maybe."

"Murder or manslaughter; if a judge like Barry that got hold of Kelly gets him, he him give him what he gave Kelly. Sizar Hendricks was with Atha that night and said there was a boy with Tyler. Might have been this boy of yours. Sizar and Atha had been on a butcher's run to the diggings and had no cattle left and were on their way home. Atha didn't see the punch coming, and Sizar doesn't know what was said or what brought it on. They were standing at the counter and Tyler was on the other side of Atha. There were words exchanged, not loudly, and Sizar wasn't looking. Next thing Atha's down and the bloke's doing a bolt. A boy ran after him. Atha's wife has put up a reward."

Cedric looked at his watch again. "Let's adjourn to the trough."

Twenty-three

At the sound of the door opening Brian instantly snapped out of his doze. From the bed where, without his coat or boots on, he had been resting for the past half hour he saw Jemmy come into the room. "Time to rise, I suppose," he sighed. He did not move. He looked at his watch. The Council meeting Cedric had gone to would not yet be finished.

Jemmy took the clothes' brush from the dressing table and brushed the front and sleeves of his jacket.

"Don't forget your boots," advised Brian.

Jemmy looked at his boots and went to a leather pouch and knelt and took out a rag. With a quick wipe the dust on his boots vanished and the sheen reappeared.

"Don't forget to comb your hair."

They were to dine at half-past six. Brian would eat almost nothing, for there would be food aplenty where he would be later, at the Sportsmen's Club dinner.

Moving to the foot of Brian's bed, Jemmy seated himself on the edge. "I was thinking ..."

"I told you what could happen if you keep that up."

Jemmy grinned.

Brian sat up, put his feet on the floor and began putting on his boots. "Go on. What were you thinking?"

"I was thinking: could we go with Mister Hoy and help him get those horses at Mount Ebony?"

"No; definitely no."

When he saw that Jemmy had no more to say, Brian went on. "Cedric's got three big strong sons, and a good tracker named Jacky Winton who'd find horses anywhere, and as many other men as he might need. He doesn't need us, and we don't need the amusement – I don't. Running horses gone wild in rough country is no fun. No man in his right mind does unless he has to. If it wasn't for that grey Arab they want, the Hoys wouldn't go near the place again."

For Jemmy, going for the Mount Ebony horses sounded like an adventure that far outweighed the fact that he had not taken a liking to Cedric Hoy. For the sake of the adventure, he could put up with Cedric.

His boots now tied, Brian stood, put on his coat and brushed the front and the sleeves.

"It's hard to say what time I'll be in tonight, but you'll be alright here on your own. There are all those books downstairs that you haven't been through yet."

"I've been through most of them."

"I might have known," Brian mumbled. "I'm pleased there are some you haven't seen yet. Don't bring me one to read to you."

There was rap on the door. Brian nodded for Jemmy to see who was there.

"It's Alfred," said Jemmy.

"Bring him in."

"I've got a note for you from my mother," Alfred told Brian.

Brian read the note and turned to Jemmy. "This is an invitation. Mister and Missus Webber, and I presume Master Alfred here, want to know if you would like to spend the rest of your stay in Fitzford with them, as their guest, at their place."

"Sleep there too?"

"That's what's indicated. It's a jolly good idea, and I think you should accept. A better place for you there than here."

"Right up till we go back to Foxhow?"

"Yes, early New Year."

"Can I – may I – keep my key for here?"

"Why not? The Royal Oak can be your second address. Usually only toffs have more than one address. No: counting Foxhow, you'll have three addresses. No: counting Quartz Creek you'll have four. There'll be no talking to you – a man with four addresses; I've never known one."

Turning to Alfred, Brian asked, "From when is this invitation to take effect?"

"Today. After dinner. Mum said if you haven't got a portmanteau, we've got one you can have a lend of. We can get it now, if you want to."

"That seals it," said Brian. "That'll give you something to do for a while. Off you go."

The boys closed the door behind them and broke into a run.

Brian heard them and went to the door, opened it and put out his head. "Walk, walk. You'll knock somebody over. You're in a hotel, not out in the street."

He sat on the edge of the bed and put on his boots, then put on his coat and started for downstairs. In the lounge or at the bar he might find somebody to talk to. There was plenty of time to kill.

Twenty-four

Brian believed that if he were a Godly man the thoughts that had come to him soon after he woke in the early hours of the morning might have been Providence-sent. Afterwards, he lay there thinking, planning. What a plan it was, if all the strands connecting it could be drawn together. Cedric Hoy would be involved, and the Webber family, and Jemmy, the object at the centre. None would know a game was being played, at least in the beginning. The first requisite was for Jemmy's stay with the Webbers to go well. The success of the plan would see Jemmy boarding with the Webbers and going to school. Brian would meet all costs. Jemmy's going with Cedric to try to catch the grey Arab would be the bait. But Cedric would have to be willing. He decided he would speak first to whoever came along first, and that might be Jemmy, for tonight they were to go to the Church of England service at the chapel in Trafalgar Street.

The morning was Christmas Eve. Dressed in his suit and bowler hat, Brian started for the cemetery.

In the cemetery he saw Hollis Bricker scything grass. Hollis told him he had been sitting away in the shade and saw him when Brian came a few days ago. Hollis spoke of the boys who had come afterwards and that one was Peter Webber's son, and that they had gone to the grave Brian had been at.

At the grave Brian took off his hat and coat and put them on the next grave and rolled up his shirtsleeves. He took out a pocket knife. Looking about to see where he might start he saw the withered posy of yellow flowers. Puzzled, he picked up the flowers then put them back. In turns, stooping and kneeling, he worked his way around the perimeter, cutting off or gouging out weeds that had sprung up from the crevices in the stonework.

The cut-off weeds became a heap in the centre of the slab. Pleased that he was finished, or close to finished, he stood and looked for weeds he might have missed.

He noticed somebody approaching – it was Jemmy, dressed in his best clothes.

"How did you know I was here?"

"I just thought you might be. You weren't at the hotel."

"A lucky guess. How's your stay with the Webbers going?"

"Good."

"You and Alfred were here the other day, I'm told. There were some flowers put here." He glanced at the posy then back at Jemmy. "Did you and Alfred put them there?"

"Yes."

"That was nice of you. Did you just happen to see me?"

"Yes. We were over there in the bush."

"What a coincidence. Anyhow, what's brought you here today?"

"Just thought I'd come and see if there was anything you wanted me to do." He looked at the tidied grave. "Can I help?"

"If you'd come earlier, you could have. I'm finished now. But you could gather up that pile of weeds and throw them over there somewhere."

All done and with hat in hand and coat over his arm, Brian, with Jemmy, started towards the road. Brian turned and gave Hollis a wave.

"I'm pleased you're enjoying your stay with the Webbers. Are you still interested in going with Mister Hoy after those horses at Mount Ebony?"

"Yes. Are we going?"

"I'm not. But I might be able to arrange for you to go. I say only 'might'. I could talk to Cedric about it. Even if he were agreeable, there are other problems. You'd have to be here in Fitzford waiting and ready at the right time."

"I'd be ready."

"There's more. You'd have to be staying somewhere, where you could easily be reached – perhaps with the Webbers, if they'd be prepared to have you for a few days, or a week or more. And after you come back from Mount Ebony, you'd have to stay with them again for a while, till we could get you back to Foxhow."

"Nobody would have to come and get me. I could get myself back. I know the way now."

"We'll talk about that later."

"Say the Webbers don't want to have me, could I stay somewhere else?"

"No. You stay with the Webbers only, or there's no deal. It's the Webbers or nothing. So while you're with them at the moment, it's important you make a good impression. Use your best manners, at all times. One other matter. Mister Hoy is not everybody's 'cup of tea'. He's a good man, one of the best – if I were in a tight corner there's nobody I'd sooner have beside me. But he's a direct man, too direct for some people's liking. He uses black powder and speaks to no man twice. His ways frighten a lot of people. You'd better think about all this before you make up your mind."

Jemmy thought about the black powder remark. He knew that in a gun black powder was more powerful than any other kind and made a louder noise. "I've made up my mind. I'm not frightened."

"I'll see what I can do. But I make no promises."

"Wouldn't you like to go too?"

"No, I'm too old for that kind of work."

"But Mister Hoy is old."

"Yes, but there's a stallion he wants – that grey Arab. His sons could do the job without him, but he feels he needs to be there. That's Cedric."

Twenty-five

Being summer, evenings closed slowly and daylight came early. As was the case on such days the chores and other activities in the Webber household were timed to end before there was need for a lamp. Kerosene had to be brought a long way and was not cheap. They were nights when the last sounds that might be heard were from magpies, sounds that often came in chorusing bursts and were like mixtures of yodelling and ringing bells and just as often might be the first to be heard in the morning, or before, from the tops of trees if a moon were to brighten a night sky.

Alfred's room had been added after the cottage was built and had no doorway opening directly into the house.

In their beds the boys lay on their backs and stared at the window that was still admitting a degree of light. They were not yet ready for sleep. They had their own thoughts. A thought that came to Jemmy was the present Alfred's sister had handed him on Christmas day, a cake of scented soap in a paper wrapper that had on it a picture of a young smiling girl with full and smooth cheeks. The present was from all the family. At that Christmas dinner he had never seen such a large amount of food on a table. He wondered if the Sportsmen's dinner Brian had gone to had as much food on the table.

"What can we do tomorrow?" said Jemmy.

"We could go eeling. But we'd have to go early, before the sun gets up. No, we can't do that. We've got to get bait first."

"We could use dogs' meat. I've caught eels before. Night-time's best, 'specially if you put a lantern on the bank or out on a limb."

"Yeah, I know. If we wake up early enough, we'll go."

Silence.

"Who were you named after?" asked Alfred.

"Nobody, I suppose."

"It's wrong, I reckon, that you're not allowed to pick your own name. If it's your name you should be allowed to pick it."

"You can't pick your own name if you're only a baby."

"I know that. I mean after you can talk. When you turn ten you should be allowed to pick your own name, the name you keep."

"What name would you pick if you didn't like Alfred?"

"Ned, of course. Who would you pick?"

"Tom, I think – after Tom Hales; he's the champion jockey of Australia, on the flat. And there's Tom Corrigan; he's the champion over jumps."

"There's a Tom in America," said Alfred, "who's got a machine that can make light without kerosene."

"That'd take some doing."

"Yeah, I know. But he can do it. It's been in the papers. Ask Dad."

"The man who might become my godfather, his name is Tom; and there's a champion cricketer named Tom Wills."

"They named me after Alfred the Great."

"What was he great at?"

"He was King Alfred. Don't you know? He drove the Vikings out of England."

Silence again.

"Want to know something else you don't know," said Alfred.

"What?"

"I've got a revolver."

Jemmy said nothing. He had learned that often Alfred made claims that did not stand up, and this could be another.

"Did you hear me? I've got a revolver – a thirty-two – six chambers."

"I heard you."

"You don't believe me, do you?"

"I'll believe it when I see it."

"You want to see it? I'll soon show you – now." Alfred sat up. "It's in the stable – hid."

Jemmy suspected another of Alfred's tricks. Alfred had made claims he could not support then would say he was only joking.

"You're too frightened to come and look, aren't you? You're not game enough."

Although Jemmy was not in the mood for Alfred's fooling, he was not ready for sleep. He sat up and faced Alfred. "If you're fooling me again, it'll be the last time."

They got out of bed.

"Don't talk loud or Letty will hear us," said Alfred. "Only put your socks on." In their nightshirts they went to the door, opened it quietly and crept out.

Alfred led the way into the stable. Their eyes began adapting to the small amount of light coming in through the few windows and the back doorway. Jemmy followed Alfred to a wooden cavity-wall between two empty stalls and sprung up, gripping the top of the highest board. He scrambled and pulled and soon was sitting up straddling the wall. He put an arm down into the cavity. "It's gone."

Jemmy sighed. Now he could go back the bed. He turned away, listening to Alfred's giggling.

"It was here yesterday," insisted Alfred.

"It might come back later," said Jemmy, sarcastically. "A fairy might bring it."

"No fairies needed." Grinning, Alfred withdrew his hand and in it held a revolver.

Jemmy turned and saw.

Crooking his arm, Alfred raised the pistol, pointing it upwards. He sat as if astride a horse and as if posing for a photograph. "Didn't believe me, did you?" He lowered the revolver and held it against his thigh as he would if he were mounted and keeping the pistol at the ready. He leaned sideways and held out the pistol. "Hold it while I get down."

Jemmy took the gun.

Alfred dropped to the floor and took back the gun.

"Where'd you get it?" asked Jemmy.

"From a man who shot himself with it."

"But how? What happened?"

"I took it after he was dead."

Alfred brought the revolver up closer to their faces. "There's five bullets in it." Using his thumb he turned the magazine, each turn making a click and at the same time exposing the rims of the bullets as each aligned itself with the barrel. With a fingernail he extracted the only spent cartridge and held it for Jemmy to see. "That's the one that killed him."

"Who was he?"

Alfred ignored the question. "If you want to fire quickly you've got to pull back the hammer, like this."

"Don't do that," objected Jemmy. "It might fire."

"No it won't; I know how to do it. You've got to wait for the sound – the click. Then it's cocked and ready."

The revolver clicked.

Alfred raised the revolver and pointed it at Jemmy's chest. "Now I've got you, and I can make you do anything I want, can't I?"

Jemmy quickly stepped backwards and to the side, pushing the point of the revolver away from him. He looked into Alfred's still leering face. "Quit it up." He began to retreat towards the doorway of the stall. Alfred's aim followed him.

Alfred's enjoyment was not yet sated. "If you tell anybody I've got this, I'll kill you."

Jemmy decided to chance making a dash.

As he ran he heard Alfred's voice from the stall. "I could get you on the run if I wanted to."

The doorway they had come into the stable by was open and Jemmy did not slow as he went through. He was on the bed sitting up when Alfred came in. Alfred silently closed the door and went to Jemmy's bed and, cross-legged, sat at the foot.

"I wouldn't have shot you," said Alfred, his voice lowered. "I was only playing around."

"I know, but the damned thing might have gone off, that's what I was frightened of."

"It couldn't go off. I didn't have my finger on the trigger; it was around the guard. Gee, you ran." He laughed. "You went like a rabbit."

"You'd go like a rabbit too if someone was pointing a gun at you. How'd you get the darn thing?"

"I'll tell you." Alfred stopped speaking and turned his head. "Someone's coming." He bounded across to his own bed and pulled the blanket over him as he buried his head in the pillow. "Pretend you're asleep."

They listened to the footsteps on the path.

The door opened.

"Are you awake?" said Peter Webber.

After making a few garbled sounds Alfred replied. "What did you say?"

"Were you over in the stable a minute ago? Letty said she thought she heard voices. Over there."

Jemmy's heart thumped.

"Nar," replied Alfred in the weariest tone he could feign.

Peter hesitated.

The boys waited.

The door closed.

The boys lay still. They heard Peter's footsteps on the path leading to the stable. Then, after about a minute, heard footsteps come out of the stable and into the house.

Alfred sat up, left his bed and sat on the edge of Jemmy's.

Jemmy pushed the blanket away from his face and sat up.

"You believe me now, don't you?" gloated Alfred.

"Where'd you get it?"

"There was this old prospector named Mick Woods and he had a camp up along the creek. Me and the other kids used to go there and hide and throw stones at his tent. I went there on my own one day and walked in. And there he was – dead on the bed. His face was in the pillow, but there wasn't much blood though. He was lying on his belly. His hand was hanging over the side and the gun was on the floor. I knew he was dead – I knew. I ran out and was going to get Dad. But while I was running I thought and I stopped and went back and got the gun. I didn't tell Dad and somebody else found him. The police went there and they said he'd been murdered. And there was an inquest, a big meeting in the courthouse. I wasn't allowed to go; I had to go to school. There was a judge and he said Mick had been murdered." He began to giggle. "Everybody was talking about Mick getting murdered. The story going round was that once he'd jumped someone's claim and the bloke caught up with him and gave it to him."

"You stole from a dead man. That's the worst thing you can do."

"No it ain't. Stealing's only when you take from someone who's alive."

"I ain't heard that before."

"It's true."

They became silent.

"Was the camp the one we saw up on the bank that first day we went to the creek and you didn't want to go up because you said it was haunted?"

"Yep."

"Do you believe in ghosts?"

"Sometimes."

There was silence again.

Alfred went back to his bed, propped himself up on an elbow and faced Jemmy. "You know what we could do tomorrow better than eeling?"

"No. What?"

"We can get some cherries – easy."

"Where? A tree?"

"No. Easier than that."

"How?"

"Tell you tomorrow. Anyway, I'll have to muck out in the morning, so we won't be able to go eeling. We can do that in the night."

Twenty-six

While he helped with the mucking out of the loose-boxes, a task that was part of the few morning chores Alfred had to do while on the last school holiday he would ever have, Jemmy asked again about where they would get the cherries. All Alfred would say was, "You'll see." The only other part of the plan Alfred had divulged was that they would do it when they took out the young-'ns, the two young horses Peter had recently broken in and which had to be ridden every day.

Near half-past nine they were mounted and about to leave.

"Walk, trot and canter," Peter warned his son. "No faster. No racing."

Where the track was wide enough to allow, they rode side by side. When the track narrowed, Alfred led.

"You'd better tell me," demanded Jemmy. "Where are these cherries? If we've got to pinch them off a tree, I won't be in it."

"They're not on a tree. They're in a cart, a Chinaman's cart, and he goes along the road where we're going. He comes about this time two days a week, the same days and one's today. I'll get them. All you've got to do it hold the horses."

"Couldn't we buy some from him?"

"Don't be mad. You don't buy what you can get for nothing. I've done it before. He doesn't know there's any gone."

Leaving the track, Alfred led into the bush. They came to where Jemmy could see through the breaks in the scrub parts of a road about fifty yards ahead. Alfred drew a halt. He stood in the stirrups and, peering through the timber, spied out the bend he believed the Chinaman would come around. They were on a slope. Down from them on the other side of the road a haze of thin smoke had settled amongst the heads of the trees. Though where it started couldn't be seen, a foot-track from the road went down to a hut where an old lady lived.

"He'll stop right there in front of us," said Alfred. "But he won't be able to see us. He'll get out of the cart, get a basket of vegetables out of the back and go into the bush. He'll be gone a few minutes. That's when we strike."

"Are you going to fill both those saddlebags?"

There was a bag on each side of Alfred's saddle.

"No, one'll give us plenty."

Alfred leaned back and unbuckled the flap of one bag. Then he unbuckled the bag on Jemmy's side.

"Why'd you bring two bags if you only needed one?" asked Jemmy.

Alfred was slow to answer. "You want the truth? Here it is." He lifted the flap of the bag on Jemmy's side.

Jemmy saw the shiny wood on the revolver handle. "Why'd you bring that? You ain't going to do a bail-up, are you?"

"I just brought it for comfort. I'm only going to shove it in my belt, that's all."

"You leave it where it is or I'm going. I'll go back to the stable on my own. I won't lag on you, but I won't lie for you either. You can tell your father what you like."

"You don't have to do anything. All you got to do is hold my horse."

"I'm out of this."

"It ain't a bail-up, I tell you. Back out if you want to. But if you do you'll get no cherries. Go on, Squib, scram. I can do this on my own."

"The Chinaman might see you and might go to the police."

"He won't see me, you idiot. Anyway, Chinamen don't go to the police. You can do what you like to Chinamen and they don't tell.

Everyone knows that."

"I don't want to be in it." Jemmy knew enough about the police to know that anyone who helps just a little bit in a robbery is said to be one of the robbers. "If I hold your horse, then I am in it. If this goes wrong, that's the end of me with Brian. He'll coach me out the day after, if I ain't in jail. I want to keep my job. My old man's on the run and I don't want to be on the run too."

"You wouldn't be on the run," scoffed Alfred. "It's only a few cherries. And we ain't gunna get caught ... What'd your old man do – pinch a horse?"

"No."

"A cow?"

"No."

“Well, what? He didn’t do a bail-up, did he?” Alfred asked, hoping.

Jemmy didn’t answer.

As eager as he was to know more, Alfred dropped the matter.’ He rose in the stirrups and moved his head about to get the best view of the bend. “He’s coming.” He dismounted, pulled the reins over his horse’s head and offered them to Jemmy.

Jemmy refused.

Alfred tied the end of the reins to a sapling sprig and began his dash towards the road. He did not take the revolver. Weaving his way he reached the bush he had hidden behind at other times. He undid the top three buttons of his shirt and tightened his belt.

The cart stopped at the head of the track that led down to the hut. Ah Chuk descended from the seat. He was neither an old nor young man. On his head was a high pointed hat made from reeds that grew at the edges of some of the Snowy’s billabongs. He wore a loose sleeveless cotton shirt and dungarees. Under the hat was a shaven head, except for the plaited tuft that grew near the back of his neck, concealing a scar, the result of a drunken prospector years before trying to remove the braid with a knife. Between the shafts of the two-wheeler was a fat old horse that long ago had forgotten how to hurry. Ah Chuk went to the rear of the cart and threw back the sheet of light canvas covering his load. He lifted out a basket with vegetables and fruit in it. He went to where the downhill track started and he disappeared.

Alfred broke from his hiding place and ran to the back of the cart. The cherries were within easy reach and he stuffed handfuls into his shirt. To his delight there was another kind of fruit, small and yellow, a kind he had never seen on the cart before. He was going back for the second handful of loquats when he heard the howl and felt the pain as Ah Chuk’s fingernails dug into the back of his neck. His shirt tightened as the hand that held him by the collar jerked him backwards.

Alfred twisted and pulled sideways then felt Ah Chuk’s arm lock around his neck, squeezing his throat. He felt Ah Chuk’s grip around his wrist and his arm being pulled up behind his back.

“What you name, boy, what you name? You rob me too much. I catch you this time. I know you come before. You very bad boy. What you name, boy, what you name?”

Alfred did not answer.

“What you name, boy? What you name?”

“Brown,” said Alfred, choking.

The arm around Alfred’s neck dropped away but not the other, the one across his chest. He stopped struggling.

“What you other name, boy? What you other name?”

“Johnny,” Alfred lied again.

“Where you live, boy, where you live? I tell policeman. You very bad boy.”

All at once Alfred twisted, pulled and let his body drop. He was free. In the instant he lunged. He felt the grab Ah Chuk made at his shoulder. He heard the sound of his shirt tearing then felt the back of it leaving his body. He ran, the fruit following him, falling on the ground.

Ah Chuk did not follow. He stood flaying the air with a piece of Alfred’s shirt. “You not Brown Johnny,” he shouted. “I know. You stableman boy. I tell your father.” After a minute he walked to where he had seen the boy vanish and peered into the bush. He saw nobody or any movement. With the cotton fragment still in his hand he went back to the cart, took an empty basket and set about recovering the scattered fruit on the ground.

Twenty-seven

It was a gentle knock and when Brian opened the door he expected to see one of the maids. Standing there was Jemmy.

"Come in, come in."

Jemmy was wearing his best clothes. Brian was dressed in his best. It was Sunday afternoon. Brian went to his bed and seated himself on the edge. Jemmy went to the bed that had been his for only one night and sat. They faced each other.

"Any special reason for the call?" asked Brian. "Nothing wrong? Horses and dogs all right?"

"Yes: everything's all right."

"A social call?"

"Yes."

"I thought you'd be out somewhere running around with Alfred."

Jemmy shook his head.

Brian thought there was glumness in Jemmy's attitude.

"You and Alfred getting along all right?"

"Good enough. But I like to get away from him sometimes. Are you going anywhere this afternoon that I could come?"

"I am going somewhere, and I suppose you could come, if you wanted. I'm going to visit a friend of mine a mile or two out – Will Kinlake."

"I'd like to go."

"Then go you shall. There'll be company there for you. Will's got a grand-son and grand-daughter about your age. They live in town with an aunt during the week and go to school. We'll get going now."

Brian put on his bowler hat and they left.

As they walked along the street Brian said, "Alfred might like to come with us."

Jemmy did not want that to happen. He did not want any more of Alfred's company today. The incident with Chinaman was still on his mind. Would the Chinaman go to the police, or to Alfred's father, or to both? If that happened, it could be the end of him with Brian. Part of the worry was that if he and Alfred were confronted, Alfred might lie and try to implicate him, and nobody might believe that Alfred had acted on his own. He thought he might get in first, tell Brian what had happened and plead that he had not taken part. But if he told Brian he could not be sure of the reaction. Brian might think it all ought to be brought out into the open before the police could be brought into it. But to lag on Alfred would mean he would be called a squealer. Time away from Alfred this afternoon was what he wanted.

"Alfred won't want to come," said Jemmy "He wants to go somewhere I don't want to go. He'll be gone by now.

They were nearly at the stable when Jemmy saw the figures of Alfred and two other boys walking away on the other side of the entrance. He was relieved and hoped they would not look back or perhaps return.

They could have ridden to Kinlake's but Brian fancied going by gig. Horse sweat and leather grease didn't suit a man's best clothes. The intention was to use one of his own horses and rent a vehicle from Peter.

"Do you particularly want to use one of your own horses?" asked Peter. "I could make you an offer; save you a few pennies."

"I'm always interested in saving pennies. What've you got in mind?"

Peter explained the offer and Brian accepted. Instead of a gig they would take the brake, a strongly built two-wheeled cart with extralong shafts, made for breaking horses to harness; and the horse would be a big reddish-bay newly broken-in gelding that Peter had not been able to handle sufficiently over the past few days.

The horse was harnessed and hitched and the drivers climbed aboard.

"He's a goer, this bloke," cautioned Peter. "He might take off a bit fast. Be ready."

Letting go of the horse's head, Peter hurried to the doorway and looked up and down the street. "All clear." He came back and released the wheel chain.

Brian took off his hat and handed it to Jemmy.

The horse remained still.

"Take the whip," Brian told Jemmy, "and just tap him lightly on the rump."

At the tap on his rump the horse lunged forward and jerked the vehicle into motion. Out onto the street they swept. Answering the right rein, and with Brian's foot on the right brake pedal, the bay swung to the desired direction. Along the street they went at more than a steady trot, faster than need be, but if the way was clear Brian thought it was best to let the horse use up some of his early steam before an effort was made to settle him down. Reaching the end of the street they went over the rise and dipped down onto the ford. Across they went, the bay still full of go.

About a mile had been put behind them when they came to shallow stream crossing the road. As expected, the bay had settled down but was still pulling determinedly. Brian eased him up and let him walk into the stream. The horse lowered his head and drank.

"The makings of a good horse, this fellow. I wouldn't mind owning him," said Brian. He took back his hat and handed the reins to Jemmy.

"Do you think of your mother much?" asked Brian.

"Yes. But not all the time. Sometimes not for days."

"I think she'd think of you a lot. I think she'd wish you were closer by than you are. I think she'd think of you every day – probably every night before she goes to sleep."

"I'm far away, but not real far. I'm just away at work, that's all. All boys have got to go away to work one day."

"Yes, I suppose they do. Is there a postman calls at the Creek?"

"Yes, every month."

"I've got an idea. There are cards you can buy and they have a little verse on the back of them. They call them Christmas cards. Have you seen them?"

"No."

"They're becoming a fashion. You can buy them at Heneberry's. Why don't you send one to your mother? All you'd have to do is write your name under the verse."

"But Christmas is over."

"That won't matter."

"I wouldn't mind doing that."

"You can to it tomorrow. Sooner the better."

The bay started pawing the water.

"He's ready to go," said Brian. "Let him walk out. Keep him at that till the top of the rise."

Shade from the roadside trees dappled the dusty track.

The frame of mind that Brian seemed to be in decided Jemmy to ask a question that he had been wanting to ask.

"May I ask you a question now?"

"Yes."

"When we were in church on Christmas Eve, why didn't you close your eyes when you prayed?"

Brian laughed. "Why would you want to know that?"

"I was only wondering. Everyone closes their eyes when they pray."

"Maybe I wasn't praying. Who says I was? And who says you have to close your eyes when you pray. If you saw me, why weren't your eyes closed. Or maybe you, too, weren't praying?"

"Oh, I was praying. I just opened them a little bit, only a few times, to see what a lot of people together looked like when they closed their eyes. That's when I saw you. Every time I looked, your eyes were open."

"I never had my eyes closed at any time," confessed Brian.

"Why?"

"Because I wasn't praying."

"If you weren't praying, why did you go to church?"

"To keep you company. You're the one who wanted to go. I'm not a praying man, at any time, but I must admit that I'm not averse to occasionally joining assemblies when people are in friendly and gentle mood, such as at Christmas time and in a church. Many of my best friends go to church. As for praying, whom would I be praying to? Who would be listening?"

Jemmy was shocked. "God, of course. He's the only one you pray to."

"You think so?"

"Yes."

"One of these days, not today, we'll have a discussion about God."

A terrible thought rushed into Jemmy's mind. He knew there were people who did not believe in God. "You believe in God, don't you?"

"I've never been able to think of a good reason for doing that. The Christian God is a matter I've done a lot of thinking about, a lot of reading about and a lot of talking about. I tend to think there is no such thing as God. But if you believe in God, it's not likely to do you any harm."

Jemmy could hardly believe what he was hearing. "But what about all the world. Someone must have made all this." He motioned with one hand and looked up at the sky.

"It was made, I agree. But how it was made is the question. You say God."

"What about the Ten Commandments? – God made them and gave them to Moses."

"Do you know that Moses was a stockman, a drover, like us?" said Brian. "I'm sure you know about the Burning Bush? When Moses saw that bush he was on a droving trip. He was working for his father-in-law and was taking the flock to 'the western side of the wilderness' – probably looking for feed. I feel a kinship with Moses; he's one biblical character I like. Once, on a droving trip, like Moses, I saw a bush that I thought was burning, but when I got to it the flames were gone and there were no burnt leaves. The flame had been like a ball going round and round the bush; at the top one moment, at the bottom the next. When I walked towards it, the fire went to another bush; it stayed there a while then vanished. I tied a handkerchief to the first bush and went back next morning. There were no burnt leaves, no ashes – nothing, only green leaves. Other stockmen have told me they've seen this sort of thing; they've called them will o' the wisps or jack o' lanterns."

"But Moses was sent by God," pleaded Jemmy.

"I doubt that.... As well as being a drover for some of his life, Moses was a leader, a thinking man, a philosopher, a man interested in governance. As for the Ten Commandments, I see nothing in them that needed to come from God. I think probably the Commandments existed in some form or other in Jewish life long before Moses. What Moses did so skilfully was draw them together in simple form. Then he delivered a masterstroke. If it were thought the rules were Godgiven, men would be less inclined to tamper with them. So that's what he did: said the rules had been handed down by God. They're great rules, no doubt about it; if adhered to, they would allow people to live at peace with one another, would allow them to live out their natural lives without fear of being robbed or murdered or enslaved. That was the appeal of the Commandments. Later, Jesus came along and added refinements."

Confused, Jemmy could think of no more to say.

They spoke little from then on and after about another half hour took the track into Will Kinlake's station, Tarrawarra.

Grace Kinlake and her younger brother, Boyd, whom the family called Boydy, were the first to hear the sound of hooves and the rumbling wheels. They ran out onto the verandah then ran back inside to tell. Out they came again, hurried down the steps and ran to welcome the visitors.

Grace had a smiling face and long loose fair hair and reminded Jemmy of the girl on the scented-soap wrapper.

Grace judged the boy holding the reins to be about her age.

Will and his wife, Charlotte, appeared at the top of the steps. The homestead was a substantial, spacious, rambling timber building that had had sections added over the years. The roof was high-gabled, which helped keep the house cool in summer. Will and Charlotte's first home on the property had been a hut.

From the steps and from the brake went cheery helloes.

"Go down to the yards and unyoke," said Will. "You know the way. There'll be tea ready by the time you come back."

Grace and Boydy walked beside the brake on Jemmy's side.

"What's your horse's name?" asked Boydy.

"He hasn't got a name," answered Jemmy. "He's not ours. We're just giving him a drive for Mister Webber."

"He's big," said Boydy.

"I know a good name for him," said Grace, "Hurly Burly."

The bay, sweating and still puffing, was unyoked. Jemmy, accompanied by Boydy and Grace, took him to a trough and let him drink. The horse was then led into the stable, unharnessed and released into a railed loose-box.

"A good horse, this fellow," Brian commented, repeating his earlier opinion. "He'd pull till he dropped. It's the thoroughbred in him."

"I'll get him some chaff," said Grace.

On the verandah when at last all were there the welcoming continued. Will and Charlotte's son, Lucas, and his wife, Thalia, had come over from their cottage. Charlotte led them into the loungeroom. Tea for the adults and lemon cordial for the youngsters was soon on the way.

Jemmy was taken charge of by Boydy and Grace and, with lemon drinks in hand, shown out onto the verandah.

"How old are you?" asked Grace.

"Thirteen. But I'll be fourteen in March."

“I’ll be thirteen in February and I’m having a party. You can come if you want to, but it’ll be in Fitzford, at my aunty’s place.”

“Thanks. If I’m in town, I’ll come. But I mightn’t be in town. I work for Mister Drury out on Foxhow. But I just might be in Fitzford in February. I might be going with Mister Hoy to catch horses at Mount Ebony.”

“My grandfather knows Mister Hoy.”

They finished their lemon drink.

“What can we do now?” asked Boydy.

“Shuttlecock,” suggested Grace.

The game was new to Jemmy and he thought it good fun. Grace made him think of his sisters. Nearly every time she ran at the shuttle or made a hit at it she shrieked. She was very good at the game, better than himself or Boydy.

They grew tired of shuttlecock.

“Let’s do something else,” suggested Boydy.

Jemmy waited. There might be another game they had that he did not know.

“What, though?” said Grace.

“Do you know any card games?” asked Jemmy.

“Sevens,” said Boydy.

“I know how to play that,” said Jemmy.

They went to the verandah and Boydy fetched a pack of cards. They had not been playing long when Grace complained. “This is boring. Let’s go for a ride.”

The boys were agreeable.

Without speaking, Grace turned and ran inside. When she reappeared Jemmy stared. She was wearing not her frock but trousers, and the strangest kind he had ever seen. The legs were narrow below the knee and ballooned out above the knee. Grace saw his surprise.

“These are jodhpurs,” she explained. “I can ride astride in these. Ladies everywhere wear them these days.”

“We’ll play follow-the-leader,” said Grace. “And I’ll go leader because I know the best places.”

There was no argument.

On foot they mustered the four ponies in a small paddock and worked them up into the stable and saddled three of them.

They cantered along bushy tracks, jumped logs and crossed streams, rested the ponies here and there, rode uphill and downhill. One spot on a hillside they came to looked out over the widest, most treeless flat Jemmy had ever seen; it seemed to stretch for miles, and on it were specks that were grazing cattle, except for one speck that Jemmy could see was a man on a horse, walking. He asked about the cattle and Grace said they were from the Monaro and were on their way to Gippsland, to the markets. There was that name again – Monaro. Jemmy knew of the Monaro, the place on the other side of the mountains that he thought always sounded as if it were almost another country. "The Monaro drovers always camp there," said Grace. About an hour later they were back at the stable.

After a lengthy farewell on the verandah, and much waving after the visitors got into the brake, the big red-bay drew away.

"You seemed to get along well with Boydy and Grace, I noticed," said Brian. "If Mister Hoy decides he'll take you to Mount Ebony, and if the Webbers are willing to have you stay with them, you could visit Boydy and Grace, in town. You might end up making quite a few friends in Fitzford."

Jemmy was disappointed that the invitation to stay longer had been refused and he asked why.

"Under other circumstances we would have stayed," answered Brian. "But Missus Webber will have cooked for you, will be expecting you."

"It's only a meal."

"You're expected at the Webbers' table and I want you to be there. You mustn't give the Webbers the impression that you're an unreliable chap. Missus Webber likes you, thinks you're a gentleman, and I want her to go on thinking that way. Don't you?"

"Did she say that?"

"In as many words, and I hope I never hear that she's changed her mind."

"It's only a meal," Jemmy complained again. "If I'm a gentleman, do I have to be one all the time?"

"I'm afraid so – that's if you're a true gentleman, the only kind that's worth being. Amongst true gentlemen there are no part-timers. No days off for a true gentleman. And you mustn't forget, if you want to go with Mister Hoy, you need Missus Webber's cooperation."

Twenty-eight

The new year had come in and on the second Monday at near 8 o'clock in the morning the Foxhow contingent was on the road, halted at present at Heneberry's store where the packsaddles were swelling every time Jemmy and one of Heneberry's apron-wearing assistants came out with the goods. The order, mostly tinned food, sugar, kerosene, flour, potatoes and onions, had been put together on Saturday and placed near the front door. The other part of the order would wait till a Braywood wagon came, probably in a few weeks.

Overhearing the young assistant joking with Jemmy about 'old Brian not allowing them to put any of the goods into the bags', Brian met him with a glare: "I don't want to be like Richard the third. I don't want to be up in those mountains crying out 'A horse, a horse; my kingdom for a horse *without a sore back*'. A horse with a sore back, laddie, won't carry anything very far. Remember that when you're loading a packer – laddie." The young man turned quickly and scuttled away.

Brian's departure from Fitzford after Christmas had never taken place till after the first Saturday following New Year's Day. Again this year, at the request of the president of the racing club, Cedric Hoy, he had officiated as a steward at the races held in Lund's paddock.

On their last night in Fitzford an incoming guest at the Royal told Brian of Grand Flaneur's win in the three-miles Champion Stakes at Flemington on New Year's Day. Brian was horrified. Bad enough that the colt had been made race over two miles in the Melbourne Cup, and so soon after running in the Derby; now, and still a three-year-old, he had been made to race over three miles. "They're racing him to death. They'll kill him."

Jemmy's expenditures for the trip had been meagre, the biggest the five-shilling postal note sent to his mother. He had enclosed the note in the card of the kind Brian had told him about. Also from Heneberry's he had bought two pencils and two large pads. One pad was of thin paper that you could see through if you put it over a picture in a book. Also he bought a rubber that could rub away pencil marks. Heneberry's was a store he liked and more than once he had gone there on his own and wandered about. Heneberry's sold even walking sticks, some of them made from what he was told was Malacca cane. There was one stick he fancied he would like to buy for Brian. The stick was made of Blackwood, but its colour was brown and near the top was a nickel band that looked like silver and your name could engraved on it; the price was high – twelve shillings and sixpence. If it were still there when he came to Fitzford again, he would at least look at it.

He thought of the fight he and Alfred had after Alfred tricked him into trying to swim under a horse's belly at the billabong. The horse had nearly trampled him and might have drowned him. Alfred had cheated a lot at the billabong that day, including in the underwater race. Alfred got the worst of the fight afterwards and threatened to tell his parents and said they would kick him out. A lot had happened during all those days. There was a lot yet to think over. He was relieved that, so far, it seemed the Chinaman had not gone to Alfred's father or the police. He still feared something might come of that. Alfred had told his parents his shirt had got ripped when it caught on a tree branch. The day at the sale-yards had been good, too. He and Alfred had helped a drover to draft sheep and cattle and make up the pens before the selling. He had not told Brian of any of his problems with Alfred. Best of all, Cedric Hoy had agreed to take him on the trip to Mount Ebony, and the Webbers would let him stay with them before and after.

The straps on the flaps of the bulging packs were buckled to the last hole and the riders mounted. The dogs rose and streaked ahead. The party had come to Fitzford with four horses but was leaving with five. A purchase had been made. The new horse was a big reddishbay that had been given the name Hurly Burly.

The ford was crossed and they made their way along the top of the bank and were nearly at where they saw the sluice men on the day they had arrived at Fitzford.

The sun found them and the air was becoming warmer by the minute. They left the river and were not far from it when Brian spoke.

"There's a smell been following us, and it's not from the dogs' meat. The blowflies tell me it's coming from that sack at the front of your saddle. What's in it?"

Jemmy had hoped he would not be asked. "Tail tips – steers'. The man at the slaughterhouse gave them to me. I didn't steal them."

"No need to tell me that. I didn't think you had. You couldn't have washed them out very well. At the next water you'd better clean them up. Did you salt the skin part?"

"No."

"You'd better do that too, or they'll be rotten before you get them home. There's salt on board. How many are there?"

"Nine."

At a creek the tail tips were washed and salted.

"What are you going to do with them?" asked Brian.

"Nothing much. I just wanted them."

"Any special reason for nine?"

"No."

Brian was too amused to argue.

Twenty-nine

There was in the outline of the approaching man on a mule, less than a quarter mile away, something so familiar that Brian saw no need to bring out the telescope. Another mule, laden, walked beside the rider. The thong Brian was working on, anchored to a verandah post, he began tying off and after that rose from his chair and stepped to the edge of the landing and waited.

Brian walked forward to greet his visitor.

Dismounting, Tom Halpen turned and faced Brian. They did not shake hands. They greeted each other with the ease of men who might have seen each other only days ago. In fact they had not seen each other in months.

Tom's grey-black, wire-like hair stood out in a way that made his head appear bigger than it really was. There was no clear demarcation between the hair on his head and that on his face. His clothes were ragged.

"And what brings you in?" asked Brian.

"Sick of the rich living – pink pigeon, white pheasant, venison, day in day out." The names were his for Galah, Cockatoo and Kangaroo. "And I've got a few picks that need drawing – if you'll let me use the forge. Also thought you could do with a hand to take the cattle up – it's near time."

Brian was pleased at the mention of a hand to take the cattle up.

"I hear you've got a boy with you," said Tom. "I've got a parcel for him. A swagman left it at Braywood, so I brought it."

The gear and saddles were removed and placed on the verandah. Leading a mule each, the men walked the animals away and turned them out.

While Brian began making tea Tom brought in the parcel for Jemmy. It was wrapped in newspaper tied with string.

"How did you come by this boy?" asked Tom.

"It's a long story. Leave it for later."

But Tom was too curious to be easily put off. "He didn't drop out of the sky. You must have picked him up somewhere."

"That I did. On the road. He's got a rough old mare that might be in foal to Kilrenny and he thinks he might get a foal that'll turn out to be some sort of white swan. The experience won't do him any harm. He'll tell you all about it – oh, he'll tell you alright. I got caught up, but I hope to move him along soon. I'm trying to set him up with Webber family in Fitzford and send him to school. He's got a brain – a clever kid but no education. I don't want to exactly tramp him; I want to do the best for him that I can. He doesn't want to go to school and doesn't want to leave here. He's latched himself onto me like death."

"How does his family fit into this? Has he got one?"

"Of sorts. His mother cooks for the men at the Quartz Creek mill, and she's got three other young-'nss at foot. His father – I suspect – is the George Tyler that did the damage to Atha Bonwick."

Tom knew Atha Bonwick and all about the trouble he had had. "How come that gives you latitude with the boy?"

"It doesn't, really. I'm gambling. I don't think his mother would mind where he was so long as he was safe. As for Tyler, he's in smoke. I don't think we'll see hide nor hair of him. The plan I've got I think could work, if it all comes together properly. By the way, he's looking for a godfather – he wants to be christened and I… put your name forward."

"Oh, did you? That was nice of you. That's just what I need, a godson."

"I'm sorry about this. I did it on the spur of the moment. I was cornered. I had to find a way out, quickly. He wanted me, but, being the way I am, I couldn't accept – it wouldn't be appropriate. If he puts it to you, all you have to do is say no."

"Thanks. I'm pleased it'll be as simple as that. And when do I meet this godson of mine? Where've you got him?"

"He's out riding through the cattle we're taking up, just to get them quiet. It's been one of his daily jobs lately. He's due back soon. You might find you like him. He's like you – got gold fever. And he plays a good game of cribbage too. He can't read a book but he can read a pack of cards pretty well. He thinks poker is a kid's game."

The laugh that broke from Tom was a roar.

When his guest gained control of himself, Brian went on. "I'll put him through his paces tonight and you'll see what I mean." He lifted a finger, indicating that he had suddenly thought of more he wanted to say. "If you see an opening to point out how lucky he would be if he got a chance to go to school, bowl it at him."

"I'll see what I can do. If I see the chance, I'll go in. He'll be begging you to send him to school by the time I'm finished with him."

"We'll see."

As he descended the hill behind the homestead Jemmy saw the two mules in the paddock. This had to mean there was a visitor. He had been told that Tom Halpen had two mules. He rode to the stable and unsaddled then turned out his horse. As he walked towards the hut he found himself becoming nervous. He had thought much about Tom Halpen since returning from Fitzford. Would Tom consent to become his godfather as Brian said he might? He reasoned that if a godfather's role was to guide a boy in religious education, the godfather would have to see the godson fairly often. Tom was a gold prospector, a man who moved around a lot and might not know where he would be from one week or month to the next. A minister might not accept a man like that for a godfather, and for the same reason Tom might not want to be a godfather. If the minister would accept Tom and Tom would accept the job, he would not care if Tom did not bother with him again afterwards. He would see to his own instruction, maybe talk to a minister or somebody like Missus Webber.

Shyly he halted inside the doorway. He looked straight at Tom.

Tom stood and faced Jemmy. "Ah, here's the man. I've been hearing about you." He put out his hand. "We've got a common interest, I believe – gold. Great stuff, if you can find it."

The appearance of Tom, so wild-looking, surprised Jemmy. There was more hair on this man than Jemmy had ever seen on the head and face of any other man.

They shook hands.

"Tom's brought a parcel for you," said Brian. "Someone left it at Braywood." He pointed at the parcel on the table.

Jemmy focused on the mysterious parcel. String was too precious to cut and as quickly as he could he picked at the knot till it came undone.

The thick scarf was fawn-coloured from wattle-bark dye.

"Put it on and show us what you look like," said Tom. "Who might have sent you a gift like that?"

"My mother," answered Jemmy, winding the scarf around his neck. "It's like one I had before."

"I've owned some scarves, but never one like that," said Tom. "That'd go around a man's neck three times. I would cut off my beard if I had a scarf like that."

Jemmy picked up the note and without unfolding it handed it to Brian. "Would you read it for me?"

Taking the note, on not a small piece of paper, Brian began studying it. He saw that his task was not going to be easy.

"Just a minute," interjected Tom. "You mustn't read another man's letter. Letters are very private things. This young man is the only one entitled to read that letter."

Jemmy didn't care who knew what his mother had to say and he tried to see the sense in what Tom had said.

"But under the circumstances…," Brian pleaded with Tom.

"I can't read," admitted Jemmy, looking at Tom.

"That has to make a difference," insisted Brian.

"Can't read?" snorted Tom. He looked at Brian. "That limits the value this fellow's going to be to you as a stockman. Can he count?"

"He's pretty good at that."

"But he'll never be able to be the manager – he won't be able to keep the books."

"He is keen to learn," answered Brian.

"He'll need to hurry. How old are you, son?"

"Fourteen, soon."

"Fourteen – mmm. My advice to you is: if an opportunity to learn reading and writing comes along, take it. But I still don't like the idea of one man reading another man's letters. I don't want to have to listen."

"You could put your fingers in your ears," suggested Brian.

"That wouldn't do – not from the way I was brought up. Letters, especially from a mother to a son, are sacred. I'll have to go outside."

Jemmy was beginning to believe Tom was a little bit mad.

Tom left.

The two settled themselves at the table.

Brian, bespectacled, lifted the already unfolded page and looked at it. The first words he was sure of and read them out. 'My dearest son'. He stopped. His forehead creased. "Your mother has a very distinctive hand. I might have to look at this letter for a while to train my eye to her style. Just bear with me." When he resumed he read slowly, haltingly, not always sure the word he saw was the one Mrs Tyler intended. Again when he stopped he looked at Jemmy. "What I think we should do is, I'll put the messages in my own words and, later, when I become better adapted to your mother's style, we'll read it word for word. That alright with you?"

Jemmy nodded.

Brian continued. "Oh, here's something. She's no longer at Quartz Creek." He paused. "...Your sisters are with her and she's at Wyballong station." He paused again. "... She says there was trouble at the mill and doesn't want you to call there for any reason ... Mister Hagley helped her get the job at Wyballong." He looked up. "Wyballong is closer to here than Quartz Creek – I reckon two-and-a-half days' ride. We could visit her." He returned to the letter. "She received your Christmas card and postal note ... She doesn't want you to send any more money ... She says she's very proud of you." He lifted his head. "Mrs Whitepipe at the station is teaching Annie to spin wool." Then he came to an item that he had little trouble in making head and tail of; after he read it he decided not to relay it, at least at the moment; it said: 'Try hard to stay with Mr Drury for as long as you can.' He put down the letter. "That'll do us for now; we'll read it again later."

Thirty

The bread was a few days old, as it often was at Foxhow by the time it was all eaten, but smothered with the nearest thing to vegetable strew Tom had seen in months, the bread was no bother.

The chores that followed were completed in short time and the table lamp lit.

Despite his uncertainties about Tom, Jemmy found the prospector friendly and not backward in talking to him. Perhaps Tom was mad so infrequently that really it did not amount to much to worry about. He decided to ask Tom about gold.

"Have you ever had a big strike – a real big one?"

"Found it and lost it," said Tom. "A reef. I'd gone in only about fifty feet when I hit it, and the further I went the better it got. The seams were thin but were getting thicker, running off like little rivers – the best gold I'd ever struck, and I was sure it would get better. It did get better, but not for long; then I struck the rubbish, the rubble, a wall of it; the reef was gone, ended, cut off as clean as if it had been done with an axe. That can happen with reefs – they break off and go wandering, maybe for thousands of years. Sometimes you can find them again, sometimes you can't. I drove up and I drove down and to the sides, but never found that broken-off bit. Maybe if I'd driven a bit farther here or there I might have found it; it might have been within arm's reach for all I knew, or it could have been half a mile away."

"Do you still look for it?"

"Not particularly. To make tucker you've got to go for the easier stuff. But I keep my eye open. I came on the first part accidentally and one day I might come across the lost part accidentally. With gold you can never tell."

"If I didn't have a job I'd go and help you."

"But you have got a job. Stick to becoming a stockman; that way you get a wage every week. Prospect in your spare time only. Do you know how to peg out a hill to find which way the gold's flowing?"

"No."

"I'll take you out one day and show you – if you can get time off." Tom did not pause. "I hear you've got quite an interest in books."

"Tom's a great reader," interrupted Brian. "He might do some reading to you if you ask him."

"Your master tells me you've got a liking for the book about the Mongols," said Tom.

"It's their horses I like. On a forced march they could do eighty miles a day – off grass; no hard feed. The book says without their horses they couldn't have conquered all that they did."

"Brian tells me you've got a mare that you think traces back to those ponies."

"Well – she looks like them, so that could mean she traces back to them, couldn't it?"

"I suppose it could."

"I'll show you the pictures in the book, then one day I'll show you my mare, and you'll see what I mean."

"There were other war horses that did a good job too. There's another book over there that'll tell about them. It's called *Wellington in Spain*. It's about the Duke of Wellington and Napoleon Bonaparte. Have you heard of them?"

"No."

"The two fought against each other. Wellington won in the end. Wellington was called the Iron Duke. Napoleon had an engraving on his sword: 'Never draw without a cause, never sheath without a victory'. Lots of stories told about their battles. One story goes that one night after a long march Napoleon couldn't sleep and went for a walk through the lines. He came on a sentry slumped against a tree, asleep. Going to sleep at your post is one of the worst crimes a soldier can commit. When the soldier woke he saw through the wisp another soldier, walking point, carbine on his shoulder, at the slope – it was Napoleon. The soldier saw his musket was gone and got to his feet and staggered over to Napoleon and fell down on his knees, sure he'd be seeing the firing squad in the morning. Napoleon handed him the carbine and said, 'We're all tired,' and turned and walked away. I don't think Wellington would have done the same if he'd come across a sentry asleep. Not that Wellington was a cruel man, he was just a different man. Weigh up the pros and cons. You're on a battle field, say, and an enemy squad sneaks past you, what could the outcome be? It could be pretty dire. If you were a general and came across a sleeping sentry, what would you do – what Napoleon did or what the Iron Duke would have done?"

"I don't know," said Jemmy. "What would you have done?"

"Like you, I don't know. I'd hate ever to have to decide."

They turned to Brian, the question on their faces.

"Ask me again the day after tomorrow," answered Brian. "Tom was a soldier once."

Jemmy turned quickly to Tom. "Were you?"

"Call me that, if you like."

"Did you fight in a war?"

"It seemed like a war."

"Tom was at Eureka – eighteen eight-four," said Brian.

Jemmy's eyes widened and he gaped. "You were at Eureka? I know all about Eureka. Everyone knows about Eureka." Then came a dreadful thought. "You weren't a redcoat, were you?"

"What do you think?"

Jemmy smiled. He knew the answer.

"Did you get a wound?"

"No. I was a soldier for a day, that's all. The battle was over in about an hour. They were professionals. We weren't. We didn't think they would attack on a Sunday. They attacked on a Sunday – got us off guard. Most of our men weren't even in the stockade at the time. We didn't win that battle, but we won the war, later, in the courts."

Brian broke in, speaking to Tom. "Why don't you show him the ... flag?"

Jemmy turned back to Tom.

Tom rose and went to where he had earlier placed a few belongings inside the door. He returned to the table and opened a battered leather-bound bible at a place where there lay a piece of blue cloth about four inches square.

Baffled, Jemmy stared at the cloth. This was not a flag.

"Always remember you've seen this," said Tom. "There's a story behind it and one day I'll tell you. I might go even further. Before I die I'd like to place it in the care of somebody who would look after it. You never know."

Still puzzled, Jemmy's mind raced. Brian had said "flag". He knew of the Eureka flag and that it was blue. In a lowered voice and as if speaking of the sacred, he asked, "Is this a piece of the flag?"

"No. None of us would ever have cut the flag. This is a piece of the cloth that the flag was made from. Put your hand on it if you like."

Jemmy put his fingertips on the cloth. "If you make me the keeper of it, I'll look after it with my life."

"No, don't do that. Don't die for a piece of rag. Live for what it represents. Spread the word. That day, a waistcoat or pair of trousers on a pole would have done. But a blue flag with a crosspiece and stars was what we had."

"Where's the flag now?"

"We don't know. The soldiers took it."

Again Jemmy put his fingers on the cloth. "I would look after if you ever asked me to."

"Well, you never know. If I continue to hear good things about you, I might make you the one." Then, abruptly, Tom's tone changed, "A thought, a thought." His eyes blazed.

Jemmy looked into eyes that seemed somehow changed. Was Tom about to go mad again?

"A thought, a thought," repeated Tom. "It's just come to me. What would impress me, if I were of a mind to consider you for custodian of 'the cloth', would be if I were to call at Braywood for stores one day and waiting for me was a letter from you, with full-stops and capital letters, all in the right places. That would impress me mightily."

Jemmy voice was slow in coming. "If I can, I will, but I don't know when."

Brian decided it was time the present conversation was let go. He looked at Jemmy. "Show Tom where the sesamoid bones are. No ... Try him on the 'fetlock test' first."

Jemmy went to his chest and took out the drawings he had copied or traced from the veterinary book by Horace Hayes. Most of the drawings and tracings were of skeletal horse parts with copied Latin and common names printed beside them. Brian had spoken the names and Jemmy remembered them all. He looked for a drawing of the external features of a foreleg and found it.

Tom rose and went to the table.

"This will test you," Brian warned. "We've caught more than a few on this one. You'll need your glasses."

"Nobody up from Braywood got it right," added Jemmy.

"What have I got to do?" asked Tom, putting on his spectacles.

"Point to where the fetlock is," said Jemmy.

"That should be easy enough," said Tom, putting a fingertip on a spot.

"No," Jemmy explained, grinning. "That's the fetlock-joint, not the fetlock." He put his finger on the lock of hair hanging down from the back of the joint. "The fetlock is only this tuft of hair underneath here, under the joint. Nearly everyone makes that mistake."

"You mean the fetlock and the fetlock-joint are two different things?" asked Tom, containing his amusement.

"Yes. One's hair and the other's bone – but they're near each other."

"That's an outright play on words meant to trick people," protested Tom. He looked over at the grinning Brian. "Worse: It's a conspiracy, a contrivance to trap me."

"Just helping you keep your wits about you, that's all," assured Brian, still grinning. "Now see how you go on the sesamoid bones. Here's your chance to redeem yourself."

"I know roughly where they are but not exactly. I know they're part of the fetlock-joint. I know that much." He turned to Jemmy. "You show me where you think they are and I'll tell you if you're right or not."

Jemmy brought forward another drawing, one of the bones and the main tendons below the knee.

"There," said Jemmy, putting a finger on a spot below and at the back of the fetlock-joint.

"Yes, I agree," said Tom. "Can you say the names of all the other bones there?"

Jemmy's finger moved quickly upwards. "Cannon-bone, radius, humerus, shoulder blade. The shoulder blade's Latin name is *scapula*." His finger went down to the hoof. "That bone there is the *Os pedis*. *Os* in Latin means bone."

"*Os* means bone in Latin – who told you that?"

"Brian."

Tom turned to Brian. "Did you tell him that?"

"I did. *Os* means bone in the Latin I was taught."

“It wasn’t in the Latin I was taught.”

Jemmy listened. This was the first time he had heard anybody say Brian was wrong. In this, was Brian wrong? If he was wrong, what else might he have been wrong in? He listened as the two men told of who had taught them Latin and why their respective teachers were above question. Tom turned to Jemmy. “Who do you want to take notice of, Brian or me?”

“… I don’t know.”

“You’ve got to decide,” said Tom.

“I don’t know.”

Tom walked to the other side of the table and put his hand on Jemmy’s shoulder. “This old coot and I have been having fun. Os does mean bone. I was watching your face. You were in trouble, weren’t you? For as long as you go on not being able to read, you’re going to be at the mercy of any mischief-maker that wants to make a fool of you. As soon as you can, you’ve got to do something about this. The way you are, a man could pick up a newspaper and say to you, ‘It says here that the world’s going to end next week.’ What he might only be looking at are the results of last week’s pigeon shoot at Yass. Can you see what I mean?”

Jemmy did not reply.

Again a change of course was decided upon by Brian. “Jemmy, fetch the cribbage board.”

They set themselves up at one end of the table.

Tom suggested they play for stakes, three-pence a game.

Jemmy shook his head.

“A penny?” suggested Tom.

Again Jemmy shook his head. “I don’t play for money.”

“But you might double your outlay, maybe treble it,” coaxed Tom.

“I’m with Jemmy,” said Brian.

“Outnumbered, am I? Then my pleasure will be beating the life out of you both, just for fun.”

Jemmy and Brian grinned at each other.

The play spread the wins fairly evenly.

“You’ve taught him well,” said Tom, referring to Jemmy.

“I taught him nothing,” replied Brian. “He’s played this well since the first time. You might be lucky you’re not playing for money.”

“I learned from the men at the mill, mostly. They used to play every night.”

Brian and Tom exchanged a glance that Jemmy didn’t notice.

“This is becoming too dull for me,” said Tom. “I’m a money player. No fun in pussyfooting, and I’m tired. Let’s finish for the night. One hand of poker for a decent stake, just for a closer? What do you say, both of you?”

“What have you got in mind for stakes?” asked Brian.

Tom stood, went to his belongings near the door and came back with a leather, rough-side out pouch. From amongst the gold inside he took out a nugget and put it on the table. “What’s that worth?”

Picking up the piece of gold, Brian made a guess. “I suppose a good smith could beat it into something the size of a couple of sovereigns.”

“Can you match it?” enquired Tom.

“I could, but that might put our young friend here out of the game.”

Tom turned to Jemmy. “This could be worth your being in. Look what you might win. If you haven’t got the ready cash, and if I won, I’d be willing to take goods in lieu of cash. Have you got a saddle or bridle you could put up?”

Jemmy shook his head. “I use Brian’s saddles, and the gear I do own, I need. I can’t risk it. You two play and I’ll watch.”

“I’d be willing to take a promissory note,” said Tom.

Jemmy shook his head again. He had never heard of a promissory note. He wondered if Tom was on the way to going mad once more.

“That leaves me with no other choice,” said Tom. “In commemoration of this occasion, the fine company and esteem in which I hold it, I’m going to put up this nugget, on its own, no matching values called for, and we’ll play for it – the winner, even if it’s me, takes the nugget. One hand of poker.”

Jemmy, bewildered, looked at Brian.

Brian understood what was happening and the part he was expected to play. “That’s a very sporting gesture,” he told Tom. “More than that: it’s generosity to a fault.”

The men turned to Jemmy.

“What’s your position?” asked Tom.

Jemmy looked at Brian.

Brian faced Tom. “He is.”

"You can have the privilege of dealing," Brian told Tom.

Tom shuffled the cards and dealt.

Picking up his cards, Tom studied them. He frowned. "Who dealt this rubbish?"

"You did," said Jemmy, surmounting his nervousness.

"Well, I didn't do a very good job."

Amongst Tom's five cards was a pair of kings, both of which he discarded along with another card and threw them on the table.

Jemmy had a pair of tens, which he kept and discarded the rest.

Brian did not have a pair, but four of his cards were hearts. He put out a heart but kept the lone spade.

Tom picked up the remainder of the pack and dealt out the number of cards required by the other players. "And three for the dealer."

With the cards he bought, Tom now had a pair of sevens. He didn't show them and threw them, face down, into the discards.

Brian showed his hand. He had bought another heart. He had neither a flush nor a pair.

Jemmy's showed his pair of tens. He was the winner. The nugget was his.

Thirty-one

Tom's eyes opened suddenly, staring. He looked out from the blankets and across at Brian. "That was a shot."

Brian was awake. In the partly dark room he answered without turning. "It was the boy. Didn't you here him go out?"

"What the hell's he shooting at this time of night?"

"A fox, I'd say. There's been one worrying the hens. He gets a shilling a head, and the skin if he wants it."

"A shilling a head, for foxes? No need for him to find a gold mine; he's found one – you."

The men lay there, contemplated rising.

They looked to the door at the sound of the latch. The door opened.

"I got him," announced Jemmy, his face aglow, a dead fox hanging from one hand, a rifle in the other. "On the run, too." He threw the fox on the floor.

"Get that stinking thing out of here," ordered Brian. He looked across at Tom. "Nothing worse than the stink of an old-man fox."

Jemmy, his face still glowing, picked up the trophy and left.

"… Have you thought any more about when you'll go up?" asked Tom.

"I'm still on it. Before the week's out, I'd say."

As understocked as Foxhow was, Brian had decided to take about a hundred and fifty cattle up to the plateau for summer grazing. The grass he would save in the best places at home would help ensure plentiful feed throughout the following winter.

Jemmy was pleased that Tom was to stay longer. He had begun to like Tom, as mad as Tom went at times, and he told good stories. Also Tom used more big words than Brian, as if he thought him clever enough to know their meanings. Jemmy had helped him at the forge the day Tom was working at drawing his blunted picks, heating them and hammering them to a point. Tom explained why he let the hot iron cool slowly in the air instead of quickly by plunging it into the water barrel. Quick cooling made iron too brittle and more likely to shatter if something very hard was hit. Tom had told him that gold came out of volcanoes and that all the gold in Australia was old gold and that many of the reefs were in disintegration and the gold scattered. If he were a young man, Tom said, New Guinea was where he would go to; he had heard that the volcanoes there were still throwing out gold and that some of the seams that had been found were as thick as a man's arm. Tom said the goldsmiths of a long time ago were the first bankers, because they had safe places to hide gold and people would pay to have it minded.

Tom had looked and listened the night Jemmy showed him the pictures in the Mongol book, and Tom had not scoffed or laughed at the idea that could be descended from the ponies of that faraway country. And he had shown to Tom, and Tom had taken him seriously. Tom did not say he believed, but did not say he disbelieved. With Jemmy present, Tom told Brian he didn't think Jem's theory was such a bad one. Then, not only did Tom become mad again, but Brian went mad with him. Brian said to him, "*Sire, your son is mad.*"

"*Mad?*" said Tom. "*The son of the king of Denmark mad? The Prince of Denmark mad? Watch your tongue, good Minister.*"

For minutes they went on in this way, with Tom calling Brian 'Polonius'. It ended when Brian said, "*Are your necessaries embarked?*" and together they burst out laughing. They did not explain themselves and soon afterward the cribbage board was brought out.

The trip to the plateau started the following Wednesday and, including the overnight stay at the hut, saw the stockmen back on Foxhow at the end of four days. It was on the way down that Tom said to Jemmy, "I hear you're looking for a godfather. If you think I'd do, you can have me."

The offer jolted Jemmy but he accepted.

"When do you want to do this?" asked Tom.

"Soon as I can."

"Let's see. I understand you're waiting on a letter from Cedric Hoy about your going with him to Mount Ebony. I'm wanting to go to Fitzford to sell some gold and buy a few new rags and stores, then I'll be heading down towards Omeo. We could go to Fitzford together. We could head off before the letter comes and let the Webbers get a message to Cedric as to where you are and let the rest take care of itself. We'd do the christening as soon after we arrive as you'd like. Would that work in with you?"

"Yes."

"All we need now is Brian's O.K. and it's a sealed deal."

Thirty-two

With the gold he sold and the sovereigns he received in exchange Tom bought new clothes, amongst other things. The clothes were the kind he would live in daily for some time to come, but, seeing they were new, he regarded them as suitable to be worn at Jemmy's christening. As well, he was bathed and barbered and was feeling pleased with himself. The Reverend Oswin North of the Church of England did the baptism before evening worship on the first Sunday after Tom and Jemmy's arrival in town. Reverend North drew Tom aside afterwards and told him that if Master Tyler did not own a Bible, an inexpensive edition of the New Testament, subsidized by the diocese, was available for nine-pence. Tom bought a copy and presented it to Jemmy. It was the first book Jemmy had ever owned. The next day Tom bought his final supplies, bade Jemmy and the Webbers farewell and left for Omeo.

Jemmy was ready for any nonsense Alfred might try to dish out. Alfred tried but was becoming accepting of Jemmy as somebody who could not be fooled with. But there had been a showdown first. They had been riding out two young horses that Peter was breaking in for a client and the boys were galloping them when Alfred came close, pulled the bridle off the head of Jemmy's mount and threw it back into Jemmy's lap. Jemmy now had no control over his horse and when he was able to ease the gelding to a halt and get the bridle back on, he did not remount and when Alfred rode up, laughing, Jemmy pulled him out of the saddle and onto the ground. They fought on the spot, at the side of the road. Jemmy soon had Alfred in a headlock. Struggling, Alfred croaked that he was a boxer and wanted to fight by Marquis of Queensberry rules.

"Never heard of them. You fight your way and I'll fight mine."

"I'm a boxer," howled Alfred.

"I'm a wrestler."

The fingers on the hand Alfred was able to get to Jemmy's face searched to find eyes. Jemmy moved his head and with his teeth latched onto a finger and he bit with all his strength.

Alfred gave up. Jemmy released him and they got to their feet. Jemmy waited, ready, in case Alfred was foxing. Alfred was pleased to see the end of the scrap and sullenly turned away. His fear now was that they might not be able to catch the horses, that had run away, or that the animals might have bolted back to the stable. If the horses went back to the stable, he would be in trouble with his father, and he was afraid Jemmy might not support him in the lie he would tell about how it all happened. Luckily they found the horses, caught them and rode them home.

The Hoys, unannounced, came for Jemmy in the early morning towards the end of the second week. They had for Jemmy to ride a fresh, grain-fed horse that they knew was reliable and sound. Cedric looked at Jemmy but neither spoke nor smiled. The other men were friendly though did not say their names. They seemed amused at taking a guest with them, which was what they regarded Jemmy as, and one so young. There was no handshaking and Jemmy was given time only to fetch his bedroll and any extra clothes he wanted. One of the men was an Aborigine named Johnny Winton, who had worked as a stockman on Mount Ebony. The Hoy men were known locally as the Black Hoys. The sons were black-headed and black-bearded and their eyes were so dark they could be called black. Their darkness, they would tell anybody, came from the Armada Spaniard in their high north Scottish ancestry. Matthew was the eldest. The two others, Paul and Samuel, were twins. Near sunset they were on the station named Mount Ebony.

There were no ebony trees on Mount Ebony, or even trees that could be mistaken for ebonies. Ebony was an African tree and its seasoned wood was black. When Simon Elderwell first saw the land he went on to acquire, the highest hill within his view was covered with the blackened, charred remains of forest timber after a fire. Simon and his brother Isaac were sons of Horatio Elderwell, the English paper manufacturer. Horatio exported paper to Australia. The brothers had been sent out to investigate the prospects for manufacturing paper in the colony. They were to take home sample logs of eucalyptus. This they did, but the hard eucalyptus wood proved unsuitable for the making of paper and the prospect of building a mill in Australia that might service all the Far East, and beyond, was abandoned. But Simon came back. He liked what he had seen of the colony. He brought with him a young grey stallion bred in England but of pure Arabian blood. He began stocking his station with cattle and horses. He had not been there a year when he was killed in a fall from a horse.

Next day the horses were left to rest and, on foot, the men walked as much of the creek as was thought necessary. Plans were made. The creek bed was thought to be the best place to try to carry out the catch. The bulk of the preparatory work had been done during previous visits by the brothers and Johnny Winton.

The first watch began later on. Two men at a time, unmounted, went to a spot where the horses coming in could be seen without the watchers being seen. There was one hole where the signs on the ground showed it was more favoured than any of the other holes. At around the time expected, the watchers saw what they wanted to see and stayed till the horses left.

Elderwell's hut and stockyards had been built not far from the creek. Most of the creek was dry at present but close to the hut the bed had become a series of waterholes. After the first good rain the creek would run again. The horses the Arab was with numbered about eight and, together, they would come to the holes around midmorning and mid-afternoon. There was other water on the property but in this dry time the grazing hereabouts was better than anywhere else and the horses were keeping to this area.

The sides of the creek were wide apart and steep. The plan was to come in behind and above the horses when they were watering and run them along the bed to where there had been set up a blind made of tree trunks and branches. The blind swung to the left and into a funnel made of more trunks and branches, at the end of which were the yards. The success of the run depended on keeping the horses in the creek bed. Cedric wanted two men, hidden, near the end where the horses were to meet the blind and be turned into the funnel. The lower side of the creek, to the left, where the horses might escape, Matthew would handle. Johnny would come in from behind. Cedric would manage the high side and give the yell when the action was to begin. If in the morning the horses came in unhesitatingly, the afternoon would be when the run would happen, when the Arab and the others would more sluggish than in the morning; they would be let drink first and fill their bellies, which would help slow them down. The run from the waterhole to the blind was about five hundred yards.

Jemmy was given strict orders; he was to go with Cedric and keep behind him and out of the way. "Don't draw level or get in front of me at any stage. You follow only – understand?"

In the morning the Arab and his companions, unconcerned, came and went. Jemmy was not asked to accompany anybody but had taken a chance and attached himself to Matthew and Paul when their watch came.

Neither Matthew nor Paul objected.

Near four o'clock Johnny and Samuel broke through the bush surrounding the hut and said the horses were coming into the creek.

The riders mounted.

Cedric and Jemmy, Matthew and Johnny, together, rode wide of the creek then except for Jemmy and Cedric, separated, each, now and again, catching a glimpse of the horses at the waterhole.

Everyone heard Cedric's cry as forward and downward the old man went, Jemmy behind him. The bank above the creek was where Cedric now needed to be.

On the other side, forward and downwards Matthew went.

In the creek bed, Johnny went forward.

All moved as fast as was safe to push their horses, though never knowing what might come up, fallen timber or rocks.

The horses in the creek bed went forward.

The rotted tree stump, no sign of it above ground, gave way under a front leg of Cedric's horse. Sideways the horse went down, rolling to one side the next second and catapulting Cedric from the saddle.

Jemmy surged past. He lay on the reins, stopped his horse within about a hundred and fifty feet and turned him. Cedric's horse was up and bolting. Cedric stood.

"Come down, come down," yelled Matthew to his father, whom he could not see.

Jemmy heard Matthew, saw him racing along the top of the bank on the other side and he saw the horses in the creek.

"Come down, come down," came Matthew's voice again. With nobody yet on the bank on Cedric's side there was the chance the horses below might see the unattended side as an escape route.

Jemmy turned his horse downwards and put heels to him.

"Come back, come back," called Cedric.

Jemmy went on. He had heard but ignored the order. He reached the bank that had to be followed and soon was level with the horses below and with Matthew on the other side.

As the horses neared the blind Matthew eased back. Jemmy eased back and so did Johnny, at the rear. The horses were needed to be let clearly see the gap in the blind on the left and think it a way of escape. If now pushed too hard they could, in their confusion and fear, make a sudden dash in a direction they were not wanted to go in.

The horses came almost to a halt and began milling.

Not the Arab but a shaggy-maned, long-tailed brown led the way, to the left, and the others followed.

Samuel and Paul ran to block the gap behind the horses. They moved out of the way when the riders came up and went through.

Side by side the three riders trotted along the makeshift lane to make sure their quarry did not attempt to come back.

"Where's the ole man?" asked Matthew.

"He's back there," said Jemmy. "But he's all right. His horse fell when we were going down to the bank."

Matthew stopped.

Jemmy and Johnny stopped.

"Lend me your horse," Matthew said to Jemmy.

Jemmy's foot had scarcely touched the ground when he felt the reins being pulled out of his hand.

At a canter and leading Jemmy's horse, Matthew started back the way he had come.

The horses secured, the gate behind them chained, Jemmy and Johnny, Paul and Samuel, looked through the rails at their prize. This was the closest to the Arab they had ever been. Not many minutes later Cedric and Matthew rode up and dismounted and joined the others. Cedric seemed none the worse for his accident. Jemmy looked at him, waiting for what might be said. Cedric did not speak nor give Jemmy a glance. All eyes were on the grey Arab, and all liked what they were looking at. The stallion's fine legs were black below the knees and hocks, and the tail and mane were black; width between the large, intelligent-looking eyes was ample and the slightly dished face tapered to a slender muzzle leading to wide, winddrinking nostrils. As for the others, they were not wild horses as in having been born in the wild. They were horses that had been allowed to run wild after the death of the man who had owned them. The handling of them, if they were to be handled, was expected to give no bother. The best of them might be taken back to the Hoys' station, in which event the others would be released and left to the pleasure of the next owner of Mount Ebony. All being well, the homeward trip would start tomorrow morning.

Thirty-three

They had eaten and the fire the men sat around outside the hut more than matched the chilly night air.

"Any ghosts on this place that anyone's heard of?" said Paul. He looked at Johnny. "A man killed here – surely someone's said he's seen or heard of a phantom rider or something."

"I never saw one or heard of one," replied Johnny.

Paul looked at Jemmy. "Do you know any ghost stories?"

"No."

"Doesn't anybody know any?" said Paul. He turned again to Johnnie. "What about that one up where you're from that we hear about, that one in western Queensland, on the plains; it gets around at night; about the size of a lantern and won't let anybody get near it? You can chase it on a horse but never catch up to it."

"That one?" said Johnny. "Yeah, I know him. Seen him plenty of times. Sometimes he goes slow, sometimes fast. The old people don't talk about him – brings bad luck if you do. They reckon he steals children. Go near him and he'll go away, and maybe come on again after, behind you or somewhere else. He's a bird."

The brothers laughed.

"He a bird alright," Johnny went on. "He makes light and insects come around and he eat em."

"A bird that lights itself up?" said Samuel. "I've never heard of a bird do that."

"He catch rat, too." said Johnny. "He flies around inside the light and rats can't see him; rats aren't frightened of light and the bird can go right up to them." He put out his hand and closed it quickly as might a bird snatching at prey with its talons.

"There's an insect that does that – light its self up," said Matthew.

"I've heard about them in the caves down near the coast – called glow-worms. If a worm can make light, I suppose a bird could. I think there are fish that can do it too – so they say."

"Mister Drury saw a light like that once," said Jemmy. "It was on a bush and he thought the bush was on fire."

"There're some strange things out there," proclaimed Paul.

The conversation about strange happenings drifted on.

Jemmy noticed that Cedric, although remaining silent, looked at everybody when they spoke but not at him when he spoke. Then he saw Cedric looking directly at him.

"Why didn't you come back when I told you?" asked Cedric.

Jemmy had been waiting for this.

All eyes turned to Cedric.

"I saw you weren't hurt," answered Jemmy. "… And my blood was up."

The brothers laughed.

Johnny grinned.

Cedric blinked. "Your blood was up. Your blood was up. Next time, whether your blood's up, down or sideways, when I give you an order, you do as I tell you. Hear me?"

"I saw you were all right and Matthew was calling and I thought there wasn't time to stop."

"There you are, father," said Matthew. "As simple as that; and it's just as well he did move. There wasn't any time to lose – if they'd got up the bank, with nobody there to keep them down, we might have lost them."

"I'd have been there soon enough if he'd come back and given me the horse."

"Maybe not, father. Seconds could have made the difference. The boy made a judgement and it turned out not to be a bad one, and he held the ground as good as any man could have. Lucky for us he was with you."

"I know that, I know that. But it's not the point."

"Well, it ought to be the point," insisted Matthew. "We got the stallion. Let's be satisfied and leave the rights and wrongs of it for talk some other time. We got what we came for, we ought to be celebrating."

Cedric looked again at Jemmy. "If there are any new lieutenants needed on any ship of mine, they don't appoint themselves – I appoint them. If ever you disobey me again, I'll skin you alive and nail your hide to the door of the Wodonga town hall."

“No, don’t do that,” quipped Samuel. “Waste of a good hide. Tan it. Hide like that would come up like kid. You’d get a dozen pairs of gloves out of him. Tie his head to the knocker and let it go at that.”

Paul chuckled. “Send a pair to Brian, as a memento.”

Cedric was not amused.

Quiet settled.

Before any further talk on what happened on the higher bank in the afternoon could resume, Matthew spoke.

“Those lights we were talking about, I think I’ve read they’re called ‘dead men’s campfires’ in some places.”

“Lots of different names for them,” said Johnny. “Depends where you are.”

Cedric looked across at Jemmy once more and stood. “Come with me.”

Jemmy rose but did not follow.

The men looked at him.

With a slight movement of his head Matthew recommended Jemmy go.

Cedric did not look back. He was out of the clearing by the time Jemmy took his first step.

“Don’t cry, mate,” said Paul, “or he’ll hit you all the harder.”

“Stuff gum leaves into your mouth,” advised Samuel. “That’s what we used to do.”

Jemmy made no attempt to catch up. He could see Cedric’s form and the sapling foliage parting as the man pushed his way through. He wondered how far Cedric was going to lead him before the worst was to happen. He watched for Cedric to break off part of a branch. He had made up his mind: he was not going to allow Cedric to beat him. The only way Cedric could do it would be to catch and hold him. If Cedric expected him to stand and be hit, the old man was wrong.

Cedric kept walking.

Jemmy kept following.

They were nearing the yards. Not once so far had Cedric turned.

Jemmy saw the saddles on the ground under a tree. It might be a stirrup leather Cedric intended using, Jemmy thought. He had tasted stirrup leather before. But Cedric walked past the saddles. He stopped at the rails and looked into the yard. He knew Jemmy was behind him.

Cedric turned his head only enough to see exactly were the boy was. "Step up," he commanded.

Jemmy did as he was told, but kept beyond arm's length.

"They're not the best lot of horses I've ever run in," said Cedric, looking into the yard. "And I'm not fussy about taking any of them – except the one I came for. But I've two minds about one: that brown there with his rump to us. See him? Now he's swinging away to the off side. See him? Make a good packer, that fellow. He's built to carry weight. Do you want him? You can have him, or one of the others, if you want; but that one is the pick of them. Might make a good saddle-horse too."

Jemmy saw the horse that Cedric meant, but his shock was such he was unable to answer.

"... Well, speak up. Do you want him?"

"... Yes."

"He's yours."

On the way back to the fire there was a private need Cedric wanted to attend to and with his hand he indicated to Jemmy to walk on.

Jemmy walked back into the gathering.

"How did you get on?" asked Samuel.

"He gave me a horse," Jemmy mumbled, still dazed.

"Gave him a horse," said Samuel, turning to Paul beside him.

"Gave him a horse," repeated Paul.

"Gave you a horse, eh," said Matthew. "Looks like you've just been made a lieutenant."

Thirty-four

With few words, as was the way with the Hoys, they, and Johnny Winton, said their goodbyes at the doorway outside Peter Webber's stable.

"Thanks for taking me," said Jemmy. Dismounted, he handed Paul the reins of the horses he had been loaned. In his other hand he held the halter lead of the shaggy brown gelding he had been given. Though he was not black, the horse had been named Ebony.

"We might call on you again one day," said Matthew as he reined away.

"You have any trouble with that one," said Johnny, "leave him here for me and I'll smooth him out for you."

Looking at Jemmy, Cedric brought up a hand to near his face in a sort of salute.

Today was the fifth since he had ridden away from the Webbers. The Webbers welcomed him as if he truly had been missed. Even Alfred seemed pleased to see him. One of the first pieces of news he was told was that Brian was in town and had requested that Jemmy come and see him at the Royal Oak. With the afternoon as late as it was, Jemmy left his visit to Brian till after dinner.

He found Brian in the lounge and after telling about how the grey Arab had been caught and that he had been given a horse, Brian suggested they go up to his room.

Brian seated himself in a chair and, pointing, indicated for Jemmy to sit on the edge of the bed.

"How are you getting on at the Webbers?" asked Brian.

"Good."

"They like having you. We've had a talk about you. How would you like to stay on with them and go to school and learn to read and write and do sums properly? A chance like this is not likely to come the way of a boy like you very often. I've given this a lot of thought. I think you should, too."

"I can live without it. I've gone all right so far."

"No you haven't. You're saying you have, but you haven't. You're full of fret. I've seen it in you often."

Jemmy's body became rigid and he felt his face tightening. The fear he had held since that day on the road, after Albury, came back. The fear was that the day would come when Brian would want to send him away, send him packing, never to see Brian again. He did not want Brian gone from his life.

"Couldn't you just have me as a worker? A lot of good workers can't read or write."

"I know that. Some of the best men I've ever had work for me weren't able to read or write. But… you've become special. I want to try to do the best for you that I can."

"I only want to work at Foxhow. I don't want to work anywhere else. I don't want to go anywhere else."

"That takes us to something else, which I'll get to in a minute. If you were to agree to this, your mother too would have to be agreeable. What I would do is, go and see her and explain what we're proposing. I'll be surprised if she's not in favour. I think, for her, what's most important is that you're with good people."

"But I'm already with good people – you. Can't we just leave it all like that? If I'm a good worker, why do you want to get rid of me?"

Brian's voice rose. "… For the very reasons I'm trying to explain to you. Listen to what I'm saying, for God's sake." He paused and when he spoke again his voice was calmer. "The other point is, in not too much time from now, I might not be at Foxhow. I'm not getting any younger and this hip of mine isn't getting any better. The day will come when I will leave. I don't want to stay on till I'm so infirm that I'll have to be trundled out in a cart. Financially, the place isn't paying what it should be. It's not carrying anywhere near the amount of stock it ought to be. I could put in a manager, an idea I've toyed with, or lease or sell up. What might become of you then?"

"Where would you go?"

"I might go to Fitzford, or Albury or Wodonga. A cottage with a few acres outside town would suit me fine. I'd still have a stallion. I'll always have a stallion."

"If you did that, you'd still need someone to help you. I could go with you."

Brian sighed deeply. "… A bit of casual labour would be all I'd need – nobody full-time."

Jemmy fell silent. Brian let him be. Then Jemmy spoke.

"If I don't do what you want me to, will you sack me?"

"No, not over this. But I'll be very disappointed. All this is sudden, I admit, but let's not close the door on it. Think it over. But I hope you don't take long. If you make up your mind to take the offer, the sooner you get going on it, the better."

No more on the matter of Jemmy's staying with the Webbers and going to school was spoken about over the two days that followed. In the hope that Jemmy would agree to the plan, Brian stayed longer than he had wanted. On the third day he said to Jemmy, "I want to start for home tomorrow. Have you made up your mind what you're going to do?"

"I want to go too."

Brian nodded and turned away.

Thirty-five

It was that time of year when foxes barked – autumn, the mating season. The bark woke Jemmy. He slid to the floor, pulled off his nightshirt and put on a daytime shirt and his pants and boots. He took the rifle beside the door and bullets from the shelf.

Foxes near the homestead at night did not always concern the dogs. It was more than the hens that brought foxes close. The dogs buried bones and the foxes might sniff them out, dig them up and make off with them.

In the moonlight, which was almost as bright as daylight, Jemmy moved slowly and without noise. He was near the forge when away from it a little he saw a form he did not expect. He stopped. The shape was of a horse and it was looking at him. Jemmy walked towards the animal. The horse did not move and watched the boy. Jemmy put out his hand and the horse, a chestnut, lifted his head. Jemmy's hand and the chestnut's nostrils touched. The head of the horse, though not its colour, reminded Jemmy of the head of the grey Arab at Mount Ebony. The forelock, mane and tail, were long and matted.

"I know who you are," said Jemmy. "You're Lanarth. I've been waiting a long time to meet you. Where've you been – hiding from me, up in those hills? Look at your poor old hooves. I'll fix them for you." He put a hand under Lanarth's neck near his head and caught hold of some of the mane on the other side. Lanarth didn't resist and walked when Jemmy walked. They went into the forge and Jemmy put a halter on Lanarth's head and let the lead dangle.

With toe-knife and hammer, then rasp, and each leg held between Jemmy's knees, Lanarth's hooves were trimmed. Finished, Jemmy led the old stallion outside and faced him. "There's a new king here now – his name is Kilrenny. But you can be the king out there. Where you've been is your land. Away you go." He drew the halter off Lanarth's head and the stallion swung away.

"Come back again. I'll fix your hooves better next time."

Lanarth cantered to the fence along the lane-side of Kilrenny's paddock. Kilrenny scented and saw the visitor and galloped towards him. Lanarth, neck arched, waited. They met and with nostrils flared and ears laid back they snorted and tried to bite each others neck. Then they set off at a gallop, along the fence, as if seeking an opening that would bring them together and allow proper battle. Jemmy watched till they disappeared on the other side of a stand of Blackwoods.

The fox he had come out to try to get would be gone, Jemmy believed, and taking the rifle from where he had left it standing he went back to the hut.

In the morning Jemmy sat up and looked across at Brian. "Lanarth was here last night. It was him, for sure. I did up his feet."

"Good boy. I heard you come in and wondered what it was all about."

"I've got a sore knee, though. I rasped it, through the hole in my pants."

"You should have put on the apron. That's what it's for. Knock much skin off?"

"Yes."

"Put some honey on it. It'll heal. How's the old fellow looking?"

"Rough, but not skinny."

The day was Sunday and, unless there was a job that needed doing urgently, it was the day Jemmy usually had off. Not that he ever found much to occupy him on such days. Brian was teaching him to plait and during the first part of this morning he did some of that. He could plait four strands round now. Though he walked with some stiffness because of the knee he had run the rasp over, when he saw not as far off as she sometimes was, he walked out to look at her, a halter over his arm and a lump of stale bread in one hand. He did not ride her these days.

As he walked he thought of Grace Kinlake. Today was the last Sunday in April and he knew this was the weekend that she and Boydy did not go out to the family station. This was the one Sunday a month that they stayed in town and went to church. He had seen Grace twice when he was in Fitzford waiting for the Hoys to call for him. He still had the soap wrapper with the picture of the girl that reminded him of Grace. At her invitation, he had been to where she lived in town with her aunt and uncle. She had invited him out to the station, but he could not go in case the Hoys came for him. There was something else he might have done today if his knee had not been sore. He might have saddled up and gone to the spot on the river where he did what nobody knew he did.

Used to the bread he regularly brought, when Bonny saw him she started towards him.

When he got back to the hut Brian said, "I saw you looking at Bonny. You picked up a hoof. Anything wrong?"

"No. Just looking. There's never anything wrong with her feet. But her belly isn't getting bigger."

"You know, maybe it is changing but you're not seeing it. You know why you mightn't be seeing it: you look too often. Why not try not looking so much? And these are early days, too. From start to finish takes eleven months. She's got another five or six months to go. Of course, no need to tell you again, there's the chance she isn't in foal. On the other hand, she might be one of those mares that fool you – they don't show up till very late. A mare I had on a ship once was the classic. If I'd thought she was in foal she wouldn't have been put on the ship. We were in the Bay of Bengal and early one morning, just coming daylight, a storm hit us and we started shipping big seas over the starboard side. We had about fifty horses on, all fore-deck cargo, topside, twenty-five head in stalls side by side on both sides. The seas on that side were hitting the horses under the belly and lifting them off their feet. If the stabling hadn't held we could have lost a lot of horses. A lascar started yelling at me and pointing. The scupper – that's the gutter running around the edge of the deck – was full of water and it was racing my way and I could see something brown in it and as it got nearer I saw it was a foal. I could use only one hand and as the foal was going by I reached out and grabbed her and pulled her in. It was a filly as it turned out – new-born. That deck took some riding but eventually I got her under canvas on top of a cargo hold and lashed her down. Later, after we got out of the storm, I went to see what I had – a live or dead foal. She was alive. But which one of the few mares on that side was her mother? I'd have staked my life that there wasn't a mare in foal on board."

"What happened after that?"

"The task was: which mare was the one? There were four possibles, and I thought all I had to do was find one with some swelling in the udder. Not one of them had an udder that suggested there could be milk in it. I carried the foal to each of them, but none showed any interest. Maybe that was understandable, in view of all that had happened. If the foal didn't get milk soon ..." Brian shook his head. "Over the next three or four hours I don't know how many times I tried. The chief officer came with me a few times. I reached the point where I saw it was no good going on and took out my knife and was just about to put it across the foal's throat."

"Why?"

"No future. No mother. No milk. Better I do this than let her starve to death. Then, this officer said to me, "Couldn't we try just once more?" Out of regard for him – he was a good fellow – I agreed. He went with me next time around. This time there was one mare whose udder I thought was a little fuller than when I last looked. So I put the foal in beside her and pushed it down towards her flank, half-expecting to see rejection. But she didn't. The foal began to nuzzle in the right spot and next thing she was suckling. We landed both mother and daughter, alive, a few days later."

There was no more to tell and Brian waited. If few or no questions were asked immediately he knew they could come along days or weeks from now.

Jemmy did not speak.

"That paddock Bonny's in," said Brian, "the feed's getting a bit light on. We might put her down on the river with any other horses that are in that paddock and we don't need. Good feed down there, and she won't be right under your nose. We'll put more cattle down there too." He broke off. "The water barrel's well down; we'd better fill it tomorrow. If I go to Albury to live, or Fitzford, and I build a cottage, I'll have a roof made of that kind of tin that runs the rainwater into a gutter then into a tank and I'll have water on tap all year round. No more fetching water from a creek, or well." Another thought came to mind. "The flats. When Chester Tweedie came the other day it was to see if I'd rent them to him, and maybe more land later on. I like the idea. We have to talk again. So, you might see a few Braywood men regularly around the place soon. The extra company shouldn't hurt us."

Jemmy said nothing.

In the afternoon he took his pencils and paper and the Capt Hayes book from the trunk and put them on the table. He put in front of him a traced drawing of a skeleton of a horse and began writing beside the bones the names as best he could remember their spellings. When he finished he checked and found he had spelt all the names correctly. Afterwards, to save paper, he rubbed out the writing. The Hayes book he kept in the chest below the end of his bunk. He was now the owner of the book. Brian had given it to him as a present. He began thinking about the Braywood men that might soon be seen on Foxhow more often.

The worry that Brian might leave Foxhow and not need him any more would not go away. He had not stopped thinking about this since Brian first mentioned it. The thoughts came not only in the daytime but often at night before he went to sleep, and sometimes they came when he woke during the night. He thought about the Webbers. He liked Mr and Mrs Webber. He thought of Alfred, whom he would have to live so closely to and whose room he would have to share. He knew he and Alfred could never become like brothers or best friends. How long could learning to read and write take? If the schooling would take no more than a few months, maybe he could put up with Alfred. He could maybe do it if he was sure he would be allowed to go back to Brian, even if Brian went away from Foxhow. But he could not see that he could be sure. He feared that once the break with Brian was made it would somehow become final. Brian could say he would take him back but could later change his mind, as he did once before, when they were leaving Albury the first time and Brian said he was taking him back to Quartz Creek. Brian seemed not yet certain whether he would leave Foxhow. If Brian sold or leased the place, or parts of it, to Mr Tweedie maybe Brian could stay on as a kind of tenant, could still have his few horses and a stallion and go to Albury every year; or if he put in a manager he would not have to leave unless he wanted to. If Brian stayed but did not need him as much as before, he would be willing to work for only his keep and perhaps sixpence or a shilling now and then. He could not accept as true that he could not go on being useful to Brian. And if work did become slack he could help Mr Tweedie's men till Brian needed him more. In view of all that had happened, and all that might go on to happen, he decided he should not risk aggravating Brian on the matter of learning to read and write. He would not, at least for the time being, speak of his wanting to read and write.

A deal happened and Braywood cattle came to Foxhow. With the cattle came stockmen, as many as three at once at times. The stockmen felled trees, split logs, made posts and rails, repaired stockyards and the roofs of some of the buildings. Jemmy noticed a happier Brian, even saw changes come to his face when the sounds of men calling to one another came from the yards and when hammering could be heard. One day Jemmy was walking beside him when Brian stopped and fixed his sight on the smoke coming from the cookhouse chimney. The stockmen, whoever they happened to be at any time, would come to the hut after dinner in the evenings and Brian would make tea for them and they would talk until late or play cards. If Jemmy turned in early he would lay there listening till he fell asleep.

One day two men, each leading a packer, rode in and asked Brian if he would allow them to camp in one of the huts for a day or two. When they told him what they were about he did not hesitate and said yes. That night, with these two men, two Braywood men, Jemmy and Brian, there were six in the hut. Jemmy turned in early, but did not go to sleep till after the two new visitors said goodnight. He heard the new visitors say they were geologists and as he listened he learned that they knew all about rocks. They said that all the land Foxhow and Braywood was on, and all the surrounding mountains, were once under the sea. And they said that where the Snowy flowed today was not where it used to be. Also they said there was talk that the state of New South Wales might be divided in two, and if it was, the capitol of the new state might be Eden, on the south coast, because Eden had a deepwater port. On this matter Brian had plenty to say. Brian saw off the geologists when they rode away and invited them to return anytime they wished. If they came and found nobody here, they were to make themselves at home.

Thirty-six

The brothers Patrick and John Keenaghan were courting the sisters Dora and Sarah Nesbitt who lived in Fitzford. The young stockmen were on their way back to Braywood after a visit to the girls and were on Foxhow. There were times at Braywood when leave without pay was not hard to arrange and the boys made use of any offer of time off. They had letters and papers for Brian.

The boys were above the river and heard the sound, of a goat bell, before they saw where the sound was coming from, close by and below them. They saw the horseman and stopped and watched. The bell, it seemed, was tied to one of the horseman's stirrups.

As Jemmy rode, at a gallop, he kept a sharp eye on the trees to his left, along the river. A bowman could be there, hidden. He was now not far from the fort. The soldiers there would hear the bell and know he was coming and would have a fresh horse saddled and ready. The message he was carrying, from Subedei to the Khan, had come a long way and had a long way yet to go. From his boot to above his head was a crooked pole with three cross-arms near the top from which ox tail-tips fluttered. At a gully he turned his horse and, at a walk, began riding back the way he had come. Where the ground above jutted out he rode up to it and out onto the ledge. Facing the river and all beyond it he shouted, "I am Jokee, son of Genghis Khan." After a rest he rode back down to the riverside and again set off with his message for the Khan.

After watching the second time Patrick and John went on their way.

From the hut Brian saw the men coming and walked out to greet them.

"You staying the night or going on?" asked Brian as the riders dismounted.

"We'll stay, if it's alright with you. We've got mail and papers for you."

"Turn your horses out – same paddock – and I'll have tea ready by the time you get back."

When they came into the hut the boys wasted no time.

"That kid of yours, Jemmy, he's gone off his head," said John.

"Right off," confirmed Patrick.

They told Brian what they had seen, and heard. They told of the strange pole with the tail-tips on it.

The pole Brian had never seen but he smiled at the story. "Not much to worry about, I think. Just a bit of play-acting. You might have done things like that when you were boys. Thanks for telling me. I'll keep an eye on him."

"We never did anything like what we saw today," said Patrick. "And who's this Joe Key he was yelling out about?"

"Oh, Jokee came into it, did he? He … was an old-time drover; not around any more. Jemmy will tell you about him, sometime. Might be a good idea not to mention the matter when you see him when he gets in. Let's keep it to ourselves, eh? Tell you what you could do for me, if you wouldn't mind: next time you're going to Fitzford, take him with you; leave him with the Webbers at the stable and bring him back when you're coming. Could you work that in?"

The boys nodded.

As always when papers came, this morning, after the Braywood boys had left, Brian intended going first to the sporting pages, to see what the latest was on the successes of Tom Hales and anything that could be found on Grand Flaneur. He did not have to go to the sporting pages to find news on Grand Flaneur. The news was on the front page of the Sydney paper. Grand Flaneur had broken down in a foreleg, and was expected never to race again. The news shocked but did not surprise nor upset him. Mentioned was that the three-year-old had never been defeated and that his last two wins were in the St. Leger and the two-miles Town Plate. He told Jemmy.

"Could a good vet cure him?" asked Jemmy.

"No. What's happened had to happen. The only surprise to me is that he lasted so long."

"Will his leg be like Kilrenny's – thick around the fetlock-joint?"

"I expect so, after all the initial swelling has gone away. At least now he's beyond the reach of any more abuse as a racehorse. We can be thankful for that much."

"Now he might go to England, to stud."

"Let's hope he does. Maybe in your time – certainly not in mine – you might see his progeny siring the best of stockhorses."

"We'll hope, eh?"

Thirty-seven

"The damned fire's broken through," said Brian, looking out the window. "Come on."

They hurried out and grabbed the shovels that stood by the doorway. Jemmy knew the fire Brian meant was at the charcoal pit and that what Brian had not wanted to happen had happened: part of the earth roof they had shovelled onto the wood to make it burn slowly had collapsed. The shallow pit was about ten feet wide. If the hole was not blocked the in-rushing air would cause the fire to burn intensely and the wood would turn to useless ash instead of becoming charcoal.

Smoke came from not only the cave-in but the many cracks here and there. There were sapling logs to the side and Brian pulled several across the hole. Then he and Jemmy shovelled soil onto the logs close to the hole. Though the smoke nearly blinded them, soon the break-out was under control.

They stood back, coughing and rubbing their eyes.

"It should be right now," said Brian. "But we'll still have to keep an eye on it. When you're making charcoal you've got to watch it all the time. One more day and it should right to open. We might kill it tomorrow morning."

"Why did we make so much? You only use it at the forge."

"I like to have a few sacks to take down to Braywood when we go. It's a small enough favour, taking into account all the favours they do us. The farrier down there can't make it – hasn't got the patience. He's always complaining about having to use wood. And I like to have a few bags over. If you've got a cow and a visitor comes, you can send him away with a pound of butter; if you've got a lot of hens, you can send him away with a dozen eggs. Us – all we can do is send him away with a bag of charcoal, if he wants it.'"

"You're all black under your eyes," said Jemmy, grinning.

"So are you."

Shovels over their shoulder they started back to the hut.

As they walked Jemmy looked up and to the east at a cloud he had noticed earlier. It was the only cloud in the sky and had a shape he thought odd. The cloud was long and slender, almost straight on both edges, thick at one end and pointy at the other. "Look at that cloud. Have you ever seen one shaped like that?"

Brian looked. "Can't recall one exactly like that. But I haven't got a good memory for clouds. It's the big fat dark ones I like best – full of rain."

"It's like a dagger."

"Yes, it is."' "How long do you think it could be?"

"About fifty miles."

"Fifty miles? A cloud couldn't be fifty miles long."

Brian began to laugh.

"What are you laughing at?"

"Nothing much. I just didn't know you knew so much about clouds."

"But a cloud couldn't be fifty miles long, could it?"

"The captain of a ship I was on told me about a cloud over him once and it lasted from Brisbane to Thursday Island – about a thousand miles."

"A cloud a thousand miles long. Phew."

The demands of the charcoal pit meant no riding away from the homestead today.

With an hour or more before dusk Jemmy slung a rifle over his back, mounted up and rode off to shoot a kangaroo for meat for the house and the dogs. Kangaroo meat in stew helped give the dish body and when minced and mixed with spices made acceptable rissoles.

While there was light Brian wanted to use it. He had gone back to the job of straightening a corner post at the yards that had been on the go since early afternoon and he was keen to finish the task today and be done with it. Jemmy now being out of sight, he let off the dogs that had been whining at seeing Jemmy ride away without them.

It was the dogs that alerted him to the visitor coming. Barking, the dogs ran a short distance towards the man. Brian stepped away from his work and looked in the direction of the excitement and saw the man. Usually a caller at this time of day meant a guest for the night. He studied the man, a man without a beard, not old and humping the usual swagman's gear.

The dogs halted, then went on.

The swagman picked up a stick.

"You won't need that," called Brian. "They're friendly."

The swagman didn't throw away the stick nor took his eyes off the dogs.

The dogs kept their distance.

Brian extended his hand as the man came up. The man gave his hand and allowed it to be shaken. He did not smile.

"Are you Brian Drury?"

"I am."

"You've got a boy here – Jem Tyler. I'm his father and I've come for him."

Unspeaking, Brian stared at the man.

"Where is he?" asked Tyler.

"He's... not here right now, but he ought to back soon, before dark or soon after. He's gone to shoot a roo. I heard a shot minutes ago. He shouldn't be long."

The men eyed each other.

"You'd better come up and have a cup of tea," said Brian.

Tyler dropped his swag at the door and went in.

"Seat yourself," said Brian.

Tyler pulled a chair out from the table and sat. The water in the black kettle was hot enough for tea and in a few minutes the caller had a steaming mug in front of him.

Brian excused himself, saying he wanted to finish a job and feed the dogs and that he should not be long. He hoped Tyler would stay inside till he came back. He was hoping Jemmy would turn up soon and he would be able to warn him.

Darkness was coming quickly and Brian went back to the hut.

"Sorry to leave you. More to do than I thought. He shouldn't be long now. More tea?"

"No," replied Tyler without looking at his host.

The dogs had been allowed in and the guest never took his eyes off them.

"Has he got any money coming to him?" asked Tyler.

"He's got a bank account and there's a monthly transfer to that from my account. He doesn't need cash up here."

"Have you got his bankbook?"

"No. He's got it."

Tyler quickly cast a glance around the hut. "In a place as small as this, you couldn't help knowing where everything's kept. Do you know where he keeps it?"

"If I did know, it wouldn't be my place to touch it."

"You tell me where it is and I'll touch it. I don't want him forgetting to bring it with him."

"If he leaves, I'm sure he'll remember to take it."

"'If he leaves'. He's leaving."

The dogs knew first. They ran to the door and waited. Brian let them out. They ran to greet Jemmy. Leaving the door open, Brian stepped out onto the verandah. Tyler followed and stood beside him.

Jemmy was within a dozen yards of the verandah when he saw his father. He stopped.

"What are you doing up here?" Tyler demanded to know. "You were told to stay at Jindabilla till I came for you. Bad enough going there for you without tramping to here. You've put us out two days – four by the time we get back on the track. Have you still got that heavy blanket I left you with?"

"Yes."

"Get it and the rest of your stuff. We're going to Queensland."

"Queensland. I don't want to go to Queensland."

"That's where we're going, so get your gear."

"I've got a mare here and she's in foal."

"Leave her. Collect her another time." He turned to Brian. "Or Mister Drury might buy her from you?"

"I don't want to sell her."

"Leave her. Come on, get your stuff."

"You wouldn't leave for anywhere at this time of day, would you?" said Brian.

Tyler ignored him. He wanted the boy out on the track and away from this old trouble-maker in short time, even if they could put only an hour behind them before making camp.

Jemmy began walking backwards then turned and ran, soon disappearing, the dogs following.

"Come back here," yelled Tyler. "The longer you muck me about, the worse it'll be for you. Come back." He waited. "I'm not going without you, so hurry up."

Brian whistled and the dogs returned and were let inside. Brian closed the door behind them and rejoined Tyler. Tyler turned to him. "I can handle this. You go in and leave it alone."

Brian decided that it might be best if he did go in. He wanted to think. He looked at the door when he heard it opening. Tyler came in.

"I can out-wait him," snarled Tyler. He went to the fire and stood with his back to it.

"Are you sure you can?" asked Brian. "I know him well enough to know that if he sets his mind for or against anything, Jesus Christ couldn't budge him."

"I'll budge him when I get a hold of him."

"You can stay as long as you like, but he won't come in if his mind's made up. He'll go bush if he thinks he has to. I know him. Are you sure taking him away right now is best for him?"

"Why wouldn't it be? I'm his father. I didn't expect he'd go against me like this, unless somebody's put something into his head."

"I've put nothing into his head against you, if that's what you mean."

"What's he told you?"

"About you? – nothing. He's kept to the drill, whatever it's been. I only know about you what a few other people know. You're in trouble with the law and there's a warrant out for you. You could get picked up. Say you do, maybe a long way from here, what would become of your boy? He'd be on his own. Anyway, if you're dodging police, wouldn't you be better off without the boy with you?"

"You mind your own business and I'll mind mine."

"Think on this. You might be in more trouble than you know. The man you hit is pretty sick and could die. If he dies, think of what the charge against you then might be. If I were you, I'd clear out now, on my own. Go, leave the boy here, and I'll make you a promise. I'll promise you I'll say nothing to anybody about your visit tonight. Take him with you and I'll give you up as soon as I can get on a horse and on my way. They got Ned Kelly – remember. I think the police would find you easier meat than him once they got a bit of information, from me."

"You'd give me up, would you?"

"Yes."

"I've half a mind to give you something to go on with here and now."

Brian knew what Tyler meant. "I wouldn't put that to the test if I were you. I think I could keep you off me long enough to make you soon change your mind. *Lay on, MacDuff.* "

Tyler was becoming more unsettled but was cautious. There could be more in this leathery old meddler than might be easily dealt with.

"Brian," came Jemmy's voice.

Brian started towards the door, Tyler behind him. They walked to the edge of the verandah and saw the dim form of the boy about twenty paces away.

"Brian, will you make me go if I don't want to?"

"No. Never."

"I'm not going with you, Dad."

Tyler descended the steps and halted. "You get up here and get your things."

Jemmy was gone.

"Stay the night if you'd like," said Brian to Tyler. "I can give you a feed. But you won't see Jemmy. He won't come in. He'll get himself a horse tonight and ride out of here to God knows where. You won't see him. Or if you're too uncomfortable under this roof, there are outhouses you can doss in. It's up to you."

Tyler did not answer and continued peering out into the darkness.

Then Tyler turned, walked past Brian and threw his swag onto his back. Again not looking at Brian, Tyler walked down the steps. "I'd sooner take my chances with the dingoes."

As Tyler disappeared Brian heard him call out. "You've made the wrong move, Jemmy. Just how wrong, you'll find out. I'll be back."

Brian waited, peering into the dark. He turned, went inside and dropped into his chair by the fire. He began to fear Tyler might engage in a cat and mouse game amongst the outbuildings. If Tyler did that, Jemmy, knowing the run of the place, would have the chance of eluding him. Brian saw no way he could help the boy. There were the paddocks that Jemmy might decide to take to. Taking to the paddocks would mean he could not be cornered. Then came the fear that Tyler, keeping out of sight, might hang around the property for a time, perhaps days, and in some other way try to carry out what he had come to do.

At the shot that rang out Brian stiffened. The sound had come from near the forge, he could tell. He rose, went to the door and opened it. His heart began pounding. The dogs raced past him. He followed in the direction he had seen the dogs go, which was not to the forge but towards the back of the stable and on the other side of the forge.

He called out, "Jemmy."

He went from doorway to doorway, peering inside, seeing nothing distinctly nor any movement.

"Jemmy."

Then Brian saw him, outside the back door of the stable and coming towards him, rifle in one hand and with the other dragging a dead fox. The dogs were with him.

As Jemmy walked up to him Brian's legs weakened and he fell onto his knees.

"I had to take the shot," explained Jemmy. "I could see him so clear, right in the doorway. He just stood there."

"Don't – don't ever – do anything like that to me again. Couldn't you, just this once, let that fox go?" He took the rifle and, pressing the butt into the ground, used the gun to help himself stand upright.

Inside the hut and with the dogs they bolted the door behind them.

They had had no dinner and at present were not thinking of food. They had not lit the lamp. There was no conversation though both were not without thoughts. They sat for a long time, mostly looking into the fire. Jemmy's eyes closed and soon he was asleep. He woke when Brian spoke.

"Why don't you take your boots off and lie on the bed and pull a rug over you. I'll keep watch. I might nod off but I'll wake quickly enough if there's need, or if I want you to relieve me."

Jemmy did as was suggested, sure that he would not fall asleep again. But he did. When he woke the fire was down and the room in near darkness. He saw Brian standing at the window near the door and looking out. He went over to him. He saw what Brian was looking at, a blazing hut, one with no others close to it.

"… Shouldn't we go and put it out?" said Jemmy.

"No. It's nearly done. Let it burn. It can't run – dew's too heavy."

Their eyes remained fixed on the blaze.

“We can build it again.”

“No need. We had no use for it, and it was falling down.”

Jemmy spoke calmly. “He’s finished with us now. He never comes back after he burns.”

Thirty-eight

Brian foresaw a possible problem he was keen to have the solution to in readiness for when it was needed. If indeed Bonny was in foal, the foaling would occur around when he usually set out for Albury. He was certain Jemmy would be reluctant to go on the trip if the foal had not yet arrived. One solution was to go to Fitzford for the season and test the prospects there for Kilrenny. If that was done, a departure from Foxhow need not take place till perhaps a month after the mare had foaled. Then, the social side of visiting Albury could still be indulged in, if wanted. They could leave Kilrenny with Peter Webber, take the Fitzford to Albury coach around Melbourne Cup time and come back a few weeks later. He decided to say nothing until Jemmy broached the matter – which, after a time, he did, and the Fitzford plan was decided upon.

The first of July was only days away. If Bonny was in foal, and if the gestation was proceeding according to the chart, the foal would arrive August.

Horses bred on Foxhow had never seen the inside of a stable at foaling time. Out in the paddocks was where it all happened. Jemmy knew this and one evening he said, "You said that sometimes snow falls on Foxhow. Does it ever come in August?"

"Yes, sometimes. But here, for some reason, we miss most of the bad snows."

"It's better if foals aren't born in snow, isn't it?"

"Yes – always better."

"Would you let me bring Bonny into the stable when she's due?"

"Fine – leave her out in the day, bring her in at night."

A loose-box was chosen but the floor was dirt and as hard as stone after years of horses standing on it. There was no straw. Over the next weeks Jemmy took a sickle and rope and rode to places where there reeds and fern and brought back bundles held across the front of the saddle and spread the material on the floor of the box. The layer was not thick but it made a better bed than nothing.

June had not ended when Brian pronounced Bonny as in foal, adding, "But I could be wrong." Weeks later he had no doubts. "She'll foal."

August came.

The increased swelling of Bonny's udder since yesterday and the sudden formation of wax at the ends of the teats told Brian the mare's time was very close. Today was the three-hundredth and forty-second since she had gone to Kilrenny. That night, in the dark between midnight and morning, Brian, without putting down the lantern, went to the bed below the one Jemmy usually slept in, the one that was Tom's when he visited. Jemmy, still in his day-clothes, woke before Brian spoke and was surprised that he had been asleep.

"Come on, stud-master, you'd better go and see what's happened down there since you last looked."

Jemmy, sat up, swung out his legs and pulled on his boots. "… Is there a foal?"

"Well, there was one horse there before and now there're two. There must be a message in that."

Jemmy ran.

Brian walked.

Bonny was standing. The foal, a colt, was sitting with legs tucked under him.

Jemmy knelt and with the back of his hand stroked the foal's shoulder. "Gee, he's small."

"He'll grow. He might never be a giant, but a good little-un is as good as a good big-un any day of the week."

"Were you here?"

"No. You were asleep and I just thought I'd come down and take a look on my own – save waking you maybe for nothing – and there he was, a bit wetter than he is now, but there he was. He'd come like a good mountain horse – quick and without fuss or bother. The old girl knew what she was doing. She had no need of us."

"His colour's nearly yellow."

"It'll darken. He'll be close to her colour one day."

The foal turned its head.

"Look." Jemmy put a finger on the only white on the colt, a spot the size of a half-crown on the forehead. "He's got snow on him already. I'll name him Kosciuszko."

A sunny morning and a home-paddock that had been rested for months and in which the feed was beginning to come away awaited Bonny and her foal. But this paddock was not to be their home for more than the next few weeks. There were other matters to be attended to and the day came when Jemmy, riding Ochre and leading Bonny with Kosciuszko beside her, took the mare and foal to a part of the property where Brian had instructed that they be put. In this area the feed there was becoming some of the best on Foxhow and, while it held, any stock put there would be unlikely to move away. Foxhow was so understocked that there would little danger of the feed becoming low before Brian and Jemmy returned from Fitzford.

September arrived and, leading Kilrenny, Brian and Jemmy set out. With them were four other horses, two mounts and two packers, and the two dogs. They took the back way, through Eilean and Wrath.

At their invitation, Jemmy stayed with the Webbers. He hoped no mention would be made of what might have happened: his coming to live with them and going to school. But one day when he was alone with Mrs Webber in the kitchen she brought up the subject. She faced him and spoke softly. "We were all sorry you didn't come to us and go to school. But I think I understand. Every boy needs a good man in his life and you think you've found yours and you have a fear of losing him." The words stunned Jemmy. Then came another shock. She put her arms around his shoulders and briefly hugged him. She was the only woman besides his mother who had ever put her hands on him in this way.

Hand-written notices of Kilrenny's availability were put on the noticeboard at Heneberry's and at Webber's stable, and Brian lost no time putting out information by word of mouth. The results were good. At the end of a month, leaving Kilrenny in the charge of Peter, Brian and Jemmy took the coach to Albury and returned three weeks later, in November and after the Melbourne Cup. The number of mares that had been brought to the stallion during Brian's absence pleased him and, taking everything into account, he confessed that his annual *grand tours* from now on might see a new pattern.

On the way home Brian made it clear that they would be going back to Fitzford for Christmas. This pleased Jemmy for it meant that his tenure with Brian was safe for a while longer. Christmas, Jemmy estimated, was about six weeks away. Then Brian made another announcement: a trip to see Jemmy's mother and sisters, still at Wybalong station, would happen before Christmas. It would be their second visit.

In the morning after their return to Foxhow Jemmy rode out to search for Bonny and the foal and found them. Bonny had remembered and came to the piece of bread Jemmy held out to her. Kosciuszko had grown. On the way in Kosciuszko often raced ahead, would come to an abrupt stop within about a hundred yards, turn and gallop back to his mother. The rocky ground they sometimes passed over did not deter when he went off on these dashes. The bigger rocks he wove between and the stony patches he sometime leapt across.

Kosciuszko's growth went on unhindered. Bonny's milk was plentiful. The rains that season were better than they had been in the previous spring and the grass kept growing and holding its lushness. Though he was growing it could be easily seen that the colt was not going to be big. The handling of him began earlier than it did for most station-bred horses. It was the nature of station breeding that horses saw very little of men till they were anything up to four years of age and ran wild for most of that time. The breaking-in of such horses was usually a rough business and most horses bucked when first ridden, some taking longer than others to give up the habit.

Because Jemmy could please himself what he did in his own time, Kosciuszko's education started early and while still a foal he was introduced to the headstall. At first he tried to shake off this strange thing on his head but soon became accepting of it. On the day after that he had his first lesson in being led. A rope was looped over his rump and passed along his back and through the headstall with the end of the line finishing up in Jemmy's hand. At the feel of the rope tightening around his rump the colt jumped forward and every time he stopped Jemmy tugged on the rope again. Soon Kosciuszko made some associations: follow when his master walked and the rope would not tighten around his rump. Jemmy hoped to be sitting on Kosciuszko's back before the colt was a year old. Saddle, bit and reins, would come much later. If all went well the colt would never buck.

Thirty-nine

As Jemmy had hoped, he was sitting on Kosciuszko's back before the colt was a year old. He had at first lain across the colt's withers a few times and, when the pony showed no objection, one day he eased his right leg to the other side and sat up. The real breaking, when it came, would go so well, he was sure. And the colt would allow all his legs to be picked up.

Jemmy had turned fifteen earlier in the year. Three days before that birthday he and Brian had set out for Wyballong station. The present his mother had sent, which had come by post but had gone first to Braywood, had arrived weeks earlier. After she had learned that the government mail service, though it took a long time, could reach her son, Margaret wrote not infrequently and just as often sent knitted gifts. Jemmy's arriving at Wyballong on his birthday was to be a special surprise for her.

That year passed and Jemmy turned sixteen, and as the time approached to take Kilrenny on tour again Brian announced that instead of going to Fitzford as he had said he would, they would go to Albury. What happened to Jemmy in Albury that year he would never have dreamed of. The episode took place at Fry's stable one morning. He was finished doing Kilrenny's box and with the gathered-up Hessian sheet with the muck in it over his shoulders he started for the dung heap out the back. He looked at the man Brian and Edgar Fry were talking to. On the way back he hung the sheet on a nail on the wall, went to Kilrenny's box and began sweeping in the straw that had found its way outside the doorway. He again looked across at the man the men were talking to and thought there was something familiar about him and that probably he had come to hire a horse and vehicle and had been here before. The man was not tall, was slightly built, had a long well-kept moustache and was dressed in a suit and bowler hat. At his feet was a small portmanteau. Brian beckoned and Jemmy put up the broom and walked over.

"Jemmy," said Brian, "do you still have that newspaper picture of this man sitting on Grand Flaneur?"

Jemmy looked at the stranger and gaped.

Tom Hales put out his hand.

Jemmy went to take the hand but drew back quickly. "I've got dung on it."

"I had plenty on my hands too when I was your age," said Hales, his hand still extended.

They shook.

"If you don't close your mouth you'll get flies in it," said Brian. "Mister Hales has just come down on the train from Sydney and wants to go over to Wodonga to catch the Melbourne train. He's going to take one of Mister Fry's gigs and wants somebody to go with him and bring it back. Do you think you could handle the job?"

Jemmy started to speak but stopped and nodded vigorously.

A horse was brought in from the yards and harnessed and hitched.

Nervously Jemmy set off with his passenger. He sat stiffly, afraid to speak but hoped Hales would speak. He wanted to drive well. He wanted Mr Hales to see that he drove well. He looked at everybody they passed and wondered if anyone knew who it was sitting beside him. He hoped a lot of people would see him and that later some might stop him in the street and ask if he was the boy seen driving the famous Tom Hales. He was sure the visit of the great jockey would be mentioned in the paper next week. By the time they reached the bridge he was calmer. The horse was driving perfectly and this had helped improve his confidence. By the time they reached the other side of the river Jemmy's nervousness was all but gone and the light conversation, when it happened, came easily.

Returning and driving down the street towards the stable he hoped Brian would be there, and Edgar Fry too. He wanted to tell them every word Tom Hales had said, and what he had said to Tom Hales, and he would tell what Hales had done in Wodonga – that Hales told him he was not going to catch the Melbourne train that day and asked to be driven to another livery stable where he hired a horse and buggy, bought provisions and set off to inspect a property on the Mitta Mitta River that he might buy. If he bought the property, he said he would start a thoroughbred stud. And he would show them the two-shilling piece Hales had given him. As soon as he could get to the vice at the forge he would file a notch into the coin so that he could never accidentally spend it.

Part Two

Forty

The dogs streaking past the side window told Brian somebody was coming. He tied off the thong and walked outside to the end of the verandah. The horseman was Jemmy, riding Ochre and leading Ebony. Jemmy had been away eight days, had gone to Fitzford for Boydy Kinlake's birthday party. They waved. As was usual, Jemmy rode on to the stable to unsaddle and turn out the horses.

Brian returned to the doorway, lowered himself into the old chair and waited. He was not only pleased the boy was back but knew there would be newspapers.

A bundle of papers under one arm, a Gladstone bag in the other hand, Jemmy came up. There were left at the stable but these would be brought up later in the wheelbarrow.

"And what's the best news from Fitzford?" asked Brian, standing.

"Pretty good news. Wait'll I tell you."

Brian led the way inside. "Good news, eh? You asked Grace Kinlake to marry you and she said, yes?"

"No, no, no," said Jemmy, annoyed. "Be serious. This is important."

Brian grinned. "Just thought I'd ask. You're seventeen now and so is she. If you like the girl, and I know you do, you'd better start letting her know – before somebody else starts talking sweetly to her."

"The best news – you won't be expecting this, so get ready." Jemmy took the rolled-up bundle from under his arm, undid the string and laid the newspapers on the table. The paper he wanted was on top and folded open at the page he wanted. "It's here in the *Border Mail*." He put a finger on a spot circled in pencil. "Missus Webber showed me. The Mechanics Institute in Albury is starting classes for teaching grown people to read and write. How old you are doesn't matter. You can be as old as Hell and they won't knock you back. I want to go."

"Am I hearing rightly? This can't be true. You want to go and learn to read and write? At last. You're willing to take yourself off and go to school?"

"I wasn't ready before, but I'm ready now."

"I'd given up hoping. You want to take yourself to school? I didn't think it would ever happen. I'd like to be there to see the sparks flying. The teacher will wonder what he's struck. You'll set the place on fire. You'll be top of the class on the first day. When you come back, you'll be reading to me, not me to you. When do you want to go?"

"As soon as I can be ready. The day after tomorrow, or the one after that. I might be away a while."

"Doesn't matter how long it takes. Go."

Brian did not get to reading the Mechanics Institute information till later on and when he did he saw that the classes were not to begin for another month. Jemmy knew this but in his excitement had forgotten to speak of it. They discussed the point and when Brian said that he had no objection to Jemmy starting out as early as he liked, Jemmy spoke again of how he would like to see where the Monaro cattlemen came from and thought he might be able to swing east somewhere, find a way through the mountains, go into the Monaro and afterwards turn west and pick up a track to Albury.

The visit to Albury offered another attraction. He would see his mother and sisters. He hoped to stay with them, if the boarding house was not too full. In her last letter she said she had left Wyballong and had rented a large house in Albury and was taking in borders; also the girls were receiving schooling. He wondered if his sisters might be attending the Mechanics Institute classes. If they were, perhaps they could all go together.

Departure morning came. His mount was Kosciuszko and Ebony his packer. He led the horses, all ready, from the stable to the hut.

Brian came out.

"Have a good journey. You'll go to top of the class first day."

Jemmy grinned. "Maybe the second day."

"Remember, don't bust your gut to get back."

"I'll be back in time to bring the cattle down."

"Doesn't matter if you're not. I'll get them down." He ran the back of his hand lightly down the side of Kosciuszko's cheek. Playfully Kosciuszko grabbed the sleeve and held on, tugging. Brian slapped him gently on the muzzle and he let go. "I still wish you weren't taking him. He's still a young-un, only a three-year-old, still a baby – like you."

"... Yes, I know, as you've said before. Don't worry. I'll take him easy. Grand Flaneur was only a three-year-old when he won the Cup – remember – and all those other races."

"A big difference between the two. Grand Flaneur was Grand Flaneur. Kosciuszko is only Kosciuszko."

Jemmy mounted.

"One more thing," said Brian. "If ever… if ever you go off like this some other time, maybe on a trip on your own, and come back and find I'm not here, see Joseph Hull the solicitor in Albury. He'll tell you what's what."

Jemmy did not quite understand what Brian meant but decided to leave working it out till later. "If I learn how to do account books, will you make me station manager when I come back? Put me in charge of Foxhow and I'll make you your second fortune."

"'Second fortune'. Help me make my first and I'll be happy enough. On your way, traveller. And remember what I told you: don't let any stranger close enough to be able to put a hand on your horse. A villain that knows what he's about could grab your ankle and empty you out of the saddle in a second. There are men out there that would murder you for a bridle let alone your horse."

Jemmy swung away.

Brian called after him, "I don't want you back till you really are a scholar."

He went back to the verandah, sat down and watched till he could see the boy no longer.

The morning became late and most of the chores Brian had intended doing had not been started, and he was not too concerned. Constantly his thoughts went to Jemmy. He saw this wing-stretching of Jemmy's as being full of all kinds of possibilities. One possibility was that although Jemmy could return, the return might be only for the purpose of putting matters in order and saying goodbye. He moped about and finally decided to plait, a task that required just enough concentration to keep his mind off things he preferred not to think about. It was plaiting he was at, and in one of his favourite nooks, on the verandah, when he noticed the rider, leading a packhorse, coming in from the way Jemmy had left. He tied off the job and waited. The dogs rose from where they were lazing and, barking, ran to meet the horseman. Then Brian saw the rider was Jemmy and walked to meet him.

"What's all this about?" said Brian. "Were you afraid the Monaro men might get you?"

Jemmy did not answer.

"What did you forget?"

"You. Why don't you come with me?"

"You wasted half a day's ride to come back to ask me that? If I'd wanted to go with you, son, I'd have spoken up."

"But why don't you come?"

"Why would I want to go to Albury at this time of year?"

"Because you like Albury. Why don't you come? I could go about my business and you could go about yours – do what you like to do: go to the races, play cards, have tea with the lady where the geese are, argue with everybody."

"Are you accusing me of being argumentative?"

"Don't joke. You know what I mean. Here on your own you might get sick. Your hip might give up on you, or you could have a fall – you've had a bad one already."

"And nothing I couldn't handle happened. Yes, I like Albury, but I'm not of a mind to pay the place a visit at the moment. Anyway, I couldn't put things in order in just five minutes."

"Yes you could, if you wanted to. The dogs could come, or we could leave them at Braywood. Turn out the horses, all of them – Kilrenny as well. The creeks are running and the feed's good and there's no urgent work to be done. You could be ready in no-time, if you wanted."

"The wagon would have to be greased and packed and horses brought in."

"No need to take the wagon. We can ride. We'll move more quickly that way."

"I'll think about it."

"There's not much time. I'll stay tonight and if you don't want to come I'll move out in the morning. Can you give me an answer before bed?"

"Yes – if I've got one."

By bedtime Jemmy had his answer. As the evening had gone on Brian found the idea of going to Albury not so unappealing. But he had reservations, one in particular. He did not want to go to the Monaro and made this clear. The trip could be the kind he had rarely done, a leisurely one – no stallion, no schedule to keep. He thought of the men, the families, he would enjoy calling on and not having to hurry away. There was something else. There was the series of articles he had been writing on the value of the Thoroughbred in the breeding of stock-horses. He had hopes of seeing these published in the *Border Mail*. They could be posted to the editor but a man-to-man discussion would be better; the pieces could be done as a series of letters, or as articles or in one, perhaps a three-quarter page spread. As for the Monaro, he saw no reason why Jemmy could not branch off at some point and go on and do what he wanted to do. They would meet up in Albury afterwards. Where they might separate could be worked out as they went along. A man could not get through the mountains from just anywhere. From Foxhow Brian knew the ways through; farther on was a different matter, but he knew men, to the north, who knew ways.

The dogs would be left at Braywood.

Forty-one

The fourth day after leaving Foxhow brought them to Gairlocky. Edward More, who held the station, knew a way through to the Monaro, a way he used when taking cattle to the railhead and markets south of Sydney. After dinner, More explained the route to Jemmy and in the morning gave him a map drawn in pencil.

It was Brian's plan not to leave his present host till tomorrow. He helped Jemmy saddle up.

All ready, Jemmy swung up onto Kosciuszko and took Ebony's lead that Brian passed to him.

"I wonder which one of us will get to Albury first," said Jemmy."

"From here, I've got the shorter distance," said Brian. "But you never know where I might tarry and spend an extra day or two if the company's pleasant. Now remember what I told you: don't let any stranger close enough to able to put a hand on your horse."

"I know, I know."

"I'll be at the Caledonian," said Brian. "If you're there before me, get to those classes straight away. Don't waste time waiting for me. But settle in with your mother first, if she's got room for you. If she's got a full house, there might be a problem. If there is a problem, book into the Caledonian."

"Don't worry about me – you look after your self," said Jemmy. "If your hip hurts much, take a rest." He grinned. "And don't let any stranger close enough to be able to put a hand on your horse. I worry about you, you know."

"No more, I'll bet, than I worry about you at times, Cheeky-face. All the lip you give …"

"Look who I learned from."

"Oh, get out with you. Go on, on your way."

"Let's shake for luck," said Jemmy.

They gripped each others hand.

"Race you to Albury, just for fun," said Jemmy.

"Go race yourself. Get on your way."

Jemmy swung his horses away.

Brian called out, "And take that young-un easy. He should still be at home in the paddock."

Without looking back Jemmy lifted a hand.

After three days Jemmy was in the Monaro. The mountains he had come through were now to the west of him.

Much of the terrain he was now seeing was similar to country that he knew, except for almost treeless expanses in some places that he suspected would be snow-covered in winter. At the homesteads he came upon he was made welcome and told about the country that lay ahead.

Mostly his daily thoughts were the same as those of the previous days; some he expanded on, some he did not spend as much time on or dismissed quickly. He had made a mental list of the people he would write a letter to after he learned to write. The first would be to Grace Kinlake. He had thought about Grace often since starting out on the trip. The teasing Brian had given him after he returned from attending Boydy's party had made him think. Like him, when Grace's next birthday came she would turn eighteen. He knew that some girls of that age got married. What if somebody did come along and propose to Grace. It could happen. No, it must not happen. The more he thought of Grace, the more urgently he felt the need to write to her. Mr and Mrs Webber were high on the list. No good writing to Alfred as nobody knew where he was. Alfred had run away about a year ago. He wondered if he might meet up with him somewhere, maybe in Albury. He was sure Alfred would have taken the revolver with him, and might now be bushranging, as he used to say he intended to do. If they met on the track, would Alfred rob him or let him go? He would write to Tom Halpen, care of Braywood, where Tom went for supplies more often than he called at Foxhow.

Thoughts about his father always crept in. He had not seen or heard of him since his visit to Foxhow. From his mother's letters he knew that she too had not seen nor heard of him in a long time. Had he gone to Queensland? The man his father had hit in the grog shop had died and the doctor said the cause was septicaemia, which Brian said was the same as blood poisoning. There had been no news that the warrant against his father had been changed.

He thought of friends in Albury he would see again. And he would watch for Tom Hales. He had heard stories of Hales having been seen in

Albury lately. One story was that Hales had gone into business with a local man named William Yeomans, who was a noted horseman and once rode the winner of a race over a distance of ten miles. They had purchased a station named Milby, north of Albury, and were running sheep and growing wheat. It was now well known that Hales had bought another property, on the Mitta Mitta River – probably the one he had spoken of the day Jemmy had driven him across to Wodonga. If he saw Hales he would speak to him. He was sure Hales would remember him.

In the early afternoon he saw ahead a rider leading a packhorse going in the same direction.

He thought that one day he would like to go on a trip to Gippsland, that place he had heard about where the grass stayed greener for longer than it did on most parts of Foxhow or Braywood. In Gippsland there were markets and railheads that took stock to Melbourne. He had heard of the market at Omeo, about a hundred miles from Foxhow. The Monaro drovers on their way past Fitzford had told him about the lush country around where the Snowy emptied into the sea. Wouldn't it be good, he thought, if Brian owned a small station in that region where cattle bred at Foxhow could be taken to and fattened for the local markets and Melbourne's. But that would mean Brian would have to run hundreds more cattle than he did at present.

The rider he had seen earlier he saw again and was closer now. Maybe the horseman was only a traveller like him, or could be a stockman on his way home. He could do with somebody to talk to. At the slow rate he was gaining on the rider he thought it unlikely he would catch him up before time to make camp. If he stirred his horses to a trot he could soon be up to him, and he was tempted. No, best stay behind. He chuckled to himself. The rider might be Alfred. No, the rider couldn't be Alfred, for this man had two horses. To own two horses you had to have means – work and money. Alfred's shyness towards work made it unlikely that he would own two horses, and the gear to go with them – unless he had stolen them.

After about another hour the rider was not to be seen. There were boulders, some higher than a man and wider than a horse, hereabouts. Maybe the rider had seen him and might be lying in wait, or wanted to avoid him for the same reasons as he had.

To make camp and a fire he needed wood.

Reaching the crest of a downward sweep he saw on the other side, half a mile away, a belt of snow-gum. He could see at the bottom of the slope a creek and he rode down to it and watered the horses. The trees might provide some shelter for the night. Good camping spots around here were not plentiful and the late afternoon air was taking on an edge.

Nearing the timber he smelt smoke, though could not see any.

When he rode into the trees he heard the tinkle of a horse bell. He came to the edge of a clearing and saw a man putting wood on a fire. Two horses, hobbled and belled, were grazing close by. The man, hatted and with a beard clipped short, looked across at him and waved.

"I saw you back there behind me," said the man as Jemmy rode up. "You camping or going on?"

"Might camp."

"Plenty of room here."

Jemmy dismounted.

"Clancy Macnamara," said the man, extending his hand.

"Jem Tyler."

They shook.

"Where're you from?" asked Macnamara.

"Over there," answered Jemmy, pointing to the mountains, "Snowy River – Kosciuszko side. Where're you from?"

"A fair way from here," drawled Clancy. "Down from Gundagai, on the Murrumbidgee, on the Overflow country. Got a place there – not enough to get a living off most of the time, but there're a lot of men got less than me."

Jemmy unsaddled, hobbled and belled his horses and turned them loose.

There was enough water in Clancy's billy to make tea for both of them. Jemmy had his tin open first and put in enough leaves for two. They sat on their packsaddles and drank. They turned their heads at the sound of horses squealing. Kosciuszko's teeth were locked on the crest of the neck of one of Clancy's horses. Jemmy put down his tea, picked up a stone as he walked threw it, hitting Kosciuszko on the rump. The surprise of the hit more than the pain made Kosciuszko release his hold.

Jemmy came back to the fire. He was apologetic. "He's always been the same. You could ride him all day, turn him out at night, dog tired, and the first thing he'd want to do is pick a fight."

"Don't let it worry you. They'll sort it out. The big grey won't stand for much nonsense. Where'd you get that little bloke?"

"Bred him."

"What way?"

"Three parts thoroughbred."

"The other part?"

"Not sure, but I think I know. It's a long story."

"More than a little bit of Timor Pony in him, I reckon."

Jemmy had never heard of Timor ponies. "He's a bit undersized, but he's all quality."

"I could believe that. If there's Timor Pony in him, he'll be tough. You could call him pony, but probably he's around half a hand or more too big to make pony, officially."

They went for more wood, enough to see them through the night and some for in the morning. It was near dark when they ate. They were tired and would bed down early. Beside the fire they took their last drink of tea.

"Do you know the stallion-man, Brian Drury, over that way?" asked Clancy.

"Doing my time with him, at Foxhow. Been with him four years. Do you know him?"

"No. Only heard of him. What are you doing over this way, if you don't mind me asking?"

"Going to Albury. Got business there."

"If you come from the other side, there was a shorter way to Albury," said Clancy.

"I know. But I wanted to see this side of the mountains. And how about you, if you don't mind me asking? Where are you headed?"

"On from here a bit. I was at a loose end and wanted to do a friend a favour."

"What do you do when you're not at a loose end, and not on your property?" asked Jemmy.

"A bit of shearing, a bit of droving, horse breaking, this and that. Droving mainly. This friend of mine – Thurston Harrison – he's got a station about a day from here. Got a valuable colt, a thoroughbred, that's got away and gone with bush horses. Worth a thousand pounds, they say."

"A thousand pounds – phew. He must have won some big races."

"He hasn't even raced yet. But he's out of a great mare named Regret and is a full-brother to Pardon that won the Sydney Aldermen's Cup a few years ago. Harrison wants to try and get him on the first run."

"That's the way to do it. If you miss the first time it's always harder the second time. Bush horses learn quick."

"You've run a few brumbies, have you?"

"One or two."

"If you're not in a hurry, why don't you come with me and lend a hand? On the way back I can put you onto a good track to Albury. You wouldn't lose much time."

"No thanks. I'd sooner keep going."

Forty-two

They were saddling up, their backs to each other.

Without turning Jemmy spoke. "You said yesterday you thought my young-un has a bit of Timor Pony in him. Where does the Timor Pony come from?"

"Timor. It's a place."

"Where?"

"It's an island, up near the top of Australia, down from Java."

"Java? I know about Java."

Jemmy turned.

Clancy continued. "An explorer named McKinnley brought some in and used them as packers when he was working in Western Australia. They were tough, good at living off not much grass and had hooves hard as iron and didn't need shoeing. A few got over this way, but you don't run into them often now. No pure-bloods around."

Jemmy's eyes widened. "My pony's got hooves as hard as iron. The Mongols invaded Java in twelve ninety-three. I know that for a fact. It's in a book. They came by sea, but the Mongols were horsemen and wherever they went, by sea or not, they took horses. I know where Java is on the map. That must be how it happened. It must have been. Does Timor belong to Java?"

"As far as I know."

"Then ponies from Java could have got into Timor?"

"I suppose so. They're close enough."

"Then Timor ponies are Mongolian ponies. They have to be. It adds up. If my fella's got Timor Pony in him, he's got Mongolian Pony in him. I've always thought so and now I'm sure. It's all in a book."

Jemmy went to the other side of Ebony, unbuckled a flap and pulled out a book.

Watching, Clancy saw in the bag the tops of a number of books.

Opening the atlas as he walked, Jemmy came back to the side Clancy was on, rested the book on the nearside pack and put a finger on a landmass in the lower right corner. "That's the top of Australia."

Clancy had no quarrel with that much.

Jemmy's finger moved swiftly upwards. "And that's Java – I know. Would you show me where Timor is?"

"Over here." Clancy put a finger on a spot in the ocean north-west of Australia.

Jemmy's finger raced again, to the top of the left of the map. "And here is the bottom of Mongolia." His finger moved downwards. "And here's China. China was ruled by Kublai Khan, the Mongol emperor who invaded Java." The finger moved again, downwards. "Here is Java, and over here is Timor and here is Australia. It's a ladder. That's how they got here. The ponies that came to Timor, then to here, were from Mongolia."

Clancy was uneasy. "I only know what ponies from Timor look like. The rest, all you've said, might be true, but I don't know." He was not sure what to make of this boy. Coming across a well-read man in the bush was not so rare, but this fellow was the first he had met that got around with a packsaddle full of books that apparently he could not read, and into the bargain gave history lessons.

"I've said all I know and I rest my case," said Clancy, wanting to end the discussion and not certain he had a case to rest.

Jemmy returned the atlas to the bag and buckled the straps. He finished saddling and, reins over his arm, turned to Clancy. "I was thinking – been thinking all the morning. Is that invitation to go with you still open?"

"As open as it was when I made it."

"I'd like to go with you."

"Mount up and we'll get going. But go easy on the history lessons."

"You said you could put me on a good track to Albury afterwards. That still stands?"

"That's what I said."

They were not out of the clearing when Jemmy spoke next. "You won't have to explain yourself to Mister Harrison, but you might have to explain me being with you."

"Shouldn't be hard. I'll just say I met this… man from Snowy River and brought him along."

Clancy was not a talkative man but he answered when the boy asked questions or made comments.

Jemmy had questions to ask, lots of them. The first were in an effort to draw out of Clancy how much more he knew about the ponies of Timor. To Jemmy's disappointment, Clancy was not able to relate any more information than he had at he camp now behind them. Clancy knew the breed and had an eye for the characteristics that might be seen in crossbreds, that was all, and he knew about McKinnley. But Clancy was prepared to listen to all that Jemmy had to say on the Mongolian Pony and to hear again how convinced the boy was that the ponies of Timor were descended from Mongolian ponies and that the ponies of Timor must have brought to the islands by Chinese invaders under the Mongol emperor Kublai Khan. 'It's plain to see,' the boy insisted again. Clancy was not sure the claim was plain to see, but he did not speak of his reservations. Jemmy told of the book about the Mongols and the pictures of their ponies and about Bonny. He now owned the Mongol book; Brian had given it to him, though it was not one he had brought with him. He now wished he had brought it, so that he could show Clancy. Including the atlas, most of the books in his packsaddle he had bought himself.

When he was not asking questions or listening to answers, or thinking up more questions, his thoughts drifted to Kosciuszko, to not only the revelation of the pony's ancestry on Bonny's side, but to the way that all this new information had come about – through meeting a stranger. He told Clancy of the eighty miles in a day a Mongolian pony, off grass, could travel on a forced march, and how the hardness of the ponies' hooves had allowed the Mongols to go to war in Russia in winter, and of the droving of the hundred-thousand horses that Jokee brought home.

Clancy was not unamused.

"You could say," said Jemmy, "in this fella of mine, there's the coming together of two great breeds – the Timor Pony and the Thoroughbred."

"Yes, I suppose you could say that: a horse of England and a horse of the East."

Jemmy asked about Thurston Harrison whose station they were on the way to, and about Pardon that had won the Aldermen's Cup at Randwick in 1876. Was Pardon a stallion and was he at stud somewhere? What other big races had Pardon won?

Clancy answered the questions and told of Pardon's end. "They put him on a steamer for Melbourne, taking him down for the Cup. The ship ran into a storm in Bass Strait and founded with a loss of nearly all hands and all cargo, including Pardon."

They made good time and reached Breadalbane station in the early afternoon. Most of the men who had answered Harrison's call were already there. Most of them Clancy knew, though he had not seen many of them in a long time. Harrison, white-haired and bearded, found Clancy a welcome sight. That word had reached as far as Gundagai surprised him.

"I'd say there are more men who wanted to come than could get here," Clancy told Harrison.

"It's not every man who can down tools and go off just as he wants," commented Harrison. "A lot of autumn shearing going on now. We've nearly got enough, though. Add my five permanents and we've got twelve, not counting me. If one or two more turn up today or tomorrow, all the better."

The following day was to be a rest day, so that the horses could freshen up. Harrison had horses for whoever wanted them, but knew most men would prefer to ride their own. Probably any man arriving from now on, if he had come far, would opt for a fresh, Breadalbane horse.

By evening two more helpers had ridden in.

Forty-three

There had not been beds for everybody, but nobody tucked inside his swag had to go without a roof over his head. Thanks to the messhut, stable and forge, no man had to wake with dew on his hair.

Breakfast was leisurely and there was much talking. Everybody had news of some kind and there was nobody who did not want to listen. Much had been covered in last night's fireside conversation but gaps had been left.

Harrison's plan for the run was to hold off till early afternoon, till after the brumbies had spent the morning feeding. With full bellies they would be at their most sluggish. Jack Affleck, the station's foreman, had, from a distance and over the past week, kept a daily on and off watch. The horses had not been disturbed and when last seen were within two miles of the homestead. There were two mobs but they never strayed far from each other. One comprised mares and foals and colts that could still be made to behave themselves and was dominated by a single stallion. The other was made up of about ten males of various ages and was forced to keep its distance by the stallion with the mares. It was into the bachelor mob that Harrison's runaway had found his way. Affleck had come in late yesterday and reported where the horses were. He had gone out again this morning and later would meet up with the others and guide them to the horses.

At morning tea Harrison addressed the men. He again thanked all those who had come to help him. "The favour you're doing me I can't pay you for, so I owe you a return favour, redeemable, plus interest, any time you want to call in debt. In the meanwhile, I want you to have a drink on me. A bottle of the best whisky I can buy for every one of you. I haven't got a supply here, but I'll catch up with you in due course, no matter where you happen to be. I won't forget. There's not much else to say that we haven't already talked about. We can't go into the finer details till we see exactly what the lay of the land is – where the devils are and all that. As much as you can, watch my hand: go when and to where I point. You won't need me telling you much, I know. I know you know the ropes, but I know this property, and I know these horses. If there's one horse that'll give trouble, it'll be the big chestnut. There'll be no time for please and thankyous. We'll try to half-moon them and work them the way we want them to go. The hardest riding will be at the beginning, when we're setting ourselves up and they're full of dash. If we can, we'll work them around the bottom of the hills and drive them out into cleared country. Keep close to them, but for hell's sake not too close, or they could break. If they break and scatter, we're in trouble. Any questions?"

There were no questions.

Harrison turned his thoughts to the boy Clancy had brought with him. The boy was the only one whom he did not know personally. He did not want the boy to go on the run. Also, he had confided in Charlie Sneddon that he thought the "runt" the boy proposed riding was not the right kind of horse for a job like today's. A horse or rider that could not keep up, or might find his way into the wrong place at the wrong time, could turn out to be more than a small problem. Today was not a day for passengers. Charlie nodded, not necessarily agreeing but allowing for the testy state of mind Harrison was in.

Harrison took his time. After most men had dawdled out of the big hut and stood about chatting and smoking he looked for Jemmy and called him aside. He put a hand on his shoulder and guided him away from the men. "Lad, there's an important job needs to be done and I think you're the man for it. I need someone to stay back here and work the gates when the horses come in. If they come in a bit fast and get too far ahead of us, if none of us is close enough to shut them the horses could turn and come back out. You can never be sure you've got them till the gates are shut behind them. If you'd do that job you'd be a big help."

Strickened, Jemmy didn't answer. He knew he was in no position to argue. As carefully as Harrison had put his words they were none the less an order.

Harrison gave a quick smile, turned and walked away.

Jemmy watched him go then slowly walked to where Kosciuszko was tethered at a fence. "Another rest-day for you," he said, patting his horse's neck. "And for me too." He untied the lead of the headstall.

He was nearly at the paddock gate when Clancy called out to him. "Don't leave him there too long. Better he be a bit empty till the run's over."

"He's not going," replied Jemmy. "Me neither."

Clancy walked to the fence. "Why, what's wrong?"

"Mister Harrison said he wants me to stay here and handle the gates."

Clancy frowned. "Handle the gates? Rats. There are kids here that could do that. Come with me."

Clancy turned and started towards where Harrison had resumed talking to Charlie Sneddon. Jemmy, leading Kosciuszko, followed.

"Thurston, could I see you for a minute?" said Clancy.

Charlie walked away.

Clancy had a question. He faced Harrison. "You want to leave the boy at the yards?"

"Yes."

"He's gone *considerable* out of his way to come and give a hand today."

Harrison knew the gates excuse would not work on Clancy. "I know and I'm grateful. But the riding today's going to be hard. It's not a day for lads."

"Where he's from the riding's hard every day, even for lads. I've been through that country over his side and I know what it's like. There's no country around here that's harder, and he's run brumbies before. He knows the game."

Suspicious, Harrison looked at Jemmy. "You've run brumbies before? Where might you have done that? Chasing a mongrel or two you might run into in the bush isn't like what we'll be about today."

"I've gone with the Hoys on brumby runs, and more than once."

"The Black Hoys?"

"Yes."

"There," said Clancy to Harrison: "You want credentials, you've got them. If he's saddled up with the Hoys, he's ridden with the best. What's more, he works for Drury the stallion-man. You know about him – I know you do; I've heard you speak of him."

Harrison looked at Jemmy. "Brian Drury?"

"Yes. And I'm still with him."

Hard-headed as Harrison was, he did not want Clancy Macnamara, of all people, thinking him a fool. He spoke sharply.

"Alright – come. But that little horse of yours won't do out there on a run like this. You'll have to take one of mine."

"This is the horse I want," protested Jemmy. "He's small but he's good, and I want under me a horse that I know. You don't know how tough he is, but I do."

Harrison had had enough of this argument. "Very well, ride him if you must. But this much I insist on: you find yourself somebody to latch on to and stay with him – don't go wandering about; and if you can't keep up, drop out and stay out. You do as you're told." He walked away.

Clancy and Jemmy turned to each other and smiled.

"He's a bit edgy today," said Clancy. "But he's a good man. If he wasn't, I wouldn't have bothered being here."

Forty-four

After the riders met up with Jack Affleck they crossed a mossy and grassy plateau and descended a short way to where, from behind a shield of boulders, they caught the first glimpse of their quarry, about two hundred yards away. The horses were at rest on the shady side of a stand of tall bushes called mimosa. On the other side of them the scrubby terrain sloped upwards. The other mob, with the mares and stallion, could not be seen. Two of the horses at the mimosa were lying down. The others stood with heads lowered, only their tails moving, swishing away the flies.

Harrison spoke quickly. "Don't give them time to think. We'll need to turn them to the right. Clancy, you go. Some of us will cut across to the left and fan out up the side. Keep close to them, son, and they'll go straight – or they ought to." In turn he pointed at five men then pointed to the slope on the other side and the men went.

Clancy was the first to leave, riding at a walk, hoping to get as close as possible before the horses either became aware of him or were not disturbed enough to view him with any more than curiosity. Every length he could better himself by to begin with, the more it would count when he had to move in fast.

It was Clancy that Jemmy at first had decided to follow but changed his mind after hearing what Harrison said. He knew that if he attempted to go with Clancy, Harrison would order him to come back. It was Harrison whom Jemmy now decided to follow.

Amongst the mimosa a chestnut with a tail that nearly touched the ground and a long, matted mane caught scent and lifted his head. Up came other heads. The horses lying down got up. At a walk they began moving away from the bushes. One stopped and turned. The others stopped and turned. They saw Clancy, still at a walk, and the men moving on the slope behind and to the side of him. The old chestnut turned and led off at a trot. The others followed.

"Now, Clancy, now," Harrison said to himself.

Clancy began his dash, cracking his whip as he went. He wanted to be galloping and gain ground before they increased speed.

Still at the rear of Clancy, the men on the wings rode as fast as the ground, timber and scrub, would allow, their horses responding as best they could, at times stumbling, sliding, passing through openings between tree trunks and boulders, at times crashing through bushes the other side of which they could not always see. Dry boughs snapped and resounded as the chests of horses or men struck them.

Once they passed through the gap coming up, the slopes on either side would be behind them.

The old chestnut leading swung suddenly to the left, plunged into the scrub and started up the slope. The horses behind him followed. Clancy rode hard in an effort to head them but could not. He pulled back, hoping they would slow and give the riders higher a chance to cut them off.

On and upwards the horses went.

The two men highest up rode their hardest but were too late.

Reaching the crest, the horses started down the other side.

One by one the riders came up and drew rein. They were almost in a line as they looked down on a descent that needed thinking about if an attempt was to be made to take it on. They watched the horses, disappearing, reappearing, zigzagging, leaping and sliding. A horse fell, rolled over and in scrambling to gain its feet fell again. If a man had been astride it, thought Harrison, a crushed leg, or worse, would have been the outcome.

Jemmy could not understand the hesitation. Time was being lost. The gap between them and the brumbies was widening with every second.

"What d' y' reckon?" said Bill Ennis, beside Harrison.

Harrison shook his head. "I wouldn't send a dog down there let alone ask a man." He sighed. "They've beaten us, boys. We can say goodbye to them for today. Luck wasn't with us."

"I'll go."

The voice had come from the end of the line.

All heard but nobody took any notice. No head turned.

"We've got 'em half-baked," said Jemmy. We mustn't let up now. They can't go forever."

"Nor can we," scoffed Harrison. "Home, boys."

Before a horse could be turned Jemmy was gone. He let out a yell and cracked his whip, hoping the horses below would hear and know that the devil was not finished with them yet and would keep them running till they wanted to run no longer.

The men watched.

A fallen tree the brumbies had skirted lay in front of Kosciuszko and he flew over it, slipping when he landed and for a moment almost sat on his haunches, stabbing the sloping ground with his front legs and throwing back his head. The jolt tested Jemmy's own balance and for an instant he rose in the stirrups and leaned back, grabbing at neither mane nor saddle and not touching Kosciuszko's mouth. The pony threw his head forward and completed the recovery. On they went, Kosciuszko sliding and leaping, Jemmy continuing to give the pony his head and occasionally reminding him with his heels that he must go on. Through the saplings they went, dodging as best they could all that came up, including wombat holes. A low dead bough struck Jemmy across the chest and the sound of the wood snapping rang out like a rifle shot. Reaching the bottom of the descent clearer ground presented itself and allowed Kosciuszko to properly stretch out.

The men at the top, not speaking, scanned the bush below, looking for a sign of either horses or the boy that had followed them.

"There," said a rider, pointing towards a break in the timber on a slope more than a quarter of a mile away. The horses were amongst light timber and climbing.

The men looked for the boy but could not see him. The way the horses were moving suggested they were being pushed. They crossed a clearing and when they reached the other side disappeared into scrub and thick timber.

"There he is," said Sid Rawes.

Jemmy came out of the thin timber that the horses has passed through, crossed the clearing and disappeared.

"I wouldn't have thought he'd have got that close," said Claude Woolcot.

"That close aint close enough," said Archie Skelly. "He's got to head 'em. Following them is no good. That Tom Thumb he's riding can't last."

"He's lasted pretty well so far," said Clancy.

"He's done well, I grant you," answered Skelly, "But he's got weight on his back and them mongrels haven't, and you know what weight can do – stop a train."

They went on watching, thinking they might get another glimpse of the horses and the boy. In the direction the horses seemed headed the hillside began to curve and the men could see nothing more that might pass as a clearing that might give them the sight they hoped for. Higher up, the tree line ended abruptly and the rest of the hill was almost bald. Near boulders that dwarfed them, the horses appeared, still moving but at only a walk. The men waited. By the time the horses again disappeared Jemmy was not seen. The riders went on waiting.

Without speaking, Harrison turned his horse and started back the way he had come. The men followed.

Forty-five

The ride back to the homestead was a glum and mostly silent affair.

At the station the men attended first to their horses, pouring water over the animals' backs where the saddle had rested and where the girth had been, breaking up patches of sweat that must not be let harden. Scratches and gashes on the horses' legs, breasts and bellies, received liberal dabs of Stockholm tar. Then the horses were turned out. At barrels outside the mess-hut the men sloshed water over their dusty, sweaty faces and wiped themselves with their shirt sleeves.

The station women were ready with tea and cake in the big hut.

Harrison was the last to walk in and did not stay. He stopped on the way out and said he would be back later.

The men drank the tea, ate the cake and blessed the ladies.

There was not much talk. What had happened was clear cut. Luck had gone against them. All knew the run was going perfectly till that cunning old chestnut in the lead decided to swing away and head up the slope. If only somebody had been able to get there in time and head him off. Each had his own thoughts about whether or not they should have followed the horses down the other side. If Harrison had led, they would have gone. They thought of the boy and how reckless he had been. If he were not back by late afternoon he would have to be looked for; the chances of him having taken a tumble were high, judging by the way he went down that side and kept going. He could be brained against a rock for all anybody knew.

Believing he could hold no more tea after his third mug, saying as much as he wanted to say and listening to as much as he wanted to hear, Clancy found no more excuses to postpone his call on Harrison. He went to the homestead and knocked on the back door. In his soiled clothes and smelling like a sweaty horse, he did not want to embarrass Mrs Harrison by having her think he expected to be admitted into the parlour. The kitchen, or even the doorstep, would serve his purpose.

Harrison answered the door. "Clancy ... Come in." He suspected why Clancy had come.

Clancy halted inside the doorway.

Harrison closed the door and beckoned his visitor to follow. In the parlour Harrison pointed to a chair and Clancy sat.

Harrison's unhappiness was clear to see. Admittedly the run was lost before the boy went off as he did. The trouble was, due to the hounding the horses got when the boy went after them, the next run would be all the more difficult. This Clancy knew. There would be a next run, but exactly when and where it would take place would have to be worked out. The men who had come to help with this one would soon have to leave.

Most of Harrison's anger was directed at himself. "I should have called him to leave off."

"I don't think he'd have taken any notice."

Harrison nodded resignedly, believing that probably Clancy was correct. "No need to tell you: next time if they get so much as a whiff of us they'll be off. We'll be lucky to get more than a quick look at them. They might have to be left a long time before we give them another go. Might have to work out a different plan." He did not speak of Clancy's persuading him to let the boy come and for this Clancy was grateful.

"When you set up the next one, let me know," said Clancy. "If I can make it, if I'm not away, I'll come."

There was nothing more worth saying and they became silent, Clancy thinking this was good time to leave.

Mrs Harrison came into the room carrying a tray with cups and a teapot and a sugar bowl covered by a doily. She placed the tray on the table, went away and came back with a plate of buttered Madeira cake. She was on her way out to the kitchen again and was passing a window. She stopped and faced the window. What she saw puzzled her. She spoke without turning. "Horses coming in."

The men rose, went to the lady and stood one each side of her. They stared.

There were horses, close together, trotting slowly, in the west home-paddock and were moving towards the yards. There was a rider behind them.

"It's the boy," muttered Clancy, "and by the look of it he's got the lot."

Harrison did not speak. He turned and led the way outside onto the verandah.

The horses moved steadily through the different yards then into the last. When the rider came through he dismounted and closed the gate.

The men and women from the mess hut began walking towards the yards. The children ran. The folk on the verandah descended the steps.

The big chestnut Harrison did not mistake. Then he saw his treasured colt.

Somebody cheered and soon everybody was cheering.

Jemmy did not remount but led Kosciuszko, walking stiffly, towards the top gateway.

Clancy slipped through the rails, went to Jemmy and plucked the reins from his hand. "I'll look after him. You go and get some tea and cake into you." He turned to Kosciuszko, saw the cuts on the legs and the long gash across his breast. He put a hand under the pony's forelock and rubbed the wet forehead. "I don't think you'll be picking a fight in the paddock tonight, little warrior."

Jemmy grinned. "I wouldn't bet a sovereign on that if I were you."

Clancy turned to the folk outside the fence. "Is there any tea left in the pot, and cake? The man from Snowy River here could do with some."

"…And a sheaf of hay for his partner," said Jemmy, putting a hand across Kosciuszko's wither.

Harrison unhooked the chain and held the gate open. He took Jemmy's hand in both of his and shook.

"You'll take your tea with me, Mister Snowy River, or whatever your name is, and if ever this colt of mine that you've brought back lines up for the Melbourne Cup, which he's bred to do, I'll remember this day."

Forty-six

To be again in Albury pleased Brian. He had been reluctant to start out but the pleasures of the trip and town this time were more than ordinarily acceptable. For one thing, the editor of the *Border Post* was keen to print his pieces. He had never been perfectly at ease in being absent from Foxhow for long periods with nobody regularly on the place. Though he had never found anything to have gone wrong during his absences, his not being there still had been a worry. This time Foxhow did have somebody there, in the comings and goings of the Braywood men. He was considering making more land available to Chester Tweedie; if he did, probably this could mean the station would not be unattended at any time. Plus, the rent paid by Chester could entirely obviate the need to run cattle of his own and this might mean retirement to Fitzford or Albury or Wodonga could more easily be contemplated. And there was this latest development in Jemmy's life. He knew the boy would shine as a student and he savoured the thought of him no longer being a scholar in spirit only but one soon to have the wherewithal to become a scholar in actuality. He realised too that these new-found wings of the boy's could mean the end of Jemmy's tenure at Foxhow. So much was yet to fall into place.

Jemmy had not yet come in and Brian's worrying, which had begun the day he farewelled the boy at Gairlocky station, had increased. There were bad men out there. Yes, admittedly there were good men too, and more good than bad, but a single bad one amongst all the others could so easily bring undone so much. Today was the eighth he had been in town. As he had done on previous afternoons around three o'clock he stepped off the veranda of the Caledonian and started across to Fry's stable to see if Jemmy had perhaps come in but not yet caught up with him. Another concern had edged its way into his mind over the past few days. Might Jemmy have changed his plans, might he have met up with somebody or come upon a chance of an adventure he could not resist and decided to put off the learning to read enterprise till another time? He was nearly to the other side when he heard the "Hey, Brian," from somewhere up the street to his left. He knew the voice and stopped and turned, put his hand up to his eyes and shaded them. He saw the rider, leading a packhorse, raise an arm and wave. He returned the wave and waited.

When near enough to not have to call out Jemmy spoke. “I’m here.”

“I can see that. What held you up?”

“I’ll tell you later.”

From the saddle Jemmy put out his hand and Brian took it, bringing up his other to fully clasp Jemmy’s.

“What did you think of the Monaro?” asked Brian.

“We ought to have land there – be nearer the Sydney markets.”

“As well as land in Gippsland, nearer the Melbourne markets, I suppose?”

“Yes. We’ll breed our cattle at Foxhow and fatten them in Gippsland for Melbourne and the Monaro for Sydney. That’s what we ought to do. And I’m told there’s even better fattening country south east of the Monaro, in from the coast.”

“Is that so, Mister Tyson?”

Jemmy grinned. He knew who Tyson was: James Tyson the cattle king. He dismounted. “I’ve got a lot to tell you.”

“When you’re ready, I’ll be waiting to hear.”

“There was a colt that might be a starter in the Melbourne Cup someday. Wait till I tell you about that”

“Is that so?” Brian’s eye went to the wound across Kosciuszko’s breast. The injury was still raw, about an inch wide but had gone no deeper than the hide, was clean and healthy and above and bellow the edges were the remnants of the last pine-tar dressing put on days ago at Lara Lake station. “What happened?” Brian’s hand went to Kosciuszko’s forehead and rubbed it.

“We got caught up in a brumby run – had to go and get a well-bred colt that had got away and gone with them. We got him. He’s the one that might run in the Cup someday.”

“Did you see what you got hooked up on?”

“No. There was a lot going on. It turned out a hard run, and we couldn’t pull out. But he did it. He went everywhere I asked him to go and didn’t put a foot wrong. You’d have been proud of him. I was. Everybody was. Tell you what else: there is Mongolian pony in him after all – that’s for sure. I got the proof. A man I met who saw him knew straight away –

straight away. But he didn't say Mongolian pony, he said Timor pony and they're both the same – I can prove it. Timor is an island up the top of Australia and that's how they got down to here. I worked it out. I'll show you on the atlas."

"Is that so? Well, I'll wait till I've had a look at this 'proof'. Even if it's true, don't forget there's Thoroughbred in him too – at least half that we know of. Don't forget that."

Jemmy dismounted.

They began walking into the stable.

"When do you plan to see your mother?"

"As soon as I fix up the horses. I'll walk. I know where the street is."

"She knows you're coming. I've been to see her. There's room for you. If there wasn't, I think she'd have pitched a tent in the yard. Another thing: I've signed you up for the course. You still want to do it, I suppose?"

Jemmy smiled.

Brian added, "The classes will be held in the evenings, three nights a week. And if that's not enough for you, there'd be plenty of work you can do at home, I'm sure."

"I'll be there. I've got letters to write, as soon as I can."

"And books to read, don't forget."

"Letters first."

"No reason why you won't be able to do both at once, after a while."

Brian looked again at Kosciuszko's wound. "He'll have a scar, a decent one – right a cross, forever."

"That won't hurt him. It can be his medal."

Printed in Australia
AUOC02n0652010617
286272AU00002B/3/P

9 781925 588064